to M.
friend and Dentist

The Day the Music Died

By

Lynn A. Eastman

authorHOUSE™

1663 Liberty Drive, Suite 200
Bloomington, Indiana 47403
(800) 839-8640
www.AuthorHouse.com

© 2005 Lynn A. Eastman. All Rights Reserved.

No part of this book may be reproduced, stored in a retrieval system, or transmitted by any means without the written permission of the author.

First published by AuthorHouse 12/15/04

ISBN: 1-4184-7956-X (sc)

Library of Congress Control Number: 2004099763

Printed in the United States of America
Bloomington, Indiana

This book is printed on acid-free paper.

INTRODUCTION

Martin Borman strode swiftly through the Fuehrer Bunker. Above, the sound of artillery and the rattle of machine guns could be heard. The young Volks army, mostly teenage boys twelve to fifteen, looked frightened. They, however, were augmented with SS troops that had been in combat since 1939 and who knew that the real fighting was still a few days away.

There was less confusion than one would expect. The various officers, Donitz, Himmler, all went about their business much the way that they had three years before in the Wolf's Lair in Bavaria, when the world was a much different place for them.

Borman found the young colonel that he had been searching for—a quartermaster colonel who was able to get supplies through war-torn Europe; able to get guns, ammunition, and fuel to combat units that needed it, in spite of allied bombing and the general chaos that was the Third Reich in its last days.

"Did you get the last shipment out of Berlin?" Borman asked.

"It went three days ago. I received confirmation not an hour ago that it had arrived."

"Good. My work here is done. I will report to the Fuehrer that all is complete and then leave Berlin for the last time."

"What about me?

You promised that when the last shipment was safe at its destination, I too could go with you."

"You shall get what I promised for your service to the Reich," replied Borman.

"Meet me here at 2200 hours and be ready to travel."

At 10:00 p.m., Borman and the young colonel arrived on the surface of Berlin in its last days. They went by foot to a small landing strip where a twin-engine Cessna was fueled and ready to go.

Both men entered the plane, and Borman, at the controls, started the engine. It began to roll down the runway. As they became airborne, keeping below 500 meters, avoiding enemy aircraft, Borman took one last look at the smoke and ash that had become Berlin, the capital of the thousand-year Reich.

"Farewell, mein Fuehrer. Farewell, mein Berlin, until next time. I will ensure that all is in readiness for you when we are needed."

The small plane disappeared south into the smoke and darkness.

Four days later, the war ended.

BOOK I: BEGINNINGS

CHAPTER I

Baltimore, Maryland

August 6, 2010

Wednesday, 1:00 p.m.

Charles Townsend III always spent Wednesday mornings on the Potomac River in his canoe. He always was home, showered, and ready for his first martini of the day by one o'clock. The drink was followed by a light lunch with his wife and son. This was a ritual that had not changed since Townsend had left the CIA five years ago.

He retired from the position of director of the CIA when an election had brought a bunch of liberal kids, with no idea of the real world or how to live in it, into power. Rather than watch the demise of the organization he loved, he simply retired.

Townsend was tall, thin, and very fit; six foot one, weighing 200 pounds even; always impeccably dressed and in superb physical condition. Townsend, much to everyone's surprise, was enjoying retirement. He would spend the mornings, still arising at 5:00 a.m., on his computer. He would research world events and talk with his many friends and acquaintances through the world by e-mail. By 10:00 each day, he would be off to a physical workout of some kind. Wednesdays it was canoeing. He would be home by 1:00 to have lunch with old friends—it varied by day as to which friend and where, but never on Wednesdays. Wednesdays were for family.

In the afternoons he would study reports and give advice to those who wanted it.

The evenings were spent in various social activities.

But not Wednesdays. Wednesdays were family days and were always spent with his wife of fifty-five years, his forty-five-year-old son Charles Townsend IV, and his grandchildren.

That's why when it got to be one thirty, the Townsends became concerned. By two they were alarmed, and by two thirty Charles IV was in a rented canoe and his mother was on the phone, first to the Maryland police, and then to the CIA office. After all, what are friends for?

It was 6:15 p.m. when the Maryland State Police officer found the canoe. He immediately called in the report and in twenty minutes, nearly a hundred men were on both sides of the river.

An FBI cadet, a volunteer from the academy, found the body at 7:50 p.m. Townsend was wedged under a tree where the river takes a bend to the south. He had been dead for several hours.

Friends and family gathered at the Townsend home throughout that night and into the next day. Condolences from the sitting president and three former presidents were received, as well as discreet notes from various foreign leaders who had benefited from Townsend's work but did not want anyone to know they had.

The family had refused an autopsy. Due to the Townsend position and power, they were able to bypass the law requiring victims found in such a manner be cut up before their family could put them to rest. It was strange that an experienced canoeist like Townsend would die like that, but these things sometimes happen to anyone.

Mrs. Townsend III was taking it rather hard. She had been sedated since they found the body on the sixth, and now it was the evening of the seventh. This meant that Charles IV had made all of the arrangements with the funeral home. In spite of the Jewish custom to always bury their dead before sundown the day they died, Charles had decided to wait two days so that all the dignitaries from around the world could get to Washington to pay their respects.

At 11:00 p.m. the phone rang in the home of Charles IV. He lived in a large, Victorian home in a wooded suburb of Baltimore, Maryland. Divorced with two sons, Charles V and Rodney James, who lived with their mother in West Virginia about 100 miles away, Charles was rather lonely but kept himself busy with his banking and international business interests.

He was quietly grieving for his father with his fifth House of Lords scotch of the evening, a favorite of the Townsend men. Charles had been as close as any living person was to his father. Charles III had been the rock that Charles had built his life around after his divorce.

Growing up had been hard for Charles IV. His father was gone a lot, never could talk about his work, and was always demanding and precise. As a teenager, Charles IV found his father remote, uncaring, and had turned to his mother. But she was even less warm than his father was, so Charles had turned to friends. He had become quite a rounder. Drug use, some dealing, and lots of alcohol had been his life. The wealth, drugs, and parties led to friends, but the wrong kind. He had attempted to find warmth with girls and women. The result was a number of scandals that his father had had to keep quiet. There was the pregnant schoolgirl who had a quiet abortion and then took a trip aboard for several months on the *Queen Elizabeth II* at the Townsends' expense. There was also the case of the wife of a Townsend family friend who had been caught in a very compromising position with young Charles. His father had bailed him out of that with an overseas assignment for the lady's husband. Of course, there were scrapes with the law as well. The Townsends, while very upset and disappointed with their son, continued to cover for him in the hopes that he would come to his senses.

Charles IV had a brilliant mind and had found school easy and a good source of parties and friends. By the time he was twenty-eight he had his Ph.D. in business from Harvard. International banking was his specialty and he was working as an assistant to the president of Chase Manhattan in the overseas area. Charles found that this assignment opened more doors to fun and frolic. It was while working here that he met his wife, Emily. Emily was a beautiful, spoiled woman. The daughter of the president of First Boston, she was used to the best and having it her way.

Charles fell hard, and she changed his life. He settled down almost overnight. They were married nine months after they met. Charles was thirty-two and Emily twenty-nine. They had two sons, Charles the V, of course, and Rodney James. However, when Charles settled down, he began to work like his father. Long hours, no sense of humor, and a certain remoteness crept in. Emily was not prepared to live like Charles' mother had; she was full of life. One day, after a flight to Rome had been delayed, Charles left the airport to return to his New York office. Walking down the street he saw Emily with his assistant eating in a restaurant. They were more then eating, and Charles followed them to a hotel around the corner and then to the room where he caught them "in the act" as it were.

Charles was devastated! He nearly killed them both and then went on a three-week binge with drugs, alcohol, and any woman he could find. He found a lot! When he woke up in Chicago after the binge, he called his father. Charles III came to Chicago and spent a week with his son. Following that week, Charles was divorced, moved to the Washington, D.C., area and became senior vice president of Citibank in charge of all overseas operations. He also became inseparable from his father. Charles reorganized his life around family values, placing his sons number-one in his life and his parents number-two. He was civil to Emily, but never had a meaningful conversation with her again.

He did not know how he would fill the void left by his father in the days and months to come. So he sat, sipping his scotch and letting a tear run down his cheek in the dark.

The phone shook him from his morose thoughts.

"Hello?"

"Mr. Townsend?"

"Yes."

"This is Alfred Plank at the Plank Funeral Home."

"Yes."

"I know it is late and I also know how bad you must feel at this moment but there is something you need to see. Could you come down here?"

"Tonight? Now?"

"Yes, I know it is unusual, but I think you will want to see this."

"I'll be there in fifteen minutes."

"Well what is it?"

"Thanks for coming, Mr. Townsend. I'm sorry to drag you down here but I wanted you to see something on your father."

With that Mr. Plank lifted the sheet that was draping his father's body.

"As you know, there was no autopsy performed because it was clear that Mr. Townsend had drowned. When I was cleaning him, I noticed two small marks in his scalp. They are very small, hardly more than a pinprick, but there are two little marks. I have never seen anything like this before.

"I became suspicious, so I began to look closer. There were the usual bumps, scrapes, etc., that one would expect after being dragged down the river. I then got out the x-ray machine that we have here to help us with reconstruction when that is necessary."

"And so…" Charles said a bit impatiently.

"Well, when I looked at Mr. Townsend's lungs, there was no water in them. He was dead BEFORE he went into the water."

"That can't be."

"I'm sure of it.

"You can have an autopsy if you want. In fact, I would recommend it. I think that whatever happened to Mr. Townsend happened before he went into the water, and those strange marks have something to do with it."

"That may be, but I still find it hard to believe. When my father retired from the CIA, he should have lost all of his enemies. They don't follow people like my father after they leave office.

"Can you take some pieces of his scalp from around those marks without letting anyone know?"

"Sure, I can do anything. I'm the best."

"Good. Do that, and don't let anyone know about our conversation tonight."

"You can count on me.

"Mr. Townsend, if you don't mind me saying so, your father was a good man, maybe even a great man. I always admired his work and his family. I hope this turns out to be easily explained."

But it was not easily explained. The mystery was to deepen.

The next two days were a blur. The famous and the infamous came to pay their respects to Charles Townsend III. Charles Townsend IV was busy being a gracious host and a perfect mourner.

The second day, Charles III was buried. There was a small reception back at Charles IV's home with about eighty close friends and family members. The evening was spent as is usual after a funeral, with condolences being offered and stories being told about fond remembrances of the deceased. The last to leave was Larry Nichols. Mr. Nichols was a close friend of both the Charles, and an international banker. He had flown to Washington for the funeral from London and had not seen Charles in three years.

"Really sorry about your father's passing. It's hard to lose a parent, and I know how close you were to him."

"Thank you, Larry. We will all miss him. But we have a lifetime of memories to share. Those of us who worked with him and knew him will always remember his continual work for what he thought was the right thing."

"Yes, that's true. I spoke with him only three weeks ago. He was working on a project that he was a little secretive about. I learned a long time ago not to ask too many questions. He was asking about transferring a large amount of gold across continental lines. Do you know anything about that?"

"No. He never mentioned any project like that with me. I thought that he was all done with international intrigues. Do you know who he was working with on this?"

"No. He just called me in London and asked questions about how it could be done. Said he would get back to me, and then I heard of his death."

"Strange, but then you know how he was. He might just have read an article in a magazine and was checking it out."

"Yeah, that's probably what it was. Anyway, good night. When you are in London, be sure to give me a ring. We can have a pleasant night on the town."

At 8:00 a.m. on the ninth, Charles received a call from Mr. Plank.

"Alfred, nice of you to call. I thought your home did a nice job with the funeral yesterday. Thanks for the special attention you pay to details. What can I do for you?"

"Well, I was just getting back to you on the piece of scalp I had analyzed by our friends at the company. It seems there was poison in the skin and hair roots.

It was a rare type of poison that is quick-acting. It could be fatal. I don't know how he would have come by it. If he had eaten it, it would have killed him long before he got into the river. I suspect he must have taken it into his system about fifteen minutes before he died."

"Do you think that is what killed him?"

"Well, it may have. I know he did not drown. But we did not have an autopsy done, so I can't say for sure. I'm only a mortician, you know. Do you want me to do further checking into this?"

"Of course! But very quietly. Can you have someone from the agency exhume the body and see what they can find out without anybody else knowing about this?"

"Yes, I can do that. Walt Willet from the company is a specialist in these areas. He knew your father and I'm sure would want to help. I'll call him. He may want to talk to you to verify that you want this done."

"That's fine. Have him call me. But please keep it quiet and do it fast!"

CHAPTER II

Tokyo, Japan

August 8, 2010

Professor Kumato left his office at Tokyo University about 5:00 p.m. He was a little man near eighty years old. What hair he had left was very thin and he was a little round-shouldered. He had been a professor here since the university was rebuilt after the war. Professor Kumato was the leading authority in Japan on the Second World War—a war in which he had just missed being intimately involved.

Kumato's father had died at Guadalcanal, his maternal family at Hiroshima. His mother had survived the war in Tokyo despite the total bombing policy of Wainwright. She never recovered as a person and had died in 1955 from the distress of the times that she had seen.

Kumato had been in training with the army at fifteen years of age. He was being trained to defend the homeland from the dread Americans at an Army base in Northern Japan when the war ended.

He, like the other boys and old men who were to defend the homeland and the emperor to the death, were considering suicide when he was discharged from the army. He had been brought up like all Japanese to believe that the world revolved around the emperor, the Sun God. His duty was to the emperor, his family, and his ancestors. Now they were gone. The emperor was in American custody, his father dead, his mother sick, his extended family dead, and his ancestors disgraced.

It had taken Kumato five years to come to grips with these events and put his world back into some semblance of order. By 1951, he had finished high school and college, where he studied economics and history. He worked for Mitsubishi as a market analyst until 1957. When his mother died in '55, he felt free to indulge himself in what he wanted to do, and that was history.

Kumato had a morbid interest in all aspects of the war. He had gone to college in Australia in 1960, then on to UCLA for his master's, and finally the University of Michigan for his doctoral work. His dissertation had been on the Japanese war strategy, a topic of some interest to American university students and historians in the late fifties and sixties.

Upon his return to Japan in 1961, he had continued his studies and expanded them into the European theater. He had become an authority on Nazi Germany in general, and the Holocaust in particular. He often consulted with Jewish authorities on various details of that horror. He had been instrumental in the capture of Eichman, although this was kept from the general public.

Kumato had never married. He spent most of his time in research and in helping young people at the university find themselves. He had mentored many young people over the years. Perhaps the search for himself after the war gave him a special insight into these young people's needs in a rapidly changing Japan. Some of these students now were high in government. They often visited him at the university. Small gatherings of students were common. The sake was shared, history retold, and good times remembered. These students were Kumato's family, and he liked it that way. It didn't hurt either when it was time for the school to receive a grant for various types of research. The school enjoyed his contacts and so he had everything he wanted for his own research and comfort, although Kumato did not require much in that line. All he needed were his books, computers to work with, and the opportunity to travel to various places to extend his knowledge of the war years.

Tonight it was growing dark, and he was in a hurry to get to his home. There, his housekeeper had prepared a lovely meal for him and three former students who were to spend another pleasant evening discussing both their and the world's past.

As Kumato hurried along, a young woman he recognized from around campus greeted him. She had not been in any of his classes, but he had seen her. She was tall for a Japanese woman, with dark, shining hair; thin, dressed in a dark blue running outfit with the ubiquitous Nike swoosh.

"Hello, Professor. How are you?" she asked.

"Just fine, my dear, and you?"

"Also good, Professor-san."

Just then she stumbled and bumped against the old professor, who attempted to break her fall. She fell against him rather heavily and then went to one knee. The professor felt a sharp pain like a pinprick but gave it no mind as he helped her up.

"You must be careful, my dear. You could break a leg or wrist like that."

"Thank you, Professor. I'll try to be more careful in the future. I am truly sorry."

Kumato continued on for another twenty paces, and then his heart stopped. He was dead before he hit the ground.

The young lady watched from behind a nearby tree. "I am sorry, Professor, you were a good man," she said to herself as she turned and jogged toward a blue Honda sedan waiting about 100 yards away.

Professor Kumato's body was found twenty minutes later by a freshman. He saw the body on the ground and stopped to help then realized that it was too late for help.

When word of Kumato's demise reached his home, the party broke up quickly. Each of the three young people left Kumato's home immediately for their own offices. They were shaken and appeared to be a little scared; at least that is what Menosee the housekeeper said to the police. But she did not know their names. They were just some of Kumato's student friends who had come to spend the evening.

The obituary said that the aged professor had died from a heart attack, and he was buried the next day. Many students were present for the funeral as well as leaders of the university. Afterward, many of the students and former students congregated in small groups of three or four. One such group met at the old teahouse where they frequented as students.

"What are we doing now?" "With whom shall we meet?" "How can we get the information that he had for us?" were the topics of conversation. The group broke up in forty-five minutes with the issues unresolved. Bukaake, who seemed to be the leader, said, "Don't do anything; don't meet with anyone until you hear from me. I'll call the next meeting of our historical society when it is safe or when I have some news for you."

CHAPTER III

Saulva, Switzerland

August 9, the day of Kumato's funeral

Molly O'Connor stretched, yawned, and rolled her long-legged body out of bed. Molly, a tall, thin blonde with rare good looks and an exquisite although thin body, surveyed the dark man in her bed.

"Molly, do you have to leave so soon? It is only 5:00 a.m. Surely you have time for at least one more embrace and we will see what else may come up." He reached for her nude body standing next to him. She spun out of his grasp and started for the bathroom.

"Not this morning, Mark. I have to be in Berlin by noon for a very important meeting with some investors from all over Europe."

Molly is a well-respected international banker at only thirty-three. Some said her good looks were why she is where she is. That, a Harvard MBA, and a command of three languages besides her native English was why she is where she is. Of course, her looks opened doors, and she understood that some doors open easier after a night of abandoned lovemaking. But, nonetheless, she was nothing if she was not good at all she did.

Molly showered, put on her makeup although she used little, and returned to the bedroom of the luxurious apartment twenty stories above downtown Saulva with a view of the lake.

Mark was still in bed. He looked hungrily at Molly but said:

"What is so important that you have to run to Berlin on a Saturday? I thought we could lounge, drink coffee, and make love most of today."

"That sounds inviting, but money is more inviting. I have been working on a big deal involving these seven players from all over Europe. They are talking about fourteen billion dollars worth of gold that they need to move from somewhere in South America to Europe. They are going to use NBD as the depository (and pay me a million), and the deal comes down in three weeks. This meeting is to put the details on it."

"Two billion dollars? That's a lot of money and a lot of gold. How can they move that much gold quietly and legally?"

"That's where I come in. They can't. It is illegal and certainly would be noted by many governments. But I have connections and know how to get it done. When this money hits the bank, I will become a senior vice president. I can never be president here, but a vice president here at NBD should get me a job as senior vice president in a large American bank, say Chase Manhattan, with a fast track to the presidency by the time I'm forty."

"Then what?"

"Then what? Then what?!"

What indeed, Molly thought. A single mother who was sometimes available had raised Molly in Lexington, Kentucky. Sometimes was when she was not in jail or busy with a man in order to pay for her habit. Molly had never had any real attention from her mother or anyone else. She never met her father. She did meet some of her mother's friends and learned at a young age what men want and when they are vulnerable to demands from a person in a position to give them what they want.

Molly left home at twelve and lived with a girlfriend. At fourteen she had moved in with an older man. It seemed her friend's mother wanted her out of the house. By the time she finished high school, she was working and had her own apartment on the run-down side of town. She received a scholarship to the University of Kentucky. She earned her BA in business in three years and her MBA in two more years.

She had started working for a regional stock brokerage house when she was in college, and by the time she finished school she was a licensed broker with a pretty good "book." She was earning $50,000 a year. In the next two years she managed to up that to $100,000. She used her knowledge, contacts, and good looks to open doors. She also learned that it did not matter which side of town you were working on, or what you were selling, men always wanted the same thing. Sometimes you could tease and sometimes you gave them what they wanted. It didn't matter because they were giving you what you wanted.

At twenty-eight she left the brokerage firms and went into personal banking. She was given a title as head cashier. While she worked for the bank, she also traded stocks and built a good portfolio for herself. She was promoted to junior vice president, and then the bank was bought out by NBD.

Molly learned Spanish while living with her mother. Admittedly it was not the kind of Spanish one used in boardrooms, but the niceties came easy. French she learned while traveling in France for three months with the president of an International Mutual Fund. Finally, German was learned from tapes after NBD bought out her bank.

With her experience and language skills, she applied for a job in the European division of NBD. Her first stop was London. She was in London for a year when NBD opened a branch in Saulva. She met for an interview with the president of the European division of NBD. This was an interview that turned into a breakfast meeting. She got the job as junior vice president, personal services, Saulva. In order to keep he job, she had to perform "personal services" for the president when he was in town.

Her personal life had been secondary to her career. Molly's sole driving force was to have enough money and power so that she could turn the tables on those who had used here. She hated men and saw them as objects to be manipulated. This, of course, did not make it easy for her to love or be loved, and while she usually had a male friend around, she had never cared for anyone. Not even Mark, whom she had been living with for the last six months.

"What do you mean, 'then what'? I will have arrived. Not bad for a poor girl from Kentucky. They will all kiss my ass. New York money, Wall Street firms, presidential candidates, and even the president will be there. No more kissing ass for me, and no more fucking some old fart that likes my tits so I can get a promotion. I will be there."

"And then what?"

"I'll be there!"

"Who will be with you, or will you be all alone?"

"Maybe you'll be there, Mark, if you are good enough."

"What do you mean, 'good enough'?"

Mark was a professional athlete, an Olympic downhill skier from the south of France. He was six three, 220 pounds of well-sculptured male body. He had the Basque dark good looks, with jet-black hair and a ruggedly handsome face.

Mark had been competing since he was twelve, and now at twenty-eight "good enough" was fighting words. He lived only to prove that not only was he good enough but he was better than anyone else. He had Olympic gold to prove that too.

"Come on over here and I'll show you good enough!"

"No, not now, but tonight when I get home, why don't you have a dinner ready with some good wine and we will see what you can do."

"That's a date. What time will you home?"

"Should be here by 9:00 if the trains are on time."

"See you then. Good luck with your gold."

Molly never kept the date.

In Berlin, seven men waited for her from noon to 2:00 p.m. before they grew anxious. They called her office but that was closed. They tried her fax and her home phone. Finally, they tried her cell phone.

"Who do you want?" a male voice answered.

"Ms. Molly O'Connor. Is this not her phone?"

"It is and she is here, but you may not speak with her."

"What do you mean? She is late for an important meeting."

"We know that. But you did not invite us and that is your mistake."

"I do not understand, Claude," the Frenchman said.

"We know what you are doing, and we want the gold. Molly will work for us if she works at all."

"That's nonsense. This has nothing to do with you."

The other men in the room were very anxious as they listened to their side of the conversation.

"Molly is not the only one that can get this done. We don't need her and we don't care who you are."

"You will care. Look out the window at the phone booth across the street from you."

All seven went to the window. There at the phone booth under the streetlight was Molly O'Connor. A man in a ski mask was holding her. As the seven looked on, the windowpane cracked. Richard Lewis, the bald, overweight American, fell to the floor with a neat hole in his forehead.

"Monsieur Claude, do you care who we are now? We know who you are, where you are, where your families are, and we can reach out and touch any of the people we have mentioned just as easily and as thoroughly as we just did Mr. Lewis.

"We will call you tomorrow at 1:30 at the place you are now and we can talk some more."

The now six men looked at one another in shock.

CHAPTER IV

Virginia

August 10, 10:30 a.m., the morning after the funeral

Charles Townsend IV is sitting in his oak-paneled office at home. His computer is on and he is talking on the phone.

"I know you need me there but it can't be helped. I need to be with my mother for a few days. Please, no more calls from the office for at least a week. If you think you need something from me, e-mail me. You have the address? I will check it regularly."

He then turned to his computer and began a conversation with an old friend of his father's in Switzerland.

"Claus, thank you for the condolence note. It is appreciated," he typed. "When was the last time you saw my father?"

Claus typed back:

"Several years ago I'm afraid. After he retired I never saw him. Before he retired I saw him little. He was not in the field."

"Did he enjoy his retirement?"

"Yes. He appeared to," Charles typed. He seemed to be busy with friends, hobbies, and some international banking. He really did not discuss his business with me. Just stuff in general comment in passing, you know."

"When was the last time he talked to you?"

"Interestingly enough, he reached me trough e-mail about once every two months or so. The last time was about ten days before his death," Claus said. "He was asking me questions about the war and what it was like afterwards. He seemed interested in what the Nazis did to control events immediately before the end of the war and what plans they had for postwar Europe once they knew the war was lost.

"I could not help him much. I was young when the war ended and did not get into the business till nearly five years after the war. I directed him to an old gentleman that trained me and is still alive. He was involved with the Nazis, Russians, some of the Allied command as well as the underground. I didn't really understand what was going on or what questions he had."

"Do you know if father followed up on that lead?"

"I think he did, but I don't know for sure."

"Can you give me his name? How can I reach him?"

"His name is Marcus Lueckeman. He lives in a Berlin suburb. He can be reached by phone, but you will have to say that I sent you. He is careful even though he has been out of the business for many years."

It was 3:00 p.m. before Charles was able to reach Mr. Lueckeman.

"Hello, I would like to speak to Herr Marcus Lueckeman."

"Who are you?"

"My name is Charles Townsend IV. I am a friend of Claus Du Blois, who gave me your number. He said you might have talked to my father Charles Townsend III in the last few weeks."

"Your father is Charles Townsend? How do I know that? What do you want from me?"

"You could call Claus. I believe you trained him in about 1950. He can tell you who I am. As far as my father goes, Claus said that he was asking questions about the Nazis and life at the end of the war. He sent him to you. Did he contact you?"

"I don't know who you are. You are a voice on the phone. I will talk to Claus and then I will contact you and we will see if you are who you say you are, and then we will talk. What is your number?"

"You can reach me though the Banc Internationale, Washington, D.C. Branch."

After the call, Charles met with his father's longtime deputy, who retired only six months ago.

"Benny, it is good to see you. Are you enjoying retirement so far?"

"I was till your father died. I will truly miss him. We would meet at least weekly and sometimes twice a week just to stay in touch and try to figure out all the mysteries that the company never let us works on. We had a good time too. Nothing like two old spies working on mysteries without any clues. We had a great time."

"Sounds interesting but maybe a little dangerous."

"No, not at all. In the first place, what we were working on was from forty years ago and had no relevance today. Secondly, no one knew we were doing anything of the kind. We were just keeping our minds alert and answering questions that have bothered us for some time.

"We even talked about writing a book or selling some of our information to anyone that might be interested. Your father mentioned the Mossad and the PLO as being possible customers. I don't think he ever talked to them but it was fun to think about it.

"It was like, you know, we were freelancing, but we had no worries. Even the data we were working with was so old no one really cared anymore."

"What was the last thing that you were playing with?"

"Your father was into Nazi gold. I think he got interested when this thing about Jews getting their families' money back from the Swiss started. He was interested in how much money was in Swiss accounts and how it got there."

"What had you done about it?"

"Nothing really, just made some initial inquires and looked at old U.S. records from right after the war."

"Do you know who else Father may have contacted about this?"

"No. I know he talked to some people in Europe. One name he mentioned was a Richard somebody. We then got on to other things, like how the Russians got the atomic bomb from us and how Hungary fell to the Russians. Things like that. He was always interested in who the players were and how they did what they did. You know, just what you would expect an old spy to be interested in."

"Thanks, Benny. Take care of yourself. I know my father thought a great deal of you. Thanks for the call."

I wonder if any of this spy business led to his death, Charles thought. Of course it did! He was murdered by a pro. Who would want him dead? Old enemies could care less about him now that he was retired. It had to be something else. Something that he knew about. Something he knew, or something he was about to know.

CHAPTER V

Saulva

August 9, evening

Mark had dinner ready and waiting at 9:00 p.m. Candles, perfumed air, and sweet music were all in place. He had spent all day preparing for a long and interesting night. He even had some Panama Red on the side table for later when they needed to catch their breath.

It was still ready at 10:00 p.m.

It was still warm at 11:00 p.m.

By 12:00 a.m., he had given up and was concerned. He called Molly's cell but received no answer. He left a message on the voice mail.

At 1:00 he tried the cell again but no answers, just the voice mail.

He called the police to see if there had been a delay in trains or a serious accident. None were reported.

At 2:00 a.m. he fell asleep.

He awoke at 8:00 a.m. and still no Molly. He tried the cell again but no use. Now he was worried this was not like Molly. In the two years they had been living together, she was never late getting home without calling. He knew that sometimes she had meetings after hours that she said advanced her career. He never asked exactly what those meetings were. But even then, he knew when she would not be home. What could he do? Who could he call on Sunday morning?

He spent the day at the gym and at the practice arena, his thoughts never far from Molly.

BOOK II: THE RUSSIANS

CHAPTER I

Kraanoyarsk, Russia

January 1, 2009

Michel Vladimir was a scientist, had been all of his life. He had showed promise as a grade school student in Odessa and had taken the science and math tests at ten. He scored well and so was directed to a special school for the sciences in eastern Ukraine. Vladimir was the son of a white Russian family that had fled Moscow during the revolution, and then Odessa during the Great Patriotic War. When the war ended, they returned to Odessa. They had three children, Michel being the baby. As the result of scoring so well on his science tests, he was now separated from his family and they only saw them occasionally. They were proud of him.

He managed to pass several other science tests during the next ten years and ended up in Moscow at the national university. He was directed to physicists and eventually into nuclear weapons. By 1975, he was the lead scientist at the nuclear facility in eastern Siberia.

Some reward, he thought, *for my abilities.* He had lost his family and never had a chance for a real relationship with a woman. Oh, the state provided "dates" for the scientists at his level. Always had, since he was in college. He would spend an evening with one of these girls, who were usually young, pretty, and scared, have a sexual encounter, and then never see her again. This was hardly a meaningful experience. In place of family, he had two very close scientist friends. They had gone through school together, were about the same age, and they had worked together for fifteen years.

Together they had gone to several conferences in the West. It was here he saw the kind of life that he wanted but never dreamed he could have. There were beautiful, fast cars, gleaming city lights, nightclubs, wonderful restaurants, and beautiful women. Over the years the troika, as they called themselves, would make about one major Western trip every two years. They visited Paris, Helsinki, San Francisco, and Chicago.

Sometime during each trip, they would bribe their watchers into letting them free for an evening or two. They would wander the streets, eat well, drink hard, and then find women that were beautiful, willing, and not scared. These trips became their reason to live.

Then the crash came. The Soviet government was over turned. They were not paid, the girls did not come, support for their research stopped, and they appeared to be forgotten. The troika would discuss their options every night over vodka.

Finally, one night Vladimir said, "If I cannot visit the West then I will live there."

"What do you mean?" Alexander said. He was a short man, a little overweight, balding, with thick glasses. "They will never let us out of Russia, nor could we afford to go."

"What are the obstacles? Let's look at this like a problem in the lab."

CHAPTER II

Kraanoyarsk, Russia

May 12, 2009

Vladimir and Alexander Yakov waited and thought about a plan. At first they considered deflecting to the highest bidder. But there was no real market. The Western powers did not need more nuclear scientists. Since the demise of the Soviet Union, Western powers needed fewer weapons, not more. China was interested, but that meant more repression and a lifestyle that was worse than they had.

It was Vladimir that met the Arab. He was drinking alone in the Astor Bar in Kraanoyarsk. That is, it passed for a bar in eastern Russia. It was dark so one could not see the dirt, had a loud jukebox, and served alcohol. The man sat next to him. After a few drinks they started to talk.

"Let me buy you a drink," the Arab said.

"Thank you. I'm drinking vodka, what else? To your health," Vladimir said as he raised the fresh glass.

"To yours," the Arab responded. "And to your country and mine."

"What country is that?" Vladimir asked.

"Azerbaijan," the Arab said with a smile.

"Why are you buying me a drink? Don't you know my people want to kill your people? How did you get here anyway?" Vladimir said, looking furtively around the room for KGB agents.

"Oh, it is safe. I have a visa. My most immediate country is Syria, and you Russians owe us so they let me in.

"Anyway, I am opposed to the war. Peace is what we need."

"Peace?" Vladimir laughed. "Peace has not helped me. It has robbed me of my livelihood. I am a nuclear scientist. A few years ago my colleagues and I were the elite in Russia. Now we are not needed, wanted, or paid."

"Well, everything brings someone good and someone evil I guess. I would think that Russia would value you since it is the strength of nuclear power that brings about the peace and maintains it. If one is not strong, one cannot maintain their land or their peace."

"Why don't you tell that to our leaders in Moscow? Then I would not have to look for work." Once more he glanced around the room and lowered his voice.

"Here, my friend, your glass is empty. Another round," the Arab called to the bartender. "A double this time."

After the liquor had been drunk and another double ordered—or was it two? Anyway, after much more liquor and a few laughs, the Arab asked:

"What did you mean looking for work?"

"Oh I am not disloyal; don't get the wrong idea. I love mother Russia and want to work for her, but she has left me. We have lost all our privileges and sometimes do not get paid. There are no supplies or equipment to carry on with the research Alexander and I were doing. We are abandoned, lost, searching for a new light to guide us, so to speak."

The Arab leaned over and whispered in Vladimir's ear, "You are the kind of man we are looking for."

"What do you mean?" Vladimir asked, his speech a little slurred from all the vodka he had consumed in the last two hours.

"Well, that depends on what you do."

"I build bombs. Nuclear bombs. Big bombs. Earth-shattering bombs," he said with a wicked smile.

"Then we could use you to build bombs for us."

"Who are us?"

"The oppressed peoples of the world. For example, say the Arab nations had weapons. They would no longer be oppressed. They could stand tall and force a solution to the problems that surround them."

"What kind of weapons?" Vladimir asked through narrowed eyes.

"Nuclear, of course," he replied.

"Do you know me?" Vladimir asked again.

"Yes, my friend, I do. You made weapons for the Soviet government and now they have forgotten you. We know how to treat our friends."

"What would you want from me? My expertise to help you build your own bombs?"

"No. We know how to build bombs. We do not have the raw material or the facilities, so having a man such as yourself would not help us much. What would help us is having a bomb, or perhaps two."

"You mean steal a bomb?"

"You do have access, do you not?"

"Well, yes, but.... How much would this be worth to you?"

"How about a ticket to anywhere in the world and a billion dollars U.S.?"

"Let me think about that," Vladimir said. "I will call you. Where can I reach you and what is your name?"

"I drink here often. We'll meet again."

Vladimir met with Alexander the next day.

"I think I have a solution to our problem, my old friend...."

"What is that?" said Alexander with a laugh. "Which problem?"

"The one where we do not get paid and are stuck here in this godforsaken city," Vladimir said with a sneer.

"What if we moved to New York or London or Paris and lived like kings? Beautiful women, fine wine, good food, and the best entertainment?" Now Vladimir was smiling broadly.

"You have been dreaming again, my friend," Alex said.

"No, not exactly," Vladimir said.

"I met a man in the bar last night who offered a ticket to anywhere in the world and one billion dollars for our services."

"You mean go make bombs for them?"

"No. *Steal* bombs for them."

"Steal bombs? How would we do that?" Alex was shocked.

"I don't know but I bet we could think of a way for that much incentive."

CHAPTER III

Astro Bar, Kraanoyarsk, Russia

May 19, 2009

Vladimir had given much thought to what he could do with the money the Arab had promised him. Alex had been interested and probably would do whatever Vladimir thought was best. But should he do this?

As he sat thinking into his vodka, the Arab sat down next to him.

"A shot of vodka for your thoughts," he laughed.

Surprised, Vladimir looked up and caught his breath.

"I thought you were a dream," he said.

"Perhaps the ultimate dream for you, my friend."

"Or my worst nightmare," Vladimir said with a sarcastic smile.

"Come, come, my friend," the Arab said cheerfully. "You have needs, we have needs. You have what we want, and we can give you what you want. What could be a better arrangement than that?"

"Treason is punishable by death. If I were dead, I could not enjoy the proceeds of my labor, now could I?" Vladimir said, looking into his vodka.

"Let me tell you, money is no object to us. You can have all you want." The Arab leaned in and whispered in Vladimir's ear.

Vladimir thought for a moment and then ordered another vodka. "I don't even know what to ask for such a thing."

"Then let me make you an offer.... My people will pay you two billion U.S. dollars for two devices ready to use. We will pay in any currency anywhere in the world."

That sobered Vladimir up. He blinked his eyes and said, "Are you serious?

"Very," the Arab said. "Isn't that enough?"

"I think that would do fine. Let me speak with my friend and see if we can develop a plan to get the merchandise to you, and ourselves into the West so we can enjoy the last years of our lives."

"Good, good. You think about it and we'll talk again."

CHAPTER IV

Kraanoyarsk, Russia

July 2009

Vladimir and Alex would walk the cold streets of Krasnoyarsk as they discussed their plan. The Arab-looking gentleman had agreed to their terms of 1.5 billion dollars for two explosive devices.

"The problems as I see them," Alex said in deep thought, "are: one, how to make the device so it can be transported; two, how to detonate the device when we want to; and three, how do we transport it? How do we get it out of Russia?"

"Let's take these problems one at a time. Like we do in the lab." Vladimir looked around as he spoke.

"First of all, we know how to build a device; we just have not been responsible for transportation. I assume we assemble the main explosive device minus one ingredient, which is added when we want to arm the device. That way it can travel. After all, that is how the government does it in bombers, etc."

"Okay, I guess that is right. We could a make thirty-pound device that when exploded would have a ten-megaton yield. We could leave out the plutonium, but make a spot for it to be inserted when they are ready to arm it."

"Okay, that would solve the first problem," Vladimir said. "Now for the second. We could leave that up to the buyer."

"No, I think that if we make it, we should be able to tell the buyer how to detonate it," Alex said firmly.

"Okay, then all we need is an explosive device to drive into the plutonium to set it off." Vladimir was dismissive.

"Plastique could do that. We shape the bomb, leaving a place for the plutonium. We then place a charge of plastique around the plutonium. We explode it with a timer, and then kaboom!" Alex smiled and then laughed.

"We can transport it in two lead-lined crates. Shipments go out of here all the time. We simply address one for a destination of our choosing."

"Where would that be?" asked Alex.

"The Black Sea is the closest point," Vladimir said thoughtfully.

"Yes, but that is too close and too guarded. We need a more open port with international movement."

"How about Gdansk? We could ship the crates to Gdansk. That would not raise eyebrows because we already send shipments there. We then meet the shipment and redirect it to a warehouse storage unit and tell the buyers where to pick it up. They can ship it themselves from there."

"That sounds good, but how can we meet it?" questioned Alex.

"We have some time off coming. We could get permission to go to Poland. We can tell them it is for a little vacation; you know, see the sights, meet some women. I think we can sell that to the chief security man here."

"That seems like a workable project," said Alex. "Now, what do we do with the money and how to we get it and how do we get out of Russia? That's the hard part. We have built bombs before but not smuggled money."

"I have been reading on the Internet about banking and moving money. What we need to do is open a savings account with a bank in Gdansk and one in Hungary. You are from there, right?" asked Vladimir.

"Yeah."

"Okay, we open an account in Gdansk and have the Arabs put the money into that account. We then move it from there to our bank in Hungary. From there we move it to a Western bank."

"Which one?"

"There is one bank in Liechtenstein that we can open an account with online without ever having to go in person. That is the one. We say we are businesspeople from Hungary and we need to transfer money from Vienna to Western Europe for our use. We then move small amounts periodically until the big one comes." Vladimir made it sound easy.

"Okay, who is going to do what?" asked Alex.

"Let's just think about this for a few weeks. And then talk about it again."

CHAPTER V

Kraanoyarsk, Russia

Late July 2009

At their next meeting, two weeks later, this time in a corner booth of the Mushroom Bar, they talked over vodka.

"I have been in touch with my sister in Budapest," Alex spoke in a low voice. "She gave me the name of a bank there. I have put in for my vacation to visit her. I think my request will be granted, and I will travel to Budapest and open an account. I will tell them that we will be doing some international wire transfers and get that all set up."

"Good," said Vladimir, glancing about. "I have the name of the bank in Liechtenstein. But I have to have a secure or at least non-traceable phone line to call and set it up."

"There are none of those in this town," Alex said annoyed.

"I know but I think that I can arrange to travel with some engineers from here to Poland. I believe they are going to a conference of some sort in Warsaw. There I can get a safe line to open an account in

Liechtenstein. I may even be able to get to Gdansk to open an account with a bank there."

"When will you know?"

"In about two weeks I should think. I am calling in favors and asking to go along as a nuclear specialist."

Once more the men met for a long walk, ending at the Mushroom Bar to discuss their plans. "I will be going to Budapest on the tenth of this month," Alex said.

"I also will be going to Poland in six weeks to set things up there."

"I think we need to talk with our Arab friend to see about some up-front money. Say 100,000 U.S. dollars. That will give you and I both some money to work with. However, we will need to be careful since no one would believe we came by the money honestly," Vladimir said.

The next week, Vladimir went to the Astro Bar on Main Street, where he had met the Arab. He had to go six nights, but on the seventh night the Arab was there. Vladimir did not approach him but waited at the far end of the bar, drinking his vodka and cursing life with the bartender. Finally around 1:00 a.m., the Arab looked to the end of the bar and offered to buy the bartender and Vladimir a drink.

"Make mine vodka," said Vladimir.

The bartender also took vodka and thanked the Arab.

The Arab then moved down to Vladimir and bought him another one. They appeared to be two drinkers sharing drinks as the morning wore on.

Finally the Arab said, "Well, are you going to be able to deliver?"

"I think so, but we will need two billion dollars U.S. and 100,000 dollars up front within the next ten days."

The Arab smiled and said, "How do I know you can and will do it?"

"Give me a way to contact you, where we can talk. I'll explain what we are going to do. Bring the money or there is no deal."

The Arab smiled wryly and said, "When you want to meet me, go to the central post office. Inside the door next to the post boxes is a writing table. Stop there. Fill out an address form with your name and address on it and then tear it up like you made a mistake or changed your mind. I will contact you.

"As for the next meeting, there is a bar and restaurant on the south side of town. It is called the Stalin Inn. I'll meet you there at midnight three days from now."

Three days later, Vladimir and Alex were in a borrowed car, sitting in front of the Stalin Inn.

"Should we go in?" Alex said.

"I don't know. It could be a trap. What do you think?"

"If it is a trap, we have come far enough to finish our days as guests of the former Union of Soviet Socialist Republics as it is. They could pick us up anytime with what we have said to the Arab."

"I guess you're right. Let's go."

The two men walked in and took a seat at a table. They ordered vodka and borscht.

When they had finished their soup, it was nearly 1:00 a.m. The Arab appeared at their table and said, "Follow me one at a time." He then walked to the back by the restrooms and opened a door marked maintenance.

Vladimir followed. Then Alex.

The door opened into a small, fifteen by fifteen room lit by a single bulb. In the center was a table with three chairs around it. On the table were two bottles of vodka, caviar bread, and sausages.

The Arab said, "Sit and eat, my friends, drink and then we talk." By 2:00 a.m. they had finished eating. The Arab said, "Now tell me, what are you going to do and how are you going to do It?"

Vladimir explained their plan.

The Arab nodded, smiled, and said, "Yes, I think it might work. It just might work. Now, how much will you sell these items for?"

"Seventy-five million each," Vladimir said in a steady voice, "and nothing less. This is a great risk for our families and us."

"Okay," said the Arab, "I can do that. What is your timetable?"

"It will take about four months, say five, to have the packages in Gdansk and ready for your pick-up."

"Okay, that is satisfactory," the Arab nodded again.

He walked to the back of the room and came forward with a briefcase. He set it on the table and opened it.

"Here is what you requested," he said with a smile. Then the smile left his face and he said calmly and slowly, "You know, if you leave here with this money, you cannot change your mind, you cannot back out; you either deliver or I will kill you very slowly.

"You understand?" The Arab looked deep into Vladimir's eyes, then Alex's.

Vladimir and Alex looked at each other then at the Arab. Vladimir spoke.

"We understand and we will deliver." He closed the case, picked it up, and they left. They got home around 3:00 a.m.

CHAPTER VI

Kraanoyarsk, Russia

August 2009

At first the late hours drew no notice. Work was slow and drinking was a way of life, but the late nights eventually began to draw the attention of the Nuclear Arms Security. It was their job to keep an eye on the scientists that worked in Bomb City. Vladimir and Alex had a history of going out together and staying out. Even when in Western countries they did this and there had never been a problem. But there was a pattern to what they had been doing the last three months. After all, how much nightlife existed in this town?

Nicole was the captain in charge of base security and he felt he needed to report this to his superior, Major Romanoff.

"So, Captain, you think you see a pattern with these two, no?"

"Yes, I do. They are always out away from Bomb City on their own till very late at night."

"What do you think they are doing?"

"I don't know. I was trained to watch for patterns. Here is a pattern."

"You are aware that they have a history of this and there has never been any hint of a problem."

"Yes."

"There is a history of women."

"Yes, I read their dossier."

"This is probably what this is. Tell you what to do. Have them followed discreetly and see what you learn. I'll bet you'll learn the address of one or more attractive ladies. If that is the case, be sure to report it to me."

"Yes, sir. I'll put two of my best men on this."

So Alex and Vladimir each had a tail assigned to them.

The tails ended up outside of the Explosion Bar one night and the Stalingrad Inn the next and so on. Their reports were boring until a certain Arab was noticed at the same bars as Alex and Vladimir.

Meanwhile, suspecting nothing, they went about their plans to set up their bank accounts.

Alex visited his sister in Budapest without incident.

He made a trip one afternoon to the Hungary Peoples Bank and opened an account with 10,000 U.S. dollars.

The use of the dollars was not unusual to the banker since they traded in U.S. currency all the time. There was a strong black market in Hungary, and U.S. dollars were what were usually used. Ten thousand seemed a little high, but this was a high-ranking scientist and he could come by his money one way or another.

As Alex was leaving the bank, Lieutenant Obrestski of the GRU was demanding to see the manager.

"Alex Yakov just was here?"

"Yes."

"What did he do or want here?"

"He opened an account." The banker was going to give away no more information then he had to.

"What kind of account?"

"A savings account. He said he wanted to start something for his retirement."

"He does not live here," the lieutenant said harshly.

"No, but some of his family does," the banker said. "He told me that when he retired, it would be to Budapest, if that were possible at the time. Otherwise, he would have the money sent to where he would be living."

"How much was the account for?"

"Fifty thousand Hungarian dollars."

"That seems large."

"Not really. He said it was his savings so far."

"Okay, I'll report your cooperation. As you may know, this man is a scientist in the special branch. As such, he is of national importance. You will keep me advised of any unusual activity in this account, yes?"

"Of course, Lieutenant. I'll put your card in the file, and if anything unusual happens to this account I'll let you know."

"Thank you."

CHAPTER VII

Warsaw/Gdansk, Poland

August 2009

The report was made regarding Alex's trip and his savings account. The report was placed in Alex's dossier and the watch on him was continued.

Vladimir made his trip to Warsaw with the engineers. He attended all the sessions and was an important speaker for one of them. The lieutenant assigned to him reported on this and also reported that one day he was sick and did not leave his room.

On that day, Vladimir had slipped out the back after midnight. He caught a ride with an army acquaintance from Bomb City a few years ago. They went to Gdansk, arriving there shortly after dawn. Vladimir paid all expenses and, after buying breakfast, asked to borrow the vehicle. Igor was reluctant, but when Vladimir said that he would drop him at a local brothel and pay all the bills for as long as he was gone, Igor said yes.

Vladimir then went to the Narodowy Bank Polski (National Bank of Poland) where he opened a savings account with 20,000 U.S. dollars. This was less unusual in Gdansk, a port city, where there was not only a black market but also drug syndicates and other kinds of smuggling going on, on a large scale.

After leaving the bank, he went down to the docks near the Gdansk shipyards. The yards are but a shadow of what they were thirty years ago. Now where once great ships were constructed there are warehouses. Perfect for Vladimir. He found a storage warehouse close to the docks, but not too close, so as to keep the cost down and to be less conspicuous. He rented a space here for 10,000 dollars for one year. He explained that he was going to start a shipping business and would have cargo stored here until his shipper would pick it up.

This was all in a day's work on the docks and so no questions were asked.

Vladimir was back at the brothel by 1:00 p.m. When he went inside to find Igor, he noticed the attentive ladies, and so spent a few hours there himself. For a few dollars more, Vladimir was allowed the use of a secure line. He called the Clariden Bank of Liechtenstein.

"Hello?" Vladimir said in thick English.

"May I help you?" the professional female voice said.

"I would like to open an account. I am a Russian citizen living in Moscow."

"I will transfer you to Mr. Terry David. He handles accounts from your country."

"This is David." A male's voice this time, in flawless Russian. "How can I help you?"

"I would like to open an account."

"We can do that. How much do you ant to deposit?"

"Eventually several million. Right now I want to open the account and have the money transferred by wire from Russia or Hungary in a few days. Is that possible?"

"Yes, I think we can do that." David liked the idea of a several-million-dollar account.

"I will assign you a number for your account and a PIN number to allow you access to the account. You will need to keep a close eye on these numbers since if someone has them, they can access the account and do what they will.

"Your account number is 32969 and your PIN is 32012581. Now, since I have not met you, you will need to give me something that I can use to identify you. What would that be?"

"Ask me the name of the girl with green eyes in New York City."

"And what is her name?"

"Aleetha Wilhelm."

"Okay, this account is open for thirty days. If there is no deposit by that time, the account closes."

Igor and Vladimir were back in Warsaw a little before dawn the next day. At the conference the next day, he looked a bit pale and maybe sleepy, but Lieutenant Evanoff put this up to the sickness the day before and so put nothing suspicious in his report.

Evanoff's report was filed in Vladimir's dossier and noted.

CHAPTER VIII

Kraanoyarsk, Russia

August 2009

Upon their return from their trips, the bar rounds continued. Alex and Vladimir met again in the Stalin Inn and talked about their successes.

"All is in place. We have two accounts now with enough funds to operate. Now we will need to place money in the account in Liechtenstein. I will transfer $5,000 to your account in Budapest and then we will move that money to Liechtenstein."

"Now we need to start hiding little bits of uranium and other bomb material so we can build the bomb."

Alex said, "I have taken care of that. There is an old locker that is not in use in the lab. It had been used to store uranium and whatever else when we were making more product than we are now. It is closed but not sealed, but no one has reason to look in there. I have made it secure for radioactive materials, and so we can begin tomorrow. We should take only small amounts that we can account for as burned up or otherwise used in production."

"Great. We start tomorrow."

That night Vladimir went online and checked his account in Liechtenstein. The money was transferred the next day from Gdansk to Budapest and then to Liechtenstein. The next night he received confirmation via e-mail.

"That was easy," he told Alex. "It went through without a hitch."

In Budapest, George Bacha, the bank manager, looked at the day's transactions and saw the movement of money into and out of Alex's account. He noticed that the money had been moved to Western Europe.

If Mr. Yakov is putting money aside, he must be planning on retiring in the West, he mused. *I am supposed to notify Lieutenant Romanoff of transactions like this. But I don't like Russians, and besides, I bet Mr. Yakov will pay well to have his secret kept.*

He placed a call to Catherine Schnoki, Alex's sister.

"Mrs. Schnoki, this is George Bacha at your bank."

"Yes?"

"Your brother Alexander Yakov opened an account with us a few weeks ago."

"Yes?"

"Something as come up and there is a small problem. Can you have him contact me? Here is my number. I know he works in top-secret areas. Tell him this is very personal and he should be sure he is on a line where he can talk when he calls me."

"Okay." She said a bit worried. "I'll tell him. Is there anything I can do?"

"No, no, this is a small matter but I do need to talk to him."

"I will let him know."

That night Catherine called Alex at home until the early morning hours. Finally she got him.

"Alex, this is Catharine."

"Yes, is there anything wrong?"

"Not with me, but our banker wants to talk to you."

"What about?"

"He did not say. He did say he needs to talk to only you, if you know what I mean."

"Yes, I will call him tomorrow. Thanks for calling me. Is all well with you, Chas, and the girls?"

"Yes, all is fine. It was good to see you last month. We look forward to your next trip."

"I do too but it will be some time before I can get another vacation. Give my love to the girls."

"Good night, Alex."

"Good night, Catherine."

The next night Alex went to the Stalin Inn and asked if he could place a call to Hungary. It was early morning here and would be late afternoon in Budapest.

"George Bacha please," he said when the phone was answered.

"This is Mr. Bacha," the voice said.

"Alexander Yakov here. You wanted to talk to me?"

"Yes, I did. Is this a private line?"

"It is the best I can get in this city."

"I guess it will have to do. Shortly after you opened your account with us, a lieutenant of the GRU came in and asked about the account. I told him as little as I could. He demanded that I keep him informed of any unusual activity in the account. Last week, as I'm sure you are aware, there was such an activity."

"Go on," Alex said, his heart sinking and his pulse rising.

"I could care less what my customers do with their accounts, but to violate an order from the GRU could cause trouble for me, if you know what I mean."

"Yes. What do you want?"

"You can make a deposit to this account of a sum similar to your last transaction tomorrow for my trouble. Otherwise, I will have to be a good citizen. Do you understand me?"

"Yes, I do. It will be done."

"Wonderful. I enjoy having you as a customer."

Later that night, Alex was drinking with Vladimir.

"So this Bacha fellow called me, and you need to transfer $5,000 to his account tomorrow or he reports to the GRU what is going on."

"I will do that online before I go to bed tonight. But that means one, you are being followed, and two, this blackmail will take a lot of our money over time. We need to do something about both."

"Why do you think they are following us?"

"I think it is our hours. They want to know what we are doing, or it could be just a routine checkup on us, or it could be a routine tail because you were out of the country."

"Where you followed in Poland?"

"I don't think so, but I was very careful about how I went to Gdansk since that was not authorized. If I had been followed, they would have arrested me by now for that side trip."

"Okay, how do we find out? What do we do?"

"I don't know. This is new to me too. I thought it had been too easy. One way is to stop using that bank."

"We need a bank like that to move money west, plus I cannot get another visa to go out of the country for nearly a year."

"Okay, so we will have to use that bank. I wonder if our Arab friend could help us. He seems knowledgeable on this sort of endeavor."

The next day Vladimir went to the post office and tore up his pieces of paper.

He found in his mailbox in the lab a note that said, "Explosion 11:00 p.m."

As soon as he had read the note, Vladimir went to the bathroom, tore it to pieces, and flushed the pieces down two different toilets.

At 11:00 p.m., Vladimer and Alex were at the Explosion Bar. The Arab came in, bought everyone in the room a drink, and sat down next to the scientists. The bartender managed somehow to keep all the other patrons away from their end of the bar as they talked.

Valimer spoke first. "The good news is that we are on schedule for making the product. The bad news is we are being followed and blackmailed."

"Already?" the Arab smiled. "Is this by the same person?"

"No," Alex said. "My banker in Budapest is blackmailing me and the GRU has followed us."

"Why are they following you?"

"We are not sure. It may be routine. They do that to all of us. Alex was out of the country, so it would be logical that he would be followed."

"Very well. I will look into this GRU thing. As for the balckmail, give me what you have on your banker and we will take care of the matter."

"How will you to that?" Alex asked.

"None of your business," the Arab said. "We will speak again soon. Keep up the good work. We are anxious for the product."

Two days later, George Bacha was leaving the bank late after a client had demanded an early-evening meeting. As he crossed the street on the way to his car, a black Mercedes came around the corner at a high rate of speed. He was thrown nearly half a block by the impact. The ambulance that picked him up never arrived at the hospital. A month later, his body was found in the river. There was not much left after a month in the Danube. Police spectulated that he had fallen in and drowned. The brusies and broken bones were thought to have been from the fall and the time in the water. There was not a lot to go on.

Alex did not not get another call from George Bacha.

CHAPTER IX

Major Romanoff had the "Arab" investigated and found that he was associated with the PLO. He had been in Russia for fifteen years and was considered a friend of the Union. The Arab's role in the past had been to be a conduit of information from the Arab world to the Russians on matters of some sensitivity. He had played a role in the hostages that had been taken in Iran, and now was supplying information to various elements of what was left of the Russian security forces on the Chechen rebels and other Moslem elements in the Russian world.

Why would he be talking with two scientists? Was he? Or was it a coincidence that he had been in the same bars as his men? The major decided to put a tail on the Arab and see what he could find out. Since this man is an operative, it would have to be handled with some care. The major selected two men, William Frownfelter and Ivan Herewaldt. Both men were fourth-generation Russians from the Germans who had immigrated to northern Russia at the Czar's invitation before 1912.

They proceeded to watch the Arab. He went from his apartment to meet various women. He ate in the best restaurants available. He spent a lot of nights in various bars, all without pattern. He also met with some army generals. He made trips out of the country to Syria, Lebanon, and Iran. Some of the bars he was in were the same ones that Vladimir and Alex were in, but there seemed to be no clear connection.

Ivan reported these facts to Major Romanoff. He read it carefully. "Did he spot you?"

"No, sir. Or at least if he did, he gave no indication that he did."

"He seems to be an interesting person. Let's continue to watch this man. I don't like him hanging around my scientists. Who knows what he is up to?"

After Ivan had left, the major received a visitor—the Arab himself!

"Good morning, Major."

Startled, Romanoff looked up. "Who are you and how did you get in here?"

"You know who I am. You have been following me for the last month."

"How?"

"Don't bother asking how. You should know that I am connected and that I am a friend of Russia. It is not friendly to spy on friends. In two minutes, your commanding general will call. He will tell you personally to stop following me. I expect you to follow his orders or two things will happen. The first is you will be reassigned to someplace cold and less nice then this town. Secondly, I will kill Frownfelter and Herewaldt. Do you understand?"

Romanoff was too shocked to answer. He simply nodded, and the Arab left. Two minutes later, Romanoff's phone rang. It was his commanding officer.

With the spies off their backs, Alex and Vladimir proceeded quickly with their work. It was not hard to obtain the plutonium a small amount at a time, and soon they had enough to make the bombs. And make the bombs they did. By August 1, two bombs were ready to be transported.

Vladimir arranged to have them placed in a shipment of military supplies being sent to Warsaw via Gdansk. The shipping date was set for Oct 15. The hard part was to be in Gdansk and arranging to have his boxes moved from the supply ship to his private storage bin in the Gdansk harbor.

Vladimir went to his boss of many years.

"Comrade, I need to ask you a favor."

"What is it?" Comrade Yelstov snapped. Yelstov was a man of nearly sixty-five, tall, with patches of gray hair around the edges of his skull. He had been in the nuclear weapons facility since the early sixties. He was tired of this job and tired of these gifted scientists who also whined to him about their problems.

"I would like to have a few days to go to Gdansk."

"You would need a pass for the time off and a visa for Gdansk."

"Yes, that is true, but you could arrange both for me."

"I could, but why should I? You really do not have time coming, and why would you want to go to Gdansk?"

"I have been writing to a girl there through my computer. You know, e-mail? She thinks she is in love with me and she is beautiful. I would like to have some time to get to know her better, if you know what I mean."

"Huh," Yelstov said, "aren't you getting a little old to be chasing pussy around the world?"

"Old but not dead. Can't you help me?"

"Maybe. What's in it for me?"

"Well, how about 500 rubles?"

"Where did you get that much money plus the money for a trip to Poland?" he said with his eyes narrowing.

"I have been saving up my rubles and playing some cards at the bars with a little luck."

"Five hundred rubles, huh? When do you want to go?"

"Around the middle of October. I thought I could catch a ride with the supply train leaving here then. It goes to Gdansk to unload, and I could meet sweet Abaya for a week. I would need a two-week leave."

"Okay, I will do this for you, but just this once. I will have the papers ready in thirty days."

Things did not go well for the train so that between supplies not being ready and various scheduling problems, the train did not go until January 15. Vladimir arrived in Gdansk January 21.

The ship, the *Red Star*, was to be in port three days. One day was for unloading.

Vladimir got to know the boson in charge of loading and unloading the ship during the cruise. The first night in port Vladimir went with Gregory Petronisky on a night on the town. They started in the bars on the waterfront then moved inland. They ended up at a high-priced brothel. Here the girls were beautiful, clean, willing to do whatever they were asked, and expensive. Vladimir paid for everything.

Gregory and Vladimir returned to the ship just after dawn arm in arm. They were buddies now.

Gregory had never had a night like that one. Drinking and bars yes. Whores? Yes, but not whores do not like these nor drinking like this. Gregory was raised in Murmesk. His father was a seaman, but his mother did not know his name. His mother worked in the shipyards doing clerking work. In order to keep her job, she had to satisfy her boss on a regular basis. For fun she hung out with sailors. They usually left her gifts of rubles when they went back to the sea. In Gregory's case, this sailor left more than rubles, but she had no idea who he was.

Gregory left school when he was thirteen, lied about his age, and went to sea. He had been at sea now for twenty-five years. He was always short of money, thirsty, and horny. Vladimir had met all his needs in a single night.

The unloading began at 11:00 a.m. Before Gregory appeared on the loading bridge, Vladimir took him aside.

"My friend," he said quietly, "did you enjoy last night?"

"I did very much," he said with a sly grin.

Vladimir returned the smile and said, "Maybe we can do that again tonight."

Gregory responded, "That blonde Samantha was beautiful and there are some things I would like to try tonight."

"Of course we can, but I need a favor and I will pay for it as well," Vladimir said with a wink.

"What is it?" Gregory asked.

"I have two boxes on this ship that need to be offloaded and placed on that transport sledge on the south side of the ship. When you unload those boxes, simply direct the men to place them there. I will need two men to push the sledge for me to a storage unit I rent across the street. I will pay you one thousand American dollars for the favor plus arrange another nice time tonight."

Gregory thought for a minute and then said, "Samantha and a thousand U.S. dollars. My friend, you have a deal."

By 4:00 p.m., the bombs were safety placed in storage, ready to be picked up by the friends of the Arab.

BOOK III: THE ARABS

CHAPTER I

Berlin

August 8, 2009

Joseph Farok was told to check the tap on Marcus Lueckemann's phone. He did not know why. Lesser operatives than he did that sort of thing. Besides, this tap was a waste of time. Lueckemann was too old, and his contacts were long since dead or had become more legend than reality. But Joe obeyed orders. That he had learned along time ago.

Joe was born to parents who were successful, middle-class Arabs. They lived outside of Amman and generally supported the king, Hussein. They also supported the PLO, who had many armed insurgents based in Jordan. When what the PLO called Black September came, they were classified with the PLO and chased from their home. This they blamed on the Jews more than Hussein.

They then moved to Lebanon and set up a family export business in southern Lebanon, once again near the PLO camps. Joe was born in the middle of this transitional time. When the Middle East exploded again, the Farok's lost more than their home.

First the Israelis, the hated Jews, bombed their home. This killed the two female siblings of Joe's, who was now five, and gravely injured his mother. Joe's father's business was destroyed. Then the Jews came in person. Joe watched his father be shot like a dog while he pleaded with a Jewish captain to allow him time to move his injured wife.

Joe was taken to the camps where the PLO families were being herded together. He was found by a distant relative and taken with them to Libya. Here he was raised to hate Jews and most foreigners who helped them steal his land and kill his family. When Joe was twelve, he joined the PLO and stared training as a fighter.

Two things happened while in the training camps. The first was that he was taught strict obedience to all orders. When he was fourteen, he was ordered to observe the rape of a young Jewish girl that the PLO had captured on a raid of a Jewish fishing village. Joe had turned away and tried to leave the painful sight. He was beaten severely, tied to a tree, and forced to watch not only her rape but also her death by slow strangulation as she cried for her mother. He was then beaten again and told that if he disobeyed again the PLO leaders would do what they had done to this Jewish girl to his female family members before his eyes. This Joe believed and he never disobeyed an order again.

The second thing was when he was fifteen he was identified as having potential for undercover work. His good looks and easy style caught the eye of

Maria, the leader of the camp. After having sex with him (his first such encounter) she had him placed in Sand Hurst near London. Here he was taught English, French, and Spanish (later he was to learn Russian). He was sent to an English finishing school and on to Cambridge, where he studied international law. After graduation, he was assigned as a junior partner to a law firm in Berlin. He was now thirty-two.

He had been working with the law firm of Khouri, Khouri and Lazaar since then. He had a good wardrobe, an upscale apartment in Berlin's fashionable side, and drove a beautiful Mercedes 500SL. To all eyes he was a successful Western Arab.

However, unknown to the rest of the world, he had become one of the PLO's most trusted agents. He had served as a courier of documents, a facilitator for the several freedom-fighter bombings against Western interests, and had a small role in the bombing of Pam Am Flight 109.

Joe had no love interest but had several women that thought he did. He had women in New York, London, Paris, Berlin, and Rome. All of these women were deeply in love with Joe and believed that he was with them; they also were all very well placed in their communities. Janet in New York was the private secretary of the U.S. ambassador to the United Nations. Jennifer was a cabinet minister in the French government of Renee de Gaulle. Elizabeth, in London, was a well-placed and well-connected stockbroker on the London Exchange. Gretchen, in Berlin, was the head of the German transportation administration and controlled all travel in the country by air, train, or sea. Finally, Rachel, in Rome, was the secretary to the Italian secret police and as such had access to all plans and documents that existed in Italy. All of these women and been carefully chosen and groomed to serve Joe's needs both personally and professionally and all of them lived to be asked to meet a need that Joe might have.

Checking the tap on Lueckemann was time consuming. First, he went to a safe house where the taps were transcribed. Each day the taps were filed by day and then at the end of the month digitized for further storage. Joe had been told to monitor personally the tapes of the last three months. This would take at least a week. So he settled in and started listening. What he was listening for was not clear. As the tapes played out and the days as well as weeks went by, Joe noticed that there were a number of calls from a professor from Japan. He was asking Lueckemann about shipments of Nazi gold. Now this was of little interest to Joe, but after the fifth conversation he began to pay attention.

It seemed that this professor was interested at first in how the Nazis moved their gold from Germany to neutral ports and then bought war supplies. As the conversations went on, the general questions were narrowed to specific shipments and then to one particular shipment. This was shipment number 213 leaving Switzerland in February of '45. As the conversations got more detailed, Lueckemann seemed less willing to talk about it. Finally, he refused and said he would only talk about it in a face-to-face meeting. A date was arranged for what was now next week.

CHAPTER II

Berlin

August 10, 2009

Joe called George Saladin in Cypress. George was his control.

"George, I have been listening to those tapes you wanted me to review. There is nothing interesting expect a professor from Japan has been asking Lueckemann about Nazi gold shipments from the war. There were several conversations, and as they got more specific Lueckemann refused to talk about them on the phone. He set up a meeting for lunch at a biergarten in the south end of Berlin for next week. I think it would be worthwhile to have a couple of our people listen in."

"Okay, you know who to work with, correct? Report back to me what you hear."

Saladin was a large man. Dark skin, droopy eyelids, and a cold stare. He had been in charge of all PLO agents in Europe for the last ten years. The

Mossad and the CIA had no idea who he was, he was in such deep cover.

Shortly after the call from Joe, Saladin received a cablegram from an agent in Eastern Europe. The cable read:

I have a contact in Russia that can make available to us a ten-megaton nuclear bomb. He said he will sell it to us for one and a half billion U.S. dollars delivered to a Swiss bank account. Can we use such a thing?

George smiled and placed a call on a secure line to the basement of a house in the Gaza Strip

He spoke to the man himself and related the offer.

"I know we can use it," the man said with a toothy grin. "I also think that it will be very hard to get the money, what with peace talks, the CIA, and world pressure shutting down our traditional funding sources. That much money would cause a stir. However, I feel we need to follow up on this. Have your man get more details, put together a team to create an operational plan, and we will see what Allah has in mind for us."

"Very good, sir. When do you want a report?"

"Two weeks should do very well."

George returned the cablegram to Eastern Europe and instructed the agent to dicker on the price and give him the exact details as to how it could be used and how and where it would be turned over to them.

He then called his three most trusted aides to a small meeting deep in the third basement of the safe house.

George started by stating what had been presented to him from Eastern Europe.

C. Albert Britt, a thin man of thirty-eight years, a bushy mustache, and eyes of stone, said:

"This is what we have been waiting for. If we could get two such bombs, we could use one for a demonstration and one to get what we demand from the Jews and their allies. We could say 'you have thirty days to create a free Palestine or we blow up a major city.'"

Eli, a much older man from the military camps in Libya, was a bit more restrained. "This has much potential, but how will we get the weapon? How can we physically detonate it? We do not have that much money, so how shall we get it? These appear to be reasonable questions to which we need the answers."

George said: "Our operatives will know how to transport the weapon and how to use it. We need to tell them where to plant it. As for the money, I think we can get that too."

"How can we get that much money? Libya barely gives us enough to keep our training camps open, and they will not support any operations from their territory anymore. The oil sheiks also only give us token sums since the U.S. defeated Baghdad. That defeat also means that Bin Laden, while wanting to help, does not have significant funds to give us either. Syria will help but only very quietly. We will need more than just a few million dollars. We will need military support to procure this weapon and use it."

"But we cannot let this opportunity pass us by!" Britt exclaimed. "This is what we have been waiting for. We can strike hard against our enemies and gain what we have been fighting for since 1948. At last, victory!"

"I too want victory, but Eli is right in what we need to consider," George said while stroking his beard. "Allow me to have the operative's report ready in two weeks. We will need to meet again at that time. However, while we are here, let's assume that we have this weapon. What do we do with it?"

Britt said, "I have already addressed that. We get two. We place them in a major Western city. We issue the ultimate demand: Here is the land we want by a given date. If the Jews and their friends do not respond positively by that date, we destroy one of the cities and then give them a new deadline. They will comply with that one."

"That has merit, my young friend, but what cities? If we destroy a city in Palestine, it will hurt us and our people. So we must go west, but how will that hurt the false state of Israel?"

"Where are there more Jews then in Palestine?" Britt said.

"New York," answered George.

"That is where the first one goes."

"The second?" asked Eli.

"Perhaps Tel Aviv or Washington or London," Britt said.

"I think it would need to be something that will destroy the Jewish state if they fail to comply."

"Let's think about this and discuss it further. Also we need to discuss the money. In two weeks from today, we will meet again."

CHAPTER III

Cypress

August 24, 2009

The same leaders meet again in the safe house.

George reported that in fact for 1.5 billion they could get two bombs, one rather small, in the ten-megaton range, and the other in the 100-megaton range. "The bombs would be delivered by diplomatic means to the city in which we want them. We will need to get them from the embassy to the site and give the third-party embassy people warning of the denotation. They can be set off by a small plastique blast that any of our trained people can use."

"So it can be done," Britt said.

"But which cities, and where do we get two billion dollars for a single operation?"

"Not a single operation," said Britt. "The Operation."

"I know where we can get the money," George said. "Our operatives in Berlin have discovered that there exists about 14.8 billion dollars worth of former Nazi gold. A professor from Japan has been meeting an old Nazi named Lueckemann. The professor believes that this gold exists and can be located. All we need to do is find the gold before this Nipponese does, and we have what we need."

"How feasible is this, and is it real?" Eli asked.

"Our agents believe that is real and that within a few days, maybe a few months, we will know where it is. All we need do then is go get it," George said.

"Okay, Arafat has agreed to the plan and has prayerfully picked the summit meeting scheduled between the U.S. president and the Jew leader in Bermuda for the demonstration bomb. This will be in February of 2010. While the nations are reeling from the loss of their leadership, we target New York for the second one. Since we have two sizes, he feels New York should get the big one."

"Allah be praised! This is the day we have prayed for," said Eli. "When can we put this in motion?"

"We start today," said George. "We have a target date of February 3 for the first bomb, one year from now. The day the music will stop in New York City."

"What about the money?" Eli asked.

George smiled and said, "Give me two weeks and we will know if we can get it from the Nazis. Surely they would want us to have it for this endeavor."

When the other two had left, George placed a call on a secure line to Joe Farok.

"Joe, we need to get going on this gold. We want to know where it is and how and when we can get it. We need it in the next six months. Can you handle that?"

"What limitations do I have?"

"None. This is top priority. Put together a team, and for anything you need, call me and you will have it. But we need results, understand? No excuses for failure."

"Got it."

"Report to me weekly."

"Yes," Joe said thoughtfully.

CHAPTER IV

Rome

August 25, 2009

Joe met with his most trusted operatives in a safe house in Rome.

"We need to know where the gold is and then we can plan how to get it. So first of all, we need a conversation with Lueckemann, and then we need a conversation with this Japanese professor. One or both may have a lead for us."

"I'll talk to Lueckemann. John, you fly to Japan and have a conversation with this professor. He teaches at Kyoto University.

"Lazaar, you put together a strike force so we can move when we know where the gold is."

Since he was in Rome, Joe called Anna lee.

"Hello?"

"Anna Lee, are you free tonight? I'm in town."

"Of course I am for you, Joe. Where shall we meet?"

"How about dinner, dancing, and a nightcap at your place?"

"Sounds wonderful. What time?"

"I'll pick you up at 8:00."

"Very well. See you at 8:00. Ciao."

Anna Lee was a beautiful woman. Tall (five foot nine), slim, with black hair and black eyes. A perfect Italian woman. Her figure was exquisite, having the right amount of curves, with breasts that were firm and high. Her black eyes were bottomless, like a clear mountain lake in early spring. She was dressed in an elegant, black, figure-fitting dress that ended just above her ankles. It fit her like a glove.

Joe sighed when he saw her. and held her for a long kiss.

"You are beautiful, Anna Lee. Why haven't I married you?"

"You tell me, Joe. Is that a proposal?"

"No, not yet, but soon."

They ate dinner at the elegant and exclusive Hotel Forum Roof Garden in the ancient city and then danced at two or three clubs.

It was 3:00 a.m. when they returned to Anna Lee's apartment.

The long slow kisses became more urgent, yielding to the eager disrobement of both of them, and then an emersion into each other's passion. They were spent by 7:00 a.m., when Anna Lee said.

"I must get showered and get to work." She rose and started for the bathroom.

Joe grabbed her and said, "We have not slept yet and I'm sure after a nap I will be hungry both for you and breakfast. Why not make a day of it?"

"I can't. You know I want to. The ministry is in a mess these days."

"Why these days?"

"It seems all this talk about Jewish gold has led to an investigation into how Der Fuehrer moved the gold. Hence my ministry has been asked to research all the records we have on various shipments of whatever from 1938 to 1946. The reports have been piling up on my desk."

"So let them pile up. We can still spend the day together."

"No, any day but today. A banker named Jim Luginbuhl from Banc Swiss is meeting me today to go over what I have. He will be in my office at 10:00 a.m."

"Call in sick."

"No, my cabinet minister has insisted that I meet with him. There has been talk about a missing gold shipment that may still be somewhere in the world. Luginbuhl has been trying to find it, and my boss,

Señor Tedeschi, says we must be very careful to appear anxious to help find this gold and return it to our Jewish friends."

"Jews, bah. Once more they cause me inconvenience. I have to return to Berlin tonight, so perhaps we can meet again next week."

"Okay, my darling," she said, bending to kiss him. "You know I have time for one more moment of passion before I must dress," she said, reaching for him.

Anna Lee left the house at 9:30 a.m. Joe was across the street from her office with a listening device when Jim Luginbuhl arrived in Anna Lee's office. He was talking about the same shipment of gold that Kumato and Lueckemann were talking about. Joe was unable to get much of the conversation due to the collateral noise in the busy building.

However, he did follow Herr Luginbuhl to an out-of-the-way café, where he met with an American blonde woman. Joe overheard Luginbuhl ask her about moving large amounts of gold across international borders and heard her agree to do it.

He followed Molly O'Connor back to Saulva without her being aware. Before he left Saulva, he contacted Abdullah and had him place a close tail on Miss O'Connor. This was a turn of events that pleased him immensely.

CHAPTER V

Cypress

October 1, 2009

Lazaar—a swarthy man, short, with a paunch that hung over his belt—was vain. He dyed his hair a jet black like it was when he was twenty-three; he was now fifty-eight, and he liked attention. For an operative he talked a lot. That was how he got the attention he craved. Usually operatives liked to not be seen, but Lazaar loved to be noticed, so he talked often, loudly, and to anyone who would listen. All the noise was his cover. He was so foolish in what he said that people came to think him a clown. A clown he was not. He was intuitive, quick thinking, cunning, and ruthless.

Lazaar had been in the "business" all of his life. His parents had survived the execution of all Arabs by the Turks in 1915. He had sworn death to anyone that was a threat to Arabs in the future. He knew anyone worth knowing on every continent and could get things done.

He assembled a group of ten experienced soldiers (terrorists) to await orders. They came from all over the world and each was a captain of a small cell of ten, giving him a strike force of 100 that could be organized and directed to anywhere in the world on ten minutes' notice. Each was a specialist. One was an explosive expert; another in clandestine operations, specializing in surveillance and assassination; another in sea operations; another in overt operations strike force; another a specialist in air power; another a weapons man; another suicide operations; the list went on. There was no army in the world that had more expertise, better-trained troops, or more dedicated men.

CHAPTER VI

Berlin

November 10, 2009

The next afternoon Joe Farok walked into Lueckmann's small storefront. He was dressed as always in a beautifully tailored suit and was impeccably groomed. Several women on the street followed him with their eyes as he locked the door to "Lueckemann's Expeditors."

Marcus looked up from his desk. His clear, Aryan, blue eyes observed Joe from over his reading glasses.

"Can I help you, young man?"

"Yes, you can. I have a few questions for you to which I expect quick and honest answers and I will be gone. Try and hide things and you will be gone in five minutes."

Marcus' old face showed no emotion. He had been threatened before.

"First, I want to know the name and address of the Japanese professor you have been meeting with."

Marcus shut his mouth and his eyes narrowed.

"What do you want that for? And how did you know about him?"

"You are a much-appreciated man. We and others keep tabs on you because of your knowledge. Now, what did that professor want?"

"What do I get for my information? If you have been 'keeping tabs' on me, you know that I am alive today and flourish, as it were, by selling what I know."

"We will pay you 20,000 U.S. dollars today and another 80,000 when this operation is successfully completed."

Mark's eyes lit up and he smiled. "What can I tell you?"

"His name is Kumato and he teaches at Kyoto University. He is writing a scholarly research paper on how the Nazis bought war supplies. In his research he discovered a missing gold shipment and he believes that the SS got the gold out of Europe for their later use. He is trying to find records of that shipment."

"Do any exist?"

"Yes. There is a Swiss banker named Kitchton that has those records. He visited me also a few weeks before Kumato did. He knows that the gold was shipped through Naples to Argentina but not where it went after that. Kumato wanted a list of former or current Nazi synthesizers in Argentina. He thought they may know about this gold. I provided that list for a price."

"You, of course, have a copy for me?"

"Of course. I can do better then that. But I will need anther 100,000 dollars for that information."

Joe nodded. "If it is good information, you may have it."

"I know which family would have been in charge of the finances for any such operation. They will know where the gold is, if it is anywhere." Marcus took a piece of paper and wrote a name on it. He then handed the paper to Joe; he placed it in his pocket.

"Thank you very much. The 100,000 will be deposited in your account at the Berlin National Bank within the hour. Another 100,000 when we find the gold.

"One more question. Does the professor know anymore than what you have told me? Did he say what he wants to do if he finds the gold?"

"I did not tell him all that I told you. He did not pay as well.

He is looking for the acclaim of finding the gold and thinks it should be returned to the Swiss for distribution to the Nazi survivors."

"How much gold is there?"

"What would now be worth about 14.8 billion dollars."*

Joe turned as if to leave the building and turned back.

"Which bank does Kitchton work for?"

"Bank of Berlin."

Joe left without another word

*In 1939, the U.S. shipped via merchant ship 148 million dollars worth of gold. That was at $34 per ounce. Today gold is ten times that figure; hence, 14.8 billion.

CHAPTER VII

Berlin

November 11, 2009

At his office Joe called John Farok and passed the information on as to where the professor is.

John was a distant cousin of Joe's, more distant than the same last name would suggest. But John too had experienced the loss of his family and their fortunes at the hands of the Israelis. John's family, cousins to Joe's, had been merchants in what was called Transjordan at the time. After the '67 war, this became the West Bank. John, his mother, father, and three sisters were made refugees, first in Jordan and then in Libya. By 1985, they had managed to immigrate to the USA, where their skills as merchants helped them reestablish themselves. John had attended the University of Kansas, where he had met hundreds of Arab students. They had invited him to attend their cultural meetings, and after four years he had been asked to join a secret society. This turned out to be a student-led American branch of the PLO.

When John graduated, he first joined the family business with his MBA. The next stop was investments. He worked for Goldman Sachs.

He continued his involvement with the PLO and based on their urgings asked for a transfer to the Goldman Sachs European office. In this capacity, he provided information to the PLO.

After hooking up with Cousin Joe at a small meeting at a safe house in Greece, he decided to become one of Joe's operatives. He was not used often, but if Joe had a job that needed a sophistication and finesse John was the man.

John had no family besides Cousin Joe, since he never married. His mother and father had died and his three sisters lived in Kansas, New York, and Florida now. He saw them only on holidays. This had become increasing difficult since John had become a practicing Moslem, while his family was Christian.

Joe next called Saul Lazaar and told him to take his surveillance strike force to Argentina and await further orders.

John was dispatched to Tokyo. He spent seven months there trying to get close to Kumato without success.

BOOK IV: CHARLES

CHAPTER I

Virginia

August 11

It took two days but Marcus Lueckemann called Charles Townsend IV.

"Your story checked out. But I do not talk on the phone. If you want to talk to me, you need to come here."

"I can do that. When and where?"

"Two days from now, the Mueller Brew House in Berlin at 2:00 p.m."

"I'll be there."

Charles made his reservations and arrived in Berlin the evening before his meeting with Lueckemann. He had dinner that night with Jeanne Southerlien.

Jeanne, an American beauty of German descent, had been an employee of both his father and the Chase Manhattan Bank. She had kept Charles III up to date on what the banks in Europe were doing. She still was undercover for the CIA. Charles IV had known her for years. Their relationship started out casually. She worked for his father and was at the house occasionally. Sometimes when Charles traveled with his father, they would have dinner. Jeanne was about Charles' age and very attractive: tall for a woman, at five foot ten, red hair, curvaceous figure with truly beautiful breasts (Charles knew that for a fact), outstanding, long legs, and a very engaging smile.

Charles had asked her for dinner when he was in Berlin with his father about ten years before. He had learned then that she was not only beautiful but also very knowledgeable and just plain smart. After that, whenever they were in the same country, they met. Dinner usually turned into breakfast.

"It's good to see you again. I'm sorry about what happened to your father."

"Thank you. It is good to see you again. It has been too long. How is your career going?"

"Oh, about the same. I am on the senior management team, but am stuck where I am. If I were free to, I would accept a job offer. Those headhunters keep bugging me about. I'm sure a move to another bank and I could get fast-tracked to either senior VP or maybe even president of a regional bank. But that would probably be back in the States and your father's company keeps me here."

"You still work for them then?"

"Yes. It pays well. The 'company' is paying for my retirement. It is exciting with the whole cloak-

and-dagger stuff and no real danger. Besides, I meet really nice men like you every once in a while." She smiled slyly.

"My dad would never let me get into his line of work. He always said follow the money, be a banker; that is where the future is. So that's what I did. But I'm afraid banking is not really exciting."

"It is here. There is a lot going on. The Common Market wants to beat the U.S. in world dominance, at least in trade. There are a lot of deals going on above and below the table."

"I bet. I suppose the company wants to know all about that, huh?"

"Yes, it does make for good reports."

"Say, do you know a banker named Richard Lewis? He lives here in Berlin and works for a Swiss bank."

"I have heard of him. He is head of records or research for the Swiss Bank Nationale. He is high-middle management. I don't have any reason to see or deal with him personally.

"Funny you should ask, though. The only reason why I can answer your question is that he was just discussed at a meeting I was at."

"Oh? Tell me more."

"Well, the Jews and Israel are putting pressure on the Swiss banks to track Nazi gold and return it to the victims or descendents of the victims of the Holocaust. Richard Lewis was given the job by a consortium of all of the Swiss banks to head this up.

There is Richard and six others that are supposed to research what Nazi gold may be in the banks vaults, then how it got there and who it belongs to."

"Sounds like a lot of research. How much effort are they really putting into this?"

"At first not much. It has been going on for a year or more. But at a meeting that I was at last week, Lewis' name came up and the president of one of the Swiss banks said something to the effect that this Lewis guy better get his ass moving on that project or he will be replaced. The Jews are really leaning and so is the world press. We need to get this issue settled. One of the VPs made excuses for him said that the records were vague and it was taking a lot of time. They have found gold that they did not know they had and that the records had been deliberately confused to make it hard to track.

"So in two weeks I have heard this guy's name twice. Why do you ask?"

"For the same reason. My father's phone logs show that he had had some conversation with him or about him before he was killed."

"Killed? What do you mean? I thought he died in a boating accident."

"No. He was murdered. Which is why I am here: to track down why someone wanted him murdered now after he retired and was no threat to anyone. He was working on immediate post-World War issues for a book with another friend and had some interest in what Richard Lewis was doing, but I do not know what. Except now it must have to do with Nazi gold."

"Interesting. Do you want to go to my house for dessert? We can talk more there," she said.

Charles smiled. "I have been thinking about nothing else for the last three hours," he said.

CHAPTER II

Berlin

August 13, 2010

Charles met Mr. Lueckemann in the back of the Mueller Brew House at half past two the next day.

"So you are Charles' son? Charles always treated me right. He never gave me any problems."

"You must have also treated him right for that to be true."

"Yes, we did a service for each other."

"What was that?"

"Right after the war, I provided him with the names and locations of many high-ranking Nazis. I also knew the whereabouts of Russian spies and what happened to large sums of money. In return, your father kept me out of the U.S. Army's hands."

"I see. He mentioned you occasionally to me. Of course, he did not talk a lot about his work at home or anywhere else. He did speak highly of you when he did talk. I understand he saw you only a few days before he was killed."

"Killed? How do you know that?"

"Never mind how I know. You were not surprised."

"No, I told him the questions he was asking would lead to trouble."

"What were the questions?"

"He contacted me about a year ago. He was searching for a shipment of Nazi gold that went from Switzerland to Argentina in April of '45. There has been no trace of that gold since it left Naples in a Red Cross ship."

"What did my father want with that? He was out of government."

"He said it was a private inquiry and that he was trying to verify that it in fact existed. He then wanted to know if I knew where it was heading or where it is today."

"Hard to say. I did some research and discovered that it was heading for Argentina to the Nazi organization there. It was to be used for getting Nazis out of Europe, funding their futures, and possibly for reestablishing the Reich."

"How much money?"

"Now about 14.8 billion in today's market."

"How many families?"

"I don't know. Probably in the area of a hundred, assuming they all got to South America alive. Many did not."

"Do you know where it is today?"

"No, and I'm not sure that it even got there. However, there are fifteen former Nazi families in Argentina. I gave him those names and what I knew about them. They have stayed in loose contact with me over the years. No one asked about them before, so I never mentioned them. They also send contributions to my work occasionally."

"Why did you think this was a dangerous line of pursuit?"

"Because the families to do not want to be found. Also there appears to be a lot of interest in this shipment of gold."

"How's that?"

"It started when this Japanese professor met with me. He was researching the flow of gold from Berlin to wherever during the war. He is an academic so I gave what information I had. Then I got a call from some friends in the PLO and they were interested in the same shipment. Shipment number 213. I thought it was strange that after fifty years two different people inside of two weeks of each other would question me about a single shipment of gold. But it got stranger. I received a visit from the Mossad and they wanted the same information. They came the week after your father. I assumed with this many people searching for the same thing it must be dangerous."

"Interesting. What is the name of the professor?"

"Kumato from Tokyo University."

"Have you heard from him since he returned to Japan?"

"No, but I did not expect to. I am expecting a copy of his book."

"Can you give me the names of the German families in Argentina, the PLO, and Mossad people?"

"I thought you might want the family's names so I made a list for you. As to the others, if I knew how to reach them I would not tell you. They find me when they want me."

"Did my father say anything else to you?"

"No, he mused about how one would explain or use 14.8 billion dollars worth of gold in today's world."

"What do you mean?"

"Well, say you had 14.8 billion dollars in gold. You can't pay for most things today with gold, so you must deposit it in a bank and write drafts against it. But how and where do you go to deposit it? You can't walk into the local branch office of any bank and say, 'I want to open an account with fifteen billion in gold.'"

"No, I guess not. You would need a bank that did not ask questions and was connected to the rest of the world. And if you had the gold in Argentina then a

Caribbean bank would be the closest place to deposit it."

"I expect so. Now, my beer is done. So am I. I met with you because I owed your father a favor. It is paid now. I have told you all I know and I do not want to be asked anymore questions, understand?"

"Yes, Mr. Lueckemann. Thank you for your help."

Alone in his room that night, Charles pondered what he knew. 14.8 billion in gold. How would you move it, and to where? There was a short list of banks that would accept such money. If the PLO was looking for it then they could go to an Eastern Bloc bank with it or one of the Arab oil countries' banks. If the Mossad had it then they would go to Israel National Bank with it, and if private individuals had it they would go to the Bahamas, the Caymans, or Switzerland unless, of course, they were Swiss!

Charles dialed Jeanne's number. "Can you come over right now, tonight?"

"Yes, but why? Do you want more of last night?"

"That is a good idea, but I have some more questions for you about this Richard Lewis."

CHAPTER III

Berlin

August 16, 2010

Jeanne arrived in Charles suite by 11:00 p.m. As they sat in the Jacuzzi tub with champagne, he asked her about Richard.

"I don't know much. I told you he was working on the Swiss Nazi gold thing."

"Anyone else working with him? How is it going? Any strange bank inquiries lately?"

"He has six others working with him. They are mostly from Swiss banks and at least one German bank. Nothing unusual that I know of. What are you looking for?"

"I'm not sure." He then told her about Lueckemann's conversation.

"Whew! That is interesting. What should I be looking for?"

"Ask yourself: If you had two billion in gold and wanted to be able to use it, how would you go about it?"

"Well, you would have to get it to a bank."

"How would you do that?"

"You would need a bank that would accept the gold bullion directly and then deposit it to your account."

"Right. And not many banks would do that. Lueckemann said that he had inquiries from your Swiss bankers, the PLO, a Japanese professor, the Mossad, and my father. So let's take each group and see where they would go with the money."

"Okay. The Swiss would go for a Caribbean bank, probably the Bahamas or the Caymans."

"The PLO would go to Syria or an oil kingdom."

"Yes, that would make good sense. Not only would they not have to answer questions they would be welcomed. The sheiks would like to have the gold and help the cause."

"Right! And the Mossad would go to Israel."

"So if one of these semi-governmental groups had the money, they would go to their supporters to handle it for them. At least initially."

"Well, if it were the bankers, they would be looking to put it where they could use it. That would mean they would need someone in Europe to help them and they would want to be fairly legit."

"That would leave only a couple of people. I would bet on a woman named Molly O'Connor. She has the contacts and the brass to try and do this, and she would use a Caribbean bank, at least for the first stopping point."

"Okay, let me talk to my friends at the company and see if they have any information. Can you check out this Molly woman?"

"I'll get on it, but first let me get on something else. You did not get me up here in the middle of the night, naked, and half drunk, just to talk about money did you?"

"No, not at all my dear. Would you like some more champagne?"

BOOK V: THE MOSSAD

CHAPTER I

Berlin, Germany

August 11, 2010

So, Mr. Townsend IV is talking to Mr. Lueckemann as well, David Steinberg thought as he removed the earphones from his head. David is a tall (six foot three) blond man with an athletic build. He used to play tight end for the University of Michigan in Ann Arbor, Michigan.

David was born and raised in southeast Michigan. All he wanted out of life was to play football in the NFL. He graduated from Grand Blanc High School and went to Michigan on a football scholarship. At Michigan he started as a freshman. At Michigan, being the football program that it is, David got offers to consider the NFL but something happened in his senior year that changed his mind.

His Mom and Dad were returning home from their thirtieth wedding anniversary trip. David was waiting at the airport in Detroit when the news of Pam Am 109 came on the CNN airport news channel he was watching. That was his parent's flight. Now, at age twenty-three, he was an orphan with only a few weeks left in college.

David was angry at first. Then lost. Then an old friend from high school approached him. It seemed his old friend had a way David could get even for Pam Am 109 and avenge his parent's senseless death: Join the Israeli Secret Service.

David was Jewish but his family had never been practicing. His friend Bobby Sillos was a very serious Jew. David had always laughed at him. Bobby was overweight, short in height, and short-sighted. David always said that Bobby was religious because no one but God would have him. David and Bobby had lost touch after high school. Now Bobby was standing, or rather sitting, in front of him suggesting a really crazy idea to David.

Bobby had left high school and gone to Hebrew University in Cincinnati, Ohio. There his computer ability was discovered and noticed not just by his professors but also by friends in Israel. He had been recruited by the Mossad as a computer expert. But now they wanted David as a field agent.

"Bobby, you are crazy," David said. "I don't want to be a spy or a secret agent. I don't know what I want to do but that's not it."

"You should think about it. I know you don't feel much like football. No studies really interested you. Have you ever really thought about Israel? Israel is our homeland. It is the only place where Jews are stood up for. It is the only place that really cares about what happened to your folks. What is the U.S. doing?"

"They say they are investigating and they will get back to me when they know something."

"Well, let me tell you that Israel is more then investigating. We know who did it and where they are, and we have plans to get them. Jewish deaths and acts of Palestinian terror do not go unpunished by Israel. It is the Mossad that makes sure of that.

"You could be part of making a difference, of doing something to stop these things from happening to other people. Things like what happened to your folks.

"Will you come and meet my boss, Benjamin? Just meet him."

Still unsure but wanting to do something worthwhile with his life, David had met with Benjamin. It had been a pleasant meeting. David was surprised by how much Benjamin knew about him. It was clear that they had done their homework on him.

David ended up being a guest of Benjamin in Israel. He saw what Israel had done to the land. He saw what terrorism had done to Israel. He met and talked to men his own age that had lost their parents and sisters and grandparents to terrorist. He saw what Israel meant to the people there.

By the end of the month that he had spent there, Israel had come to mean something to him. He was ready to consider the Mossad.

He had enlisted and after two years of training and briefing had been assigned to a surveillance team in Germany. While being an agent sounded exciting, it was boring. David's team consisted of three men and one woman. Their job was to monitor all phone calls and personal contacts that a man named Marcus Lueckemann had.

Lueckemann was an old Nazi. He had served the party well, but by the end of '44 the handwriting was on the wall. So Marcus had left Berlin and moved to southwest Germany, where he fell into Allied rather than Russian hands.

By 1946, denazification was going strong, and the Allies came for him. He, however, had been busy. During the war, he had served as a communications expert. His job was to assist communication with German spies all over the world. This, of course, entailed knowing them and many Russian and other nation's spies as well. Marcus had been a good listener. Through listening and being generous with schnapps and vodka to the inner circle of Der Fuehrer, he had come to know much about not just the inner workings of Nazi Germany but Russia, Italy, and most of Western Europe. In return for his freedom, Marcus talked about who and what he knew. To the Americas first, then any ally that wanted his time.

While he had answered all their questions, he did not tell them all he knew. Because of his contacts and his freedom, he came to know a great deal about postwar Europe and Europe just before the end of the war. He had helped several former Nazis escape both before the war ended and while he was "sharing" with the Allies. He knew many of the secrets of Nazi

Germany and much about how reconstruction took place.

He knew Adenauer, de Gaulle, Eisenhower, Churchill, and even Zurkoff on a first name bases.

As a result, the Mossad and found that tapping his phone and monitoring his contacts was a useful thing to do. Already it had been instrumental in capturing three war criminals and locating several other persons that the Mossad was interested in. In the past this assignment had been a plum and had taken three active teams to work. Now it was just one team of usually new recruits, to give them some operational experience, just to keep an eye on things.

David had found the job boring, although he was surprised at how many well-known people did talk to Marcus Lueckemann. Among them a year ago had been Charles Townsend III, director of the CIA. He had called to ask Marcus some questions about the gold and cash reserves of the Third Reich and the German government in the years 1944 to 1947. David had typed up the report and then passed it along to Rome, where his superiors were located.

At about the same time, Marcus had talked to a Japanese professor who was doing research on the same topic for a book he was writing. Marcus had agreed to meet the professor. David had passed that report along too but then it was out of his hands.

Now Charles Townsend IV was calling to discuss what his father had wanted. David had read of his father's death in a boating accident and had felt bad for the man. He did not know because he knew how much losing a parent hurt.

What David did not know was that last year his superior had assigned a second surveillance team to cover the lunch meeting and then a third to follow the professor when he returned to Japan, and Sophia Scalso was sent to Washington to talk to Charles III.

"Sophia, I need to know what or why Charles Townsend was asking about this. What did he want? How does he know about this?"

CHAPTER II

Washington, D.C.

July 16, 2009

Sophia arrived in Washington, D.C., on Monday. She took a room at the Watergate and made a call to the Israeli embassy.

"Is Ari in?"

"Yeah, this is Ari. What do you need?"

"Ari, Sophia. I need to meet you tonight. I'm staying at the Watergate. Can you meet in the bar for drinks, say about 8:00?"

"Yeah, see you there."

At eight Sophia was camped out in a corner of the Watergate lobby bar. The tables were scattered around a room full of large plants to give a sense of privacy to the quiet drinkers.

Ari Kassell walked in five minutes past eight. He was tall, well-built, near fifty, with thin hair and deep, black eyes. The kind of eyes women love to gaze into.

Sophia remembered the last time she had drunk from those eyes. It was in Paris in a small hotel off the Champs-Elysées. They had spent the better part of a week making love and had hardly left the hotel. That was three years ago, and they had not met or spoke since. That was how it is in this business. You take what you can when you can, not knowing where you will be next or what you will be doing or if you will be alive.

Ari spotted her and walked over. He eyed her appraisingly and said:

"You are more beautiful then I remember. They do have room service here."

Taking a deep breath Sophia handed him her key.

Three hours later, lying in bed, spent, relaxed, and thoroughly satisfied, they ordered dinner and drinks in the room.

Over dinner, Ari said, "What brings you to Washington?"

"I need to check out Charles Townsend. Can you get me an appointment or, better yet, a private casual meeting with him?"

"Sure, I can do either. He is retired from the CIA now and dabbles in various things of interest from his home in Virginia."

"It would be better if I could meet him by accident."

"He canoes every Wednesday in the Potomac River north of D.C. in Virginia. He is always alone and he is there from about nine to twelve p.m. it is a ritual to him."

"This is Monday. Do you have to be anyplace to be during the next two days?"

"Yes, the bedroom. Let's go." He bent down and gave her a deep, exciting kiss, caressed her breast, and led her back to the bedroom.

Wednesday at 10:00 a.m. Sophia was on the banks of the Potomac. When she could see the canoe coming around a bend, she dived in and swam to the center of the river, where she began to flounder.

Charles Townsend, seeing an apparently drowning woman, pulled alongside and offered her a paddle and then a lift into the canoe. He took her to the river's edge.

Sophia was a beautiful woman with lovely, firm, round breasts, great legs, and a dazzling smile. None of these features were lost on Charles.

"Here you go. What were you doing out there?"

"I was driving by, saw the beautiful river, and thought I would take a dip. But the current was stronger than I expected, so I ended up where you found me. I was probably more scared then in real danger." Her nipples were obvious through her thin bathing suit.

"You are cold. Where is your car?"

"Upriver a ways. I have some things in the car for a small picnic. I was going to eat after the swim. Would you like to share it with me?"

Charles hesitated and Sophia turned on her eyes and said:

"I would appreciate it. Besides it will give me a chance to thank you for saving my life," she said with a warm smile.

They walked about a quarter mile upriver to her rented car parked off the road in some brush. The trees and brush gave the site privacy, and the river made it lovely.

Sophia handed Charles a bottle of Chardonnay and asked him to open it while she "put something on."

Sophia walked to the rear of the car and pulled out of the trunk a pair of jeans and a warm, woolly sweater. Before she put them on she toweled herself and then stripped off the suit.

Charles tried to be a gentleman but could not help but sneak a peek at the dressing, strikingly attractive woman.

They ate and talked, finished the bottle of wine, and Sophia handed Charles another one. After glasses were poured Charles said.

"Why did you want to meet me?"

"What do you mean? I was in trouble and you helped."

"No. That is not true. You are truly beautiful and have not hesitated to use your beauty to gain my attention. The picnic was planned for two people with lots of wine. This is a planned meeting. What do you want from me?"

"Okay. I guess I should have known you would see through this. But I wanted to talk to you in private and in more relaxed setting than an office.

"I am Sophia Scalier. I am a Mossad agent. I tell you that because without a doubt when you return home you will check me out and find this information on your own.

"Ever vigilant, we have a running tape on Marcus Lueckemann's phone. You talked to him two weeks ago about a shipment of Nazi gold that when to South America. We would like to know why, since you are retired, you were asking about this. We also want to know what you know about this gold, since we believe that it is Jewish."

Charles hesitated, thinking about what he should or should not say to this beautiful foreign agent.

"The Mossad has improved the appearances of their agents, I will say that. When I was working, they were all big, burly, and rather ugly men. You know that I cannot share information with you."

Sophia smiled. "If you were still working, I would not have asked. If this were a state secret, I would not have asked. But you are retired. This is international money, and I think this is something you are doing for personal reasons and has nothing to do with your government. Therefore, you have no reason not to share information on this topic with me. In addition, Israel is your country's greatest ally in the East."

"Well, that's all true. But I'm afraid I know little. I was approached a month ago by a woman. A friend of my son's, or at least an acquaintance from banking. Her name was Molly O'Connor and she works for the National Bank of Detroit in Saulva. She asked me if I would be willing to help her, or at least provide information to her on how to transport or transfer large amounts of gold bullion.

"When I asked her what she wanted this information for, she said that she was working with some clients who think they have discovered a sunken treasure ship, and they wanted to recover and secure most of the gold or silver that was there before they made the find public.

"I, of course, I told her to have her friends recover the metal and place with the nearest bank.

"She said that the wreck was in arguably territorial waters, and they wanted the profit from their years of searching rather then giving it to some tin-pot dictator to hide in Switzerland.

"So I gave her some suggestions as to which banks in the Caribbean would be most accommodating to her. As we talked, she said that her friends were German. When she left I got to thinking about this and thought that perhaps we were talking about some German gold or even Nazi treasure. In the company we always heard rumors about lost treasure from the Nazis.

"So I called Marcus Lueckemann to see if he could supply any information that might be helpful.

"He told me that during and at the end of the war, Nazis moved large amounts of gold and other valuables through neutral shipping to neutral countries that were favorably disposed toward Germany. He thought that it was possible that one or more of these ships may have sunk. If someone could find the ship or ships, there would be lots of gold. He also said that such gold would be claimed by the current German government as stolen property to be returned to Germany. He also thought that Israel would make a demand on the funds, depending what form they were in, saying that it was stolen Jewish money.

"Having that information, I began to nose around other major banks to see if anyone and approached them. They had not. Or at least that is what they said. So, after a few months I lost interest. But it was good to talk to old friends."

"Interesting," Sophia said. Then she leaned over and gave Charles a deep, passionate kiss. "Thank you for sharing this information with me. I know you did not have to. If you find out anything else, will you call me? Here is a number I can be reached at. I do know how to show my gratitude."

Wednesday night, she was on a plane back to Rome.

CHAPTER III

Rome

September 10, 2009

The report that was filed pursuant to the luncheon between Marcus Lueckemann and Professor Kumato stayed that

Marcus Lueckemann was approached by Professor Kumato of Tokyo University and asked specific questions regarding transfers and locations of large amounts of German gold toward the end of the war. Kumato said he was writing a book tracing the path of Nazi gold. He was interested in Jewish claims to large gold deposits in Swiss banks and what happened to Nazi gold that Kumato felt was unaccounted for.

This piqued the interest of the powers that be at Mossad, especially that Charles Townsend III would be asking similar questions at this particular time. The Swiss were not forthcoming at all. Casual contacts with Townsend through a mutual friend had also proved unproductive. Something was going on and no one was telling the Mossad. This made the Mossad very nervous as well as curious.

Adam Levine had been called at that point and sent to Japan. He was to make contact with Professor Kumato and see if he could find anything out about his work. Andy had arrived in Tokyo and signed up for a class on post-World War II Europe at the University of Kyoto from Professor Kumato.

During the course of the class, Adam had got to know Professor Kumato rather well. In fact, he became a regular at the Tea House with the other disciples of the good professor.

The class itself dealt with economic stabilization, the Marshall Plan, creation of Capital and finally the revitalization of Europe. The second semester was to cover economic reconstruction of both Europe and Asia.

Conversations with the professor let Adam know that he was indeed knowledgeable. Adam had brought the conversation around to gold several times, but Kumato had steered clear of giving any information away.

"I know what you are saying about the Marshall Plan meeting food needs and helping to create capital," Adam said one night as he and several other students sipped tea and enjoyed each other's company.

"I also understand how necessary that all was. I think we can use this as a model for the development of capitalism in the former Soviet Union and her

Eastern European allies. But where did the money all go?

I mean, Germany was functioning. Hitler was building weapons, feeding armies, and running an economy right up until May 7 of '45. How was he doing it? What was he doing it with? If on May 1 there was a functioning economy and on May 8 there was not, where did the money go?"

"That, my dear Adam, that is a good question. Where did the cash go in the Great Depression on Oct 1929? It just disappears!" said the professor with an oriental shrug.

"I am writing a book that I think answers that question, but it is a secret for now. There is much interest in this book both from academic circles and from non-academic sources, let me assure you. You would be surprised who has approached me about information like this. It is for me to know now, and later I will tell the world when I am ready. Believe me, it will cause quit a stir when I publish my book."

Adam was ordered to break into the professor's office and home to try and find his notes. Adam did break into the professor's home, but the notes were not there. They must have been in his office.

After a semester with no results, the Mossad tried an end run. In late January 2010, Bradley Albert, a senior operative for the Far East, approached the president of the university, Bukkake, and through him several other high officials in Japan's academic circles.

"I will level with you, gentlemen. My name is Bradley Albert and I am with the Mossad. We have reason to believe that professor Kumato knows the whereabouts of a missing shipment of Nazi gold. Israel, as you are aware, feels that this is Jewish money and belongs in Israel. We want to be there when it is found. I am prepared to offer to the University of Tokyo five million dollars for the professor's research before it is released to the public."

"Five million dollars," Bukkake said. "That is a lot of money. We could do a lot with that. But the research is Kumato's. He would have to share it."

"I don't think he wants to do that," said Bradley.

"I have talked with him and he sees himself as publishing a book about postwar Europe and using the location of the gold as the selling point of the book. He has been very guarded about facts that will be in the book. Can you do something to help me get this information?" Bradley said. A little of the desperation he felt seemed to creep into his voice.

"What would that something be?" Suomato, a senior professor in Kumato's department, said.

"Well, you could pressure him for details."

"That will not work. He is and always has been extremely reclusive about his research and publications."

"Well, then you could help me locate the data without his knowledge."

"What do you suggest? We steal the information?"

"You can use any word you want but I need to get the data."

"We could never do that. Thank you for your kind offer but we must decline, and furthermore, I will need to report this conversation to the Ministry of Education."

"Ten million dollars," said Bradley quietly.

"What did you say?"

"Ten million dollars. I will up my offer to one hundred million dollars for the information in the next ten days."

The five men looked at each other.

"I will deliver it to you, Mr. Bukkake. I will deliver it personally to you. You can split it among yourselves or give it to the university. Do what you want, I don't care. All I want is to know where the gold is."

"Well, maybe we can locate the information for you. Give us a day or two to think on this and we will see." Bukkake and his friends had temporized for a few weeks and told Bradley that they would help him.

"But it will have to be in our time and our methods," Bukkake said.

"I will agree to that as long as it is done by the end of the summer. It is May now. By the end of August, I must have the information I seek."

Adam was the young man that found the professor on the campus lawn after his "heart attack."

After seeing to the body, Adam went straight to the professor's office. He was there about twenty minutes, when he had visitors but slipped out the back door without being discovered by those visitors—but not empty-handed.

Adam had found some notes on the hard drive and sent the file to his own computer in Europe before he deleted the file. He also found a paper file with several interesting names. One of them was Charles Townsend III and the other Raoul Latino in Paraguay.

Interrupted, Adam took these names with him and left the building. He then returned to Europe and turned his information over to Roberto Gilardi, attorney-at-law, who was, in fact, Moshe Sharon, the head of all Mossad European operations. Adam was then returned to the surveillance teams in Europe. The Mossad had their information before the end of the summer.

When the news that Marcus had received a call from Charles IV was passed to Rome, David was summoned.

CHAPTER IV

Rome

August 15, 2010

David met on a Tuesday at 9:00 a.m. with two men and a woman. They were introduced to him as Roberto Gilardi, Sophia Scalso, and Benjamin Weiss.

"We called you here to discuss what it was you found in Japan and how we think Marcus may fit in with this," Roberto said.

"First of all, are you aware of why we wanted you to follow the professor?" asked Roberto. He was a tall, slim but powerfully built man. Always perfectly groomed and dressed, he gave every appearance of being a successful attorney. Roberto's real skill was interrogation. He had eyes that could bore through you and make you want to confess to anything just to make him stop looking at you. He also had a mind that grasped and held every detail. This meant that if you were lying, he would trip you.

"No," David said. "I learned in my first round of training to not ask questions and gather all the facts I can from any situation."

"Well, what would be your guess? The professor was interested in the immediate postwar economy of Europe in general and Germany in particular. That was his specialty and he was writing a book about it. He visited Lueckemann to get information on the German economy; probably on gold reserves and how they were handled. The CIA must have thought something was up since Townsend called. My guest is it involves either war criminals or money. Since the U.S. is really not interested in war criminals, I guess money. Since we are interested in it, it must be Jewish money. Reading the newspapers, I would guess it may have something to do with Jewish gold."

"You are good, David, and right on. We believe that there is a large amount of Jewish gold floating around, and Lueckemann knows something about it, as did the professor. Allow me to introduce you to these people. They both work for us under deep cover.

"This is Sophia Scalso. Her day job is director of the Swiss Banc National here in Rome.

"The gentleman is Ben Weiss. His day job is deputy to the Ministry of Finance of Germany. He has worked for the ministry for thirty years. He has worked his way up to the office of deputy. He is the highest non-political appointment in the ministry.

"Ben, please go first and fill David in on what you know."

Ben was a little man with small, round glasses and seemed to perch lightly on his nose. He was in his late fifties. He wore a faded gray suit that had seen better days. David thought that if he were at Michigan today, he would have a pocket penholder and a calculator tied to his belt.

"Well, David, Roberto came to me shortly after the lunch with Professor Kumato and Lueckemann. He said he wanted me to find out all that I could about how the German economy ran during the war and just after the war. I dug through the records, and there are a lot of them. Germans keep records on everything. The information that I was looking for was not on computer but stored in boxes in the basement of the ministry. True, some research had been done by students and scholars from time to time, but nothing like real thorough categorizing of the records. It took me three months and raised suspicions in the ministry. What I found is this:

"Germany ran its wartime economy through Switzerland. This is not new, but no one knows the extent of it. Almost all German gold reserves were kept in Switzerland. Germany would send its gold to Swiss banks; they used them all just to keep everyone involved. When they needed materials such as oil, rubber, and natural materials for weapons and the public use in general, they would pay for it with their Swiss gold reserves. These reserves came from gold mines that they plundered, what the Weimar Republic had, and what they stole or exhorted from the Jews throughout Europe. Some was stolen and some was paid to them for exit visas.

"The gold was transferred by train from Berlin to Saulva. Most of the gold was delivered before 1943. But a lot of Jewish gold arrived in '44. When gold was needed abroad, Germany would have the gold loaded on a train and sent to Italy, usually Naples, where it was loaded on the boat of a neutral nation and sent to the country they were bargaining with."

"How did it get to Naples? How was it put on a boat of a neutral and where was it delivered?" David asked.

"Good questions," Roberto said. It would seem that the pope arranged the passage from Switzerland to Naples. This kept the shipments away from Allied eyes. The pope also told Argentina, a Catholic nation not unfriendly to the Nazis, that it was the church's gold they were trying to get out of Europe, away from Mussolini and Hitler. The gold was delivered to South America, usually Argentina, Paraguay, or Peru. These countries acted as intermediaries to process it to Japan, the Middle East countries, and to various scoundrels in other parts of the world that would provide anything to anyone for a price."

"The interesting part," said Joseph, "is that by 1944, there were three large consignments of gold in Swiss banks waiting to be used. In November, the first one was shipped to South America. This, according to records, easily paid for the Ardennes Offensive. The second one was shipped to Argentina in February of '45. This was to be escape money for the high Nazi officials and was probably not authorized by the Fuehrer. The third was shipped in April of '45. No authorization and no destination; it just disappeared.

"It is this shipment that Kumato was inquiring about, and also Townsend in a roundabout way. He did not know there were three shipments. He was asking about a lost shipment of Nazi gold. He also asked about how one might go about shipping large amounts of gold today. Lueckemann could be of little help in either inquiry, although we believe he knows more than he is letting on. Perhaps he is hoping to sell the information.

"Now we need to turn the story over to Sophia. We asked her to review the Swiss bank records on gold. Sophia, what can you tell us?"

Sophia was a typical Italian beauty. Dark, olive-colored skin, large breasts, high cheekbones. She too was perfectly dressed and used just enough make up to set off her beauty. She had hazel eyes that a man could drown in.

"I researched all the Swiss business with Germany that came through Italy. I was able to confirm what Ben has said and to zero in on the missing shipment. I tracked it to Naples, just as the others did. It too was protected by the pope and was bound for Argentina. A man named Raul Latino was to meet the shipment. The gold left Switzerland April 7, 1945, and arrived in Naples on April 25. It was shipped by sea in an Argentine ship, with the bill of lading signed by a papal representative, and was bound for Argentina. We know that it arrived safely there May 6, 1945, and then we lost it.

"One more thing you should know. When I was researching this, I spoke with one of the clerks that had been with the Swiss Nationale for fifty years: William Ingram. He is the only one that really has access to such records. It is kept secret since no one wants the public to know the extent of collaboration that went on with Nazi Germany. He said that it was strange that I was asking about this since just the week before a man named Jim Luginbuhl from the Saulva branch called and asked detailed questions about this shipment as well. He said that he was researching the Jewish gold and treasure issue. Funny how no one asks anything for fifty years then twice in one week.

"I checked out Luginbuhl. He is legitimate. He is a young assistant in Saulva and he is working on records for the Jewish settlement. But how would he find out about this?"

Roberto turned to David and said, "I have another job for you. I want you to go to Argentina, track down Raul Latino or his children, and see what he can tell us.

"Joseph, find out all you can on Luginbuhl," Roberto directed.

CHAPTER V

Saulva, Switzerland

August 16, 2010

Benjamin left Rome for Saulva the next morning. He checked into the Hotel Intercontinental and called the Swiss National Bank. He asked for Mr. Luginbuhl's supervisor, Stephanie Rolland.

"This is Joseph Wierbach from the Amas Bank and we are considering adding several assistants to our operation here in Saulva. Mr. Luginbuhl works for you I understand?"

"That is correct. I did not know he was unhappy."

"He's not. But we may be interested in a man like him that we could train. We may be looking for a departmental supervisor also. We have heard good things about your work as well. Are you interested in leaving the Amas Bank?"

"Well," Rolland was flattered and greedy, "that would depend on the offer."

"Well, tell me," Terrence asked, "what exactly does your department do?"

"We research all operations for the bank. We are given assignments and then report back to the appropriate office when we have the data they need."

"I understand that one such issue is the matter of Jewish money from the Germans during the war."

"Yes, we are researching that, but I can't talk about it."

"Of course not. You would need to make a report to your supervisors not to me, but I assume this is a major piece of research that you are responsible for?"

"Yes. Yes indeed."

"If my bank were engaged in research, not just a financial matter but one of international significance, I could assume that you and your people could do this and do it well?"

"Why, of course."

"Tell me, can you cooperate with other banks?"

"Of course, that is what we are doing now. There are seven Swiss banks involved in this research and we are the lead bank."

"So you are responsible for not only the research but also the coordination of the work?"

"Yes."

"That's a lot of responsibility and must require a lot of skill."

"Well, it is a lot of work."

"Does Mr. Luginbuhl work in this area as well?"

"Yes, he is crucial to the operation. He has done most of the deep research and been involved in coordinating the various work groups."

"You would give him high marks?"

"Oh yes, he is one of the best young men I have in the department. He is a hard worker and builds a good network."

"Do you know who all he is working with."

"Well, I can get it. There is a man named Richard Lewis from an American bank and four or five others."

"Thank you. You have been most helpful. I will call in a couple of weeks to set up a more formal interview."

Ben's next stop was the Banque Contonale De Saulva. The building was a twenty-story structure built before the war, meant to make a corporate statement of strength and security. Ben wandered in and checked out the lobby. It was the usual large bank. The main floor was all teller windows and manager cubicles. In the back was a door leading to the vault and safe deposit boxes. Outside the main floor was a bank of elevators and a directory. Ben looked up the location of a couple of offices and then pushed the button on the elevator.

He arrived at the fifth floor office of personnel. He walked in and introduced himself to the young, bouncy girl at the front desk as Douglas Buckner from the Republic Bank headquartered in Grand Rapids, Michigan, and asked to see the personnel manager.

He watched as the busty young woman in a short skirt made her way quickly to the back of the room. She returned in a few minutes with an older gentleman in tow. He introduced himself as Ronald Polsgroet. He was tall, thin, and very carefully dressed in a conservative manner with a suit and tie. The suit coat was buttoned. His eyes were apprising and calculating.

Benjamin said:

"I am Douglas Buckner. I am an attorney in the United States." He handed him his card. "My client is a bank named Republic headquartered in Grand Rapids, Michigan. We are interested in opening a research department to aid our customers. The bank has a large number of customers that have roots in Europe, specifically in the Netherlands. Some of these families have been customers of the bank since before the turn of the last century. They have business, or, I should say, their families have business interest on the continent. They have been requesting that we have available to them persons that can do research on old accounts and old business contracts, some of them dating back to the very early 1900s. They engaged me to seek out a person or persons that would be able to do a good job with such an assignment. Do you have any recommendations? Of course, we are willing to pay you for your time and expertise in personnel matters."

Polsgroet's face was tight as Joseph spoke, but when he got to the money part it softened into a board smile. "Well, what sort of compensation are we speaking of?"

"I believe the usual amount is 10 percent of the first year's salary and a bonus of 10,000 U.S. dollars for the search. We are, however, interested in specific information on potential employees."

"I see. Well, I believe I could help you. What would you like to know?"

"We are aware that your bank as been engaged in the research of the Jewish money that the Nazis moved out of Germany to Switzerland in the thirties and forties."

"Yes, we are doing that."

"We also understand that your bank is the lead bank along with several others."

"Yes."

"The skills that your research team has developed in this project would be the same skills that we are looking for. Can you tell me who is on your team for this project and who would be the most competent persons?"

"I think I can do that. However, these records are confidential. I should not speak of them."

"Mr. Polsgroet," Joseph said, reaching into his coat pocket and pulling out a check, "here is a retainer check for 5,000 U.S. dollars made payable to you. The other 5,000 will be given to you when we begin interviewing. We believe your cooperation to be worth this expense to ensure that we get the best available people. Our starting salary for this position will be 60,000 for the three persons we hire. Ten percent of that is another 18,000. We do need your help."

"Of course," Polsgroet smiled slyly. "Let's see what we have." He turned on his computer and punched up some information. "We have the following persons for our bank working on the project:

Robert Morris

George Kitchton

Gerald Rhoten

Mr. Rhoten is the team leader. They are coordinating with two other banks. Their personnel are not listed here, of course."

"Do you have performance reviews on these people?"

"Yes." He punched a few more keys, and a new screen appeared and then two more were screens followed. "They all have excellent reviews. There is a note in the file on this project stating that the bank is very happy with the work they are doing. 'Both the timeliness, quality, and confidentiality you have displayed in this project is praiseworthy' is one line. It appears that those in power here think quite highly of these three."

"Excellent. Can you make copies of their personnel file for me?"

Polsgroet hesitated. "You are not supposed to have these."

Joseph raised his eyebrows and said, "I thought we had an agreement."

"Yes, yes, but If anyone finds out about this...."

"Just print their files off on blank paper. I will put them in my briefcase and no one but I will see them. Once I do the initial screening, my clients will build their own file."

"Okay." He punched some more keys, and the files were printed out and handed to Joseph. He thanked Polsgroet for his help and said that he would stay in touch as to what the bank was doing and left.

Ben stopped at a little coffee shop a block from the Bank, pulled out the files, and studied them.

Morris was thirty-eight, born in Saulva from a Swiss banking family. His father had been a mid-level official at the Swiss National Bank. He went to college and earned an MBA and then joined the bank ten years ago. He first worked in customer service but showed potential for research work and had been moved to the auditor's office. Here he monitored Swiss National Bank operations and personnel. He had caught three managers embezzling from the bank and had received commendations and bonuses for his efforts. Two years ago he was assigned the "Jewish project" and had been there ever since. There was no information in file as to what or who was involved in this project, except he reported to one of the three executive vice presidents.

George Kitchton had a little different background. He is fifty-eight and close to retirement. He too is Swiss born, in Bern. Educated in France at the Sorbonne and then came to the bank. He was seen as a fast riser, but his star burned out and he was shuffled from one department to another. Reviews were mediocre. He was assigned this project after being a trust officer. There was record of a customer complaint about some inappropriate joke he had told the costumer's wife. He was a customer with twenty-five million on account with the bank, so George was moved.

The last man, Gerald Rhoten, forty-five, was born in Lausanne. His mother was Swiss but his father was American. He was educated in America and worked for an American bank, Michigan National, before coming to work for the Swiss National. He had been in three areas of management and had excellent performance reviews. Gerald appears to have been chosen for this assignment because of his informal international connections. His father had been an attaché to the American embassy, and when he retired settled in Lausanne.

All three worked on the fifteenth floor of the headquarters building. There were also photos of all three in their personnel files.

Ben decided that it was probably a good idea to meet these men and see what they knew about gold shipments to Italy during the war.

About 4:00 p.m., Ben went back to the bank and waited in the lobby. George was the first one of the three to come out of the elevator. Ten minutes later, Morris and Rhoten came out together. Ben followed them to the parking lot and as they were about to separate he spoke to them.

"Gentlemen, my name is Benjamin. I know you are two of the three men that are working on the 'Jewish project' for your bank and I would like to talk to you."

"We cannot talk to anyone about that," Morris said. "If you want information you need to talk to Herr Schmitt, who is vice president of the bank. He will make any statements that need to be made."

"I do not want official statements. I have a couple of minor questions to ask that will satisfy my curiosity."

"Sorry," Rhoten said and turned to go.

"No, you do not understand. I need some questions answered and you will answer them."

"Now see here," Rhoten began but stopped when he saw the gun Ben had in his hand.

"Now, step into your car, Rhoten. You too, Morris. Get in the front and I will get in the back. I only have a few questions. It will be easier for you to answer me than to die."

The men obeyed the directions.

"Now, I want to know why, Herr Morris, you were in Italy asking about gold shipments from Switzerland to Italy by the Nazis." Noticing Morris' hesitation, Terrence screwed on the silencer of his gun and leveled it at Morris' eye.

"We discovered that Nazi's were shipping gold by train to Naples, and from Naples were shipping the gold to South America to pay for war supplies. This was fairly routine until 1945 when a shipment of gold left Italy, arrived in Argentina, and disappeared. I was tracking it to see if it was Jewish gold or not."

"What did you find out?"

"A man named Raul Latino was the German agent in Argentina. He signed for the gold but has not been heard from since."

"Now, Rhoten, what other banks are innovated in this?"

"Two others: Amas Bank and Deutsche Bank of Saulva."

"Any foreign banks helping you?"

"Not formally, but the Chase Manhattan is giving us a little informal help."

"Thank you, gentlemen. See, that was not so hard, was it?"

Ben left the car and went off down the street. At 9:00 that evening, he paid George Kitchton a visit at his home. George lived in a suburban home with his wife. His two children were grown and did not live with him.

He answered Ben's ring. George was a tall man, a bit on the heavy side but not really fat. He had a goatee and eyes that were hard to read.

"Yes?"

"My name is Benjamin. I need to speak to you immediately."

"What about?"

Terrence showed him his gun and said, "Take me to a room where you and I can speak privately."

The color left Kitchton's face but he opened the door and led the man to a room off the family room, where his wife was watching TV.

"We will be out in a minute, dear," was all he said.

Once in the private room, Ben laid the gun on a nearby table.

"Now, I am going to ask questions, and you are going to answer them or I will call your wife Sandy in here and do things to her you cannot imagine.

"Do you believe me?"

Kitchton nodded.

"Now, you work for Luginbuhl on the 'Jewish project,' correct?"

"Yes."

"Why did he go to Italy to find out about a shipment of German gold?"

"He wanted to track it to see if it was Jewish or not."

Terrence picked up the gun and said, "One more lie and we talk with Sandy."

"Okay, leave her out of this. I was only trying to make her life better. Don't hurt her, please," Kitchton said, his voice shrill.

"Answer the questions," Benjamin said slowly and evenly.

"We found a shipment of gold, about 148 million at that time, which was shipped in early '45 to Rome via train. This was how it was always done. This shipment was not authorized by the Reischbank but was authorized on Barman's signature alone and a quartermaster's signature."

"What was the quartermaster's name?"

"Klaus, Edward Klaus."

"Go on. What happened to the shipment?"

"It disappeared. It arrived in Rome and was placed on a ship bound for Argentina. It arrived in Argentina, and a man named Raul Latino signed for it and then it disappeared."

"So why are you interested in this gold? It is not related to your project."

"It was an unauthorized shipment. It was fifty years ago. It did not go to the bottom of the sea. It is somewhere. We thought we could find it and maybe keep it for ourselves."

"How are you planning on doing that?"

"If we can find it, we will need to ship it to a bank, and then we can draw on it."

"Do you of all people think that a bank would accept that much gold with no questions asked?"

"In the Caribbean they will. We have a connection with an American, Molly O'Connor. She has made arrangements to have the Bank of Cayman accept the funds, no questions asked. She knows the president and has assured him that if he accepts what is now almost fifteen billion in gold that we will not transfer the gold out of the bank but leave all the relevant accounts with him for at least ten years. That will give him a chance to earn at least 100 million for himself or his bank."

"Do you know where the gold is?"

Kitchton hesitated.

Terrence studied his pistol and then stood and walked to the door.

"No, please, I'll tell you," Kitchton said, again desperate.

"We found that Raul Latino had received the shipment and had it moved by train to Paraguay to an abandoned mine, where the gold was stored as was the custom. We also learned that Klaus had escaped Berlin in the end, along with Barman. They both made it to South America.

"We are trying to locate the mine now."

"How are you doing that?"

"We have an adventurer named Jon Loszin, a Polish fellow. He said that for 500,000 dollars he would find whatever we wanted found. If he has to kill people then it will cost more. He left for Paraguay a month ago and we have not heard from him yet."

"Who else is working on this with you? There is Luginbuhl, Rodham, this O'Connor woman, and who else?"

"We worked with three other bankers on the research and raising the capital for Loszin and other expenses. They are Jeff Seymour, Tony Martin, Mick Goblet, and an American Richard Lewis."

"How are you structured?"

"Share and share alike. We have all put up all the money needed and we will all share the rewards."

"When to do expect to hear from your Polish fellow?"

"Soon, but we do not know when. We thought we would at least get a report soon, and we have contacted his people in Warsaw to see if we can get an update on what he is doing."

"When you get that update, I want it. Here is my address. Mail it to me here the same day you get it."

"I can't do that."

"Your son George Jr. lives in Athens, does he not?"

"Yes."

"If you want him, his wife, and your grandchild to stay healthy then you had better do it. It had better be the same day and it had better be accurate, or before you die you will hear of your son and his family's death as well as watch your wife die very painfully. Do you understand?"

Kitchton bowed his head, a tear running out of one eye. He whispered yes.

Benjamin was on the midnight train for Rome.

CHAPTER VI

Weiss met with Rex at 10:00 a.m.

"Rex, what is going on with Jim Luginbuhl?"

"He has been acting funny since the shooting. He has been watching for tails and not gone into work."

"Have you tapped his phone?"

"No, do you want me to?"

"Yes. I want to know who he is talking to and what he is planning. Where has he been the last week?"

"He has not been to work and only out of the house a couple of times. Once to a pub and once to the grocery store near his house."

"What did he do on these trips?"

"The grocery store was a food run. He talked to no one, bought his food, and left. At the pub he did meet someone. A woman. Dark, attractive. They appeared to be acquainted. My man said he thought they were going to fuck in the back of the pub."

"Anything else unusual?"

"Yeah, he said that for all the touching that was going on, Luginbuhl looked scared. He kept looking around and did not seem to enjoy this beautiful woman."

"Did you have her followed?"

"No. You did not tell me this was a full-court press. What are you looking for and what do you want me to do?"

"I do want the full-court press now. On all of these bankers. And a full report on all of their contacts and families. Get me a full report by tomorrow at my hotel."

The next morning Rex and Weiss poured over three weeks of surveillance reports. "Do you see any patterns? Or anything unusual?" Weiss said.

"Not yet. We will need to chart all contacts from the first week and then see what reoccurs or what is new."

"Let's get to work."

They created charts for all seven bankers and their families. The walls were lined with each one. In some cases pictures were stuck next to contacts. When they were done, they had an accurate picture of their men.

"What do we have now?"

"I don't see anything on most of these guys. Their families look clean. So whatever is going on probably does not involve them directly. Most of their contacts have been between themselves, other Bank functions, or social and recreational activities with their families. Not a lot of friends outside the circle of family and work."

"Any reoccurring contacts? Road trips?"

"Luginbuhl and Loszin have met with that O'Connor woman weekly at out-of-the-way places in Berlin. I think you know what that is about."

"Did your boys pick up anyone else following any of these three?"

"Not for sure. Bernie reported that he thought he saw someone following O'Connor, but he could not be sure. He just noted it."

"Let's see what else we got. Richard Lewis did make contacts with a shipping firm that does business with his bank. He met with them before he was killed."

"Loszin met with the finance attaché to the Argentinean embassy, and Person C did the same with the Paraguayan embassy."

"They were touching their basses all right. They must have been ready to pull the trigger on this adventure when they had a big problem created. Now they are laying low. I guess the only thing to do is to get Loszin where he can talk and see what he has to say. I think we can use force to get the answers we want."

"How should we do that?"

"We could use his house since he doesn't leave there. They must be watching his house too. Have your man check out his house. I want to know if it is bugged and who, if anyone, is watching him."

The next Monday after an uneasy week, Rex and Weiss met over breakfast again.

"What do you have?"

"The house is bugged and there are two men watching him at all times. Across the street, they have a listening post set up as well."

"Do you know who?"

"A private company like ours. They do a lot of work for independent terrorist organizations."

"Who?"

"Mostly the IRA and the PLO and some spin-offs from those groups."

"So the PLO is in on this," Weiss said thoughtfully.

"Could be the IRA too. Who does not want several billions of dollars to help their cause?"

"Can you find out who they are working for?"

"Sure."

"I guess we can't use his home. We will need to grab him."

"That we can do, but his tails will know it. That will spook them into taking some action."

"Or they will simply start killing people to cover the trail."

"True. Once we grab him we will need to get all of them to try and keep them alive. We could do that and take them to our island. They would be safe there until this was settled."

"Well, how do we get him without spooking the tails?"

"Maybe just keep our own tail on him and see who he meets with. If he is going to deal with someone, he will need to talk to them."

"What do we want to know?" Rex said.

"Where the money is. I don't care about any of them. Let the PLO or the IRA do what they want; it is none of my business. In fact, if his family is in danger it may make him easier to deal with. I think if we offer him some of the money we should get a deal with no effort.

"I want him grabbed next time he leaves his apartment, and transported to our island in the next forty-eight hours. When you do that, keep close tabs on his associates and also on what his tails do. Follow them if you can."

Wednesday at 3:00 a.m. Weiss' phone rang.

"Weiss."

"We have your delivery. It can be met at dawn at the agreed upon place."

Weiss dressed quickly and took his private plane to a small island in the middle of Lake Saulva. Here, in a bunker deep beneath a hunting cabin, Loszin was tied to a chair.

"What do you want?" Loszin said as Weiss walked into the room.

"Information, and I want it now. There is no time to waste. The men that were following you no doubt have already reported your disappearance, and whatever actions they may take are without a doubt underway. I would assume that your associates and your families are in grave danger. Time is crucial."

"What do you want? I'm just banker," Loszin said, still trying to bluff.

"Bullshit," Weiss laughed.

"You know the whereabouts of 1.5 billion dollars worth of Nazi gold. Someone else knows you know it too and has grabbed your banker friend O'Connor and killed Richard Lewis to make his point.

"Now tell me where the gold is and what the arrangements are for getting it."

Loszin hesitated, surprised at what Weiss knew. "Who am I talking to?"

"That doesn't matter. Answer my question. Mosses, get the needle ready. We do not have time to waste."

"No, wait, please, no drugs. No pain."

"If I tell you what you want to know, what do I get?"

"If you give me accurate information in a timely enough fashion so that I can recover the gold before your other friends do, I will pay each of the six of you one million U.S. dollars. That is the only offer I will be making."

"Okay. That is good enough. How do I know I can trust you?"

"You don't. But you do not have much choice now do you?"

"Okay."

"The gold was shipped to Argentina and then moved by train to an old mine in Paraguay outside x."

"How do I now where? I have a map. It is in a safe deposit box in the bank. However, plans are already set for moving it."

"O'Connor arranged for a train to make a run up to the mine and pick up the gold. We have paid off the caretaker, an old Nazi named Mueller. There is sufficient equipment to load the train. It will then be transported to Argentina and placed on a ship. An American ship named the *Wolverine*. The gold will be transported to Grand Cayman and deposited in the bank of St. George. From there we will be able to wire the cash anywhere in the world."

"How were you going to get it?"

"O'Connor had it all arranged. She was coming to the last meeting with us when she was kidnapped or made her own deal with someone. I was to tell her where the gold was and give her the necessary papers. She, in turn, would give us the passwords for the banks and other shipping data. She was to be paid two million dollars for the help."

"Do you know where she is?" Loszin asked quietly.

"Of course not. If I did I would have simply killed or ignored you."

"How do I get the map and what is the password for Mueller?"

Loszin told him, "A beaten man now."

"Okay. You have been helpful. Now we are going drug you and beat you and deposit you back on the streets. Your story will be that we picked you up and tried to hold you for ransom, but you jumped from the car and escaped. We need three days after that. You can tell the truth to whomever, it will make no difference."

Wednesday at noon, Weiss met with Rex in his apartment.

"What happened when Loszin disappeared?"

"When Loszin did not appear in the morning as usual, they got anxious. They waited around then made a call on their cell. We tracked it to a PLO front organization office. They asked for directions. Since it was now 9:00 a.m., they were told to go in and get him. They knocked on the door, and when Mrs. Kathy Loszin answered they pulled their guns and went in. Once inside, they searched the house and terrified the two women that were there. They were wondering where John was too but had decided that he had gone to work early. He was not at the office.

"The two were then instructed to take the women to one of their safe houses. That was when we went in. They were surprised to see us and we made short work of them.

"We then took the women to our safe house, where Loszin is now. We grabbed him as soon as you dropped him figuring that he would be dead in a few hours if we did not. But what do we do next?"

"Anything happen to the others?"

"I'm affair so. Kitchton was grabbed right out of the bank at 11:00 a.m. They got his wife at home and took them to their safe house. There they questioned poor George, who knows nothing. When they brought his wife in and started to beat her, he told them about his conversations with you. It did no good. They still raped her and beat her badly. Their bodies were dumped in the river by 2:00 p.m.

"Between noon and 3:00 they got the other four. They did not bother with their families, but all of them are now dead. Which leaves only Loszin, who I'm sure they want dead too. There are three men staked out at his home and another two at his office."

"Okay. I don't care what happened to those scum. They tried to steal Jewish money and make themselves rich. That is a dangerous game, and they paid the price. However, I do feel a little sorry of their families.

"Pick them all up and take them along with Loszin to Grand Cayman. Set them up there with a million each in their bank accounts. Don't let them know who you are, but tell the families what happened to their husbands and tell Loszin that he owes them to take care of them.

"Kill the men watching Loszin. That will keep out friends at the PLO busy for a while, chasing Loszin and maybe buying us a day or two."

Weiss then went to his office at Travel Brokers and cabled (encrypted) what he had learned about the whereabouts of the gold to Rome.

CHAPTER VII

Rome

October 10, 2010

They met in Gilardi's office overlooking the Piazza di Popolo. Each gave their report of where they had been and what they learned.

"Well," Gilardi said, "this is interesting. Some young Swiss bankers are trying to get rich by stealing stolen gold. Does this have interest for us?"

"I'm not sure how," David said. Weiss and Sophia nodded. "Let them steal from the Nazis. What do we care?"

"What if it is Jewish gold?"

"We can never prove that, and anyway the Swiss banks will be paying for all the Jewish gold we can identify."

"Why were our contacts in Buenos Aries murdered, and by whom?"

"It could be a coincidence. Maybe someone wanted them dead and we happened to simply get in the middle."

"Possibly but I have learned in this business that there are no coincidences. I think someone wanted them dead to keep you away from them. You just got to Kruse a little quicker than they thought you would or his son would have been dead too."

"How do we find out what is going on? Maybe someone else is looking for the gold. I don't think those bankers would be into this kind of murder. I doubt they would order it and I doubt that they would have contacts that would know how to get that kind of job done."

"I will call Tessa and see if he has found out anything in Argentina. As far as Townsend and our banker friends go, we will just have to wait. Maybe we should have a talk with O'Connor and see what she knows."

"I don't see the point. If anything develops in Saulva or the U.S. we will know about it. What we need is a lead from South America."

"Let's sit tight for a week and see what develops. We'll meet here next week, same time and same place."

The next Thursday Gilardi had news. "I received a cable from Tessa last night. He said that they have learned that all of our known contacts with Nazi backgrounds have been murdered. That includes your friend Edgar Kruse Jr., David. There was no attempt to be subtle either. It was, in every case, efficient and bloody. They believe that a gang of Argentinean hit men did the murders. But they think the hits were ordered by the PLO."

"Why? They would like the Nazis, not want to kill them."

"Unless they were trying to shut down a trail. A trail that led to two billion in gold. If the PLO wants that gold, we have a reason to be interested now."

"Sophia, I want you to check in with our insider in the PLO in Athens and see what you can learn.

"I want David to go back to Argentina and see what you can find out.

"Weiss, keep your eye on our bankers."

Sophia called David Albert that afternoon and made arrangements to have dinner with him the next night.

They met at the Olympic Restaurant. It was dark and expensive. Sophia was dressed in a dark, tight dress that left her neck and shoulders bare. It was almost as expensive as the diamond earrings she wore.

They met in the bar. David slipped his arm around her and whispered in her ear, "I have been having wet dreams about you. It is good to see you again."

They embraced and Sophia whispered back, "Dreams can come true you know."

After a few drinks and time to catch up on each other's activities, they moved on to dinner. From dinner they moved to dancing and from dancing to a small, private, exclusive hotel, where they shed their expensive clothes and worked on those dreams.

Afterward, they sat naked on a sofa, cuddling and sharing a bottle of champagne.

"That was worth waiting for," Sophia said.

"Indeed! Well, what do you want to know this time? It is strange to think that I would betray my country for a fuck, but you are worth it."

"Now Dave, it is not exactly betraying, nor is it merely a fuck, is it?"

"Does that mean that you care about me?"

"Of course I do. I could fuck anyone for information, but you are special."

Dave laughed and said, "Does that mean that after we are out of this spy business we can be together?"

"I could happen. But that will be a long way off I'm afraid. What I want to know is why you are killing former or current Nazi sympathizers in South America."

"I did not know we were. All the Nazis I know are our friends, and we have worked with them on several projects that are detrimental to Israeli interests. In fact, they helped us in Munich at the Olympics."

"No, this is special. It seems that there may be two billion or so in Nazi gold hidden in South America. We believe that your people want this gold and are trying to shut down the trail that leads to it. Have you heard about this?"

"Well, I have heard that we are trying to get a lot of gold out of South America."

"Do you know why?"

"Not exactly. This is pretty hush-hush but we want the gold to buy some weapons."

"Two billion buys a lot of weapons."

"Or one big one?"

"What do you mean?"

"We have a contact with a former Russian nuclear scientist who has a warhead that is for sale."

"For two billion?"

"That is about the price."

"What are you going to do with it?"

"There is a special-ops group that is set up to use it. They are in training, but I do not know where or how they are going to use it."

"Do you now who does?"

"Is that someone else that you will be fucking? And will you tell him that he is special too?"

"I may have to fuck him but he won't be a special as you," she said as she slipped her hand up the inside of his thigh and gave his balls a slight caress.

"Well, this one will be interesting since it is Glenda Durst. Do you do women too?"

"If I have to. But you know I prefer men." Now her hand moved to his awakening shaft and began a light stroke. "Can you arrange for me to meet her?"

His hand found her right breast began to caress the nipple. "Can I watch?"

"That might be arranged. Where and when can I meet her?" His shaft was now fully erect, and she played with it and it became little harder. Sophia laid her head down on his thigh so that she was looking into his eyes with his erect penis between them.

David groaned and grasped her beautiful breast a little harder.

"How about I introduce you tomorrow? But I do want to watch."

"What time and where?" These words were slightly muffled since her mouth was full.

CHAPTER VIII

Saulva, Switzerland

October 25, 2010

Weiss returned to Saulva and simply played a waiting game. He had an old reliable contractor do background on the bankers, but there was nothing there that he did not already know. He then had them placed under surveillance with reports to him every morning at 8:00. Nothing much happened for more than a month.

"Good morning, Rex," Weiss said amicably. "What is new today? Same old same old?"

"No. I'm afraid we have something today." Rex was all business. "Yesterday the O'Connor woman was kidnapped off a train bound for Berlin from Saulva. She was taken by car to Berlin, where, incidentally, your seven bankers were to meet her. There, one of the bankers was killed. So now there are six."

"Who was killed?"

"A Richard Lewis."

"And then?"

"Molly was removed from the train and taken to Munich. The bankers called the police and then went home."

"What do you think happened?"

"I don't know. You have not told me what is going on. Only follow these people and report was my contract."

"I can't tell you much except I believe that the bankers are trying to steel a large amount of gold and Molly is supposed to help them. Evidently someone else found out about the gold and wants Molly to help them."

"How much gold?"

"Billions."

Rex gasped but said nothing else.

"What do you want me to do now?" Rex said.

"Do you know where the girl is?"

"Yes."

"Keep tabs on her. Find out who grabbed her and keep an eye on the bankers. I will pay my old friend George Kitchton a visit and see what he can tell me."

Wednesday morning as George got into his car to go to the bank, he felt a gun being pressed to his head. "Keep driving," was all Weiss said.

"George, my old friend, did you try to move the gold without telling me?"

"Did you grab her?" George said truly frightened.

"Her?"

"Molly O'Connor. Did you grab her and then kill Dick?"

"No. The only people I am going to kill are your son in Athens, your wife, and then you."

"Why?"

"Because you were supposed to keep me informed on what was going on and I have not been told a thing by you. Turn left at the next street and follow it to the park up ahead.

"Now turn into the park and take the first road to the left.

"Good. Now pull over in that clump of trees on the right.

"You have one chance and one only to tell me what is going on, or I make a call on this cell phone and in twenty-five minutes you can hear your son die.

"Now talk!"

"I know little." George was starting to cry and had a pleading look in his eyes. "We had a meeting scheduled with his O'Connor woman. She was supposed to make the arrangements to get the gold into the Caymans. From there we were going to be able to move cash to our own bank accounts. This was supposed to be the final meeting.

"She was late. We called her cell phone. A man answered and told us to go to the window. There we could see Molly. He had a gun to her head. The man said he wanted the gold and expected us to help him. Luginbuhl said no, and before we could look at each other Dick ... Richard was shot through the head. The shot came through the window and shattered it. He was dead."

"What did you tell the police?"

"Nothing. Just that he was shot as he stood by the window."

"Who wanted the money?"

"I don't know. He did not say. He was supposed to contact us this afternoon and tell us what to do with the money."

"Where are you supposed to be contacted again?"

"We have a meeting this afternoon in Bern at the Banque due Swiss Nationale."

"What are you going to do?"

"I don't know. Loszin said that we can get a deal with him and at least get some the money for us.

Maybe a million each. So he was going to try and convince them to try and cut a deal."

"Do you have the money yet?"

"It is not in our possession. We have a man in South America that has it ready to go."

"Who and where?"

"Only Jim knows that."

Weiss retuned Kitchton to the bank. "Keep me informed ... or else," he said by way of a good bye.

BOOK VI: PLO

CHAPTER I

Cypress

July 2010

George Saladin was very upset with Joseph Farok.

"Why have you taken so long? I told you, no more than six months. It has been eight and no results! Why?"

"We have been careful. He has had Lazaar trailing the German families in Argentina and has learned much about their operations. We also have been working on Kumato but without much success."

"Have you learned where the gold is?"

"Not yet."

"Do you know that it exists for sure?"

"No. But we think it does. We have located a mining village in Paraguay that could be where the gold is."

"Eight months and you know nothing?

"Joe, do you enjoy your current life."

"Yes," Joe said with dread.

"Well, you have exactly forty-five days to tell me where the gold is or it will change drastically. Do you understand?"

"Yes, sir," Joe said quietly.

He returned to Berlin by train and placed a call to John.

"We must have results now!

"You have two days to get the information I need and then I will send someone to help you."

"Okay," John said, "I will have the information you want, but it will not be subtle."

"I don't care about that. I want the information."

CHAPTER II

Tokyo, Japan

August 2010

John decided to try a more direct approach. He contacted the president of the university and arranged a meeting for the next day.

"We are looking to fund research on how Nazi Germany related to Palestine. My employer wants to make up to a million-dollar endowment for that research. We have heard of Professor Kumato and believe that he has the expertise for such a project. Can you arrange for me to meet him?"

"Of course," the president said with a smile. "A million-dollar endowment would make him look good to the board of regents, which had a meeting coming up in the next month."

Twenty minutes later, Kumato was in the president's office. John explained what he wanted and Kumato said that he was busy. Too busy for such a project. After some arm-twisting, he still refused and then left.

The president said, "I have other fine researchers that could do an excellent job for you."

"No, my employer wants Kumato."

"Let me talk to him some more and maybe he can be persuaded. Give me a couple of days, and then we can discuss this further? Say Thursday at 11:00, here again. Afterward we can go to lunch and celebrate our collaboration."

During the two days, John set up a tap on Kumato's phone and broke into his office. He searched Kumato's paper files and found nothing. He then tried to search the computer files but was unable to gain access to the computer. He then put the computer online and connected with a computer expert in the Libya base camp.

"I need access to the files on this machine. Can you break into it for me?" John asked.

"But of course. Leave the machine online and I will get the information you need. I will contact you in ten hours."

By the next night John had the codes needed to gain access to Kumato's computer.

He broke in through the second-story window on the back side of the building. He reached the window from a tree. Once inside he moved quickly down the hall to Professor Kumato's office. The doors were unlocked, both outer and inner, and he was on the computer in minutes. John scrolled through the file until he found the file marked Hitler's Gold and then copied it. He next searched the cabinets for additional files. He found two disks that appeared related and he copied those too.

He was back in the hallway, moving toward the window, when he was challenged by the night watchman, a boy of about twenty, working as a night guard to pay his way through college. John stopped at the challenge. The boy came up to him armed with only a radio and asked who he was and what he was doing there at 3:00 a.m. John smiled and said, "Just checking on an experiment that I have been working on."

"All the labs are in the basement. Why are you on the second floor? Can I see some ID?"

As he spoke, he reached for his radio. Before he could thumb the key he was dead. John and thrown a well-placed back of the arm to his throat.

The boy's eyes rolled in his head and he hit the floor.

John proceeded to the exit window and was back in his apartment in ten minutes.

He copied the file to his computer and then went online. He made contact with his base in Europe and transferred the data through a secure, encrypted line.

He then began to review the material for himself. Most of it was dry notes on various personalities and transactions that had taken place between Nazi Germany and various suppliers of war materials. He saw how Kumato had traced the money from

Germany to Switzerland to the Vatican and then on to the suppliers. *Interesting,* John thought, *similar to our network. The more things change the more they stay the same.*

He then noted that a shipment of gold had left Switzerland in the spring of '45 and had not arrived at suppliers. Of course, by then, it was useless anyway. But this shipment seemed to disappear from all overt records. Kumato had traced it and with, Luginbuhl's help had found that it went to Argentina and from there to Paraguay. Noted for further follow up was a list of names in Argentinean and one in Paraguayan. John printed the names out and reported to Joe.

Joe then called Lazaar:

"Have your team in an active mode by tomorrow morning. I have some people for you to talk to."

By three that afternoon, Joe had received an encoded message from George. "Good work," he said.

"I think that gives us what we need to know."

"Saul will be talking to the names provided by tomorrow. I hope that in the next three days we will have the answer to your questions."

"Good. Now, we do not want anyone getting to the gold before us. The world has forgotten this shipment. Let's leave it that way. You need to erase Kumato's disk, records, and Kumato himself."

"I will take care of that today."

Kumato always left the school at 4:30 p.m. and walked across the campus to his home on the far west side of both the city and the campus. As he walked across the campus, he was bumped by a dark, good-looking woman.

"Excuse me," she said and moved on.

"That is all right," Kumato said. "We all are careless at some time." By the time he reached the far side of campus he was feeling weak. So weak in fact that he could not stand up. The last thing he saw was the ground coming up to meet him.

John in his hotel room watched the news report. They were making a big deal about the dead night watchman and now the death of Kumato. They treated it as a coincidence since Kumato was believed to have died from a heart attack. He had had a history of heart problems.

At 3:00 a.m. John retuned to campus. Security was much tighter this time, but he made it in without being seen. He then proceeded to the professor's office. He turned on the computer and instructed it to delete all files. He then inserted the two disks that had been in the cabinet and cleaned them too. Next a small package of C4 was attached to the computer. John then scattered a highly flammable powder throughout the office. Down the hall, more powder. John went to the basement, where he placed another C4 package and more powder. He then left the building....

At 3:30 a.m., there was an explosion, and a very fast-moving fire ensued. At 4:30, the TV news reported that he result was the total destruction of the history research building. Two night watchmen died in the blaze. Both students.

George received the news of the death of professor Kumato and the destruction of the history wing of the university from Joe with a wry smile.

"Well, that cuts off that link and gives us the information."

"What is on the disks that we received?"

"The names of a group of Nazis and their families in Argentina. We assume they know where the gold is."

"When will we know if the gold still exists and where it is?" George asked calmly.

"Not until Lazaar 'talks' to the Germans."

John Flew home to Paris.

CHAPTER III

August 2010

Lazaar's Army, as he liked to call his men, arrived in Buenos Aires in teams of two. Thomas the electronics expert and Steff the explosives man arrived first. Their first job was to secure two safe houses. Local support people provided one, while the other was rented by Thomas and swept for "bugs." They also reserved a room in the Marriott downtown for the next two men to arrive.

This time it was two soldiers. By soldiers, Lazaar meant weapons specialists. There were four of them on the team. They set up camp in one of the safe houses.

Lazaar came next along with the communications man Eli. They set up camp in the Marriott suite. Part of Eli's job in communications was to arrange for beautiful women for Lazaar to communicate with.

A week later, two more weapons specialists arrived and were housed in the other safe house.

Finally, two air specialists arrived. These two men could fly anything anywhere and were essential for transporting the team in operation situations.

It took six weeks but they were all in country with all their equipment ready to start the operation. Lazaar reported to Joe.

"All is ready. Do you have any directions for us?"

"Not yet. I will be sending you a list of families to be observed. No contact, only observation. That is where we start. I will FedEx the information to you at the hotel. You should have it by tomorrow."

The package arrived. It was a list of six families. All German, all arrived in Argentine between 1938 and 1946.

Lazaar gathered his men at the local safe house, and after Ari assured them it was all right to conduct the meeting Lazaar started. "We have six families that need to be observed. No contact. Ari and Eli, I want you to research these families find out all you can. Steff, you and the others spilt up and begin following all six families. In a couple of weeks, we will match up what we have learned with what you have seen and we will go from there."

Steff Parvizi set up a command bunker in the second safe house. He assigned one family to each of the six men working for him. They had freedom to choose who to watch in each family and when to watch. Each man reported daily to Steff, who kept the notes of contacts on is laptop.

Two weeks later he met with Lazaar, Thomas, and Eli. "Here is what we have on each family." He laid out the reports.

"The Valentines have three generations living in a compound. They are engaged in import and export. The old man seems to control the family. His son is Karl and he is the figurehead of the company. His only child is a beautiful daughter, twenty-three years old. She appears to be doing what any young pretty twenty-three-year-old does. The business appears to be straightforward. Karl and the old man need closer watching. They have had contact with the other five families in the last two weeks. It appears that they are close with them. Again it is the old people that are the closest, but the second generation is close, while the third acts like cousins in an extended family.

"The Klaus family are financiers. There is the old man, Edgar, and his son Edgar Jr. Edgar is not married but has many female friends that he appears the spend a great deal of time with. They live in a large mansion on the south side of town. They deal with import and export finances.

"The John Winfield family also has three generations. However, in the third generation two sons live in the States. Their father Wolfgang lives here with his father Sebastian. The sons are bankers. One works in Wells Fargo Bank in San Francisco and the other with Bank of America in Denver, Colorado. They have regular contact with the family but are not close to them. Both are married with one child each. Their wives are American. Wolfgang's wife is a society personage here in Argentina, rather a high-profile socialite.

"Karl Kershner is a widower. He has a son, Adolph, and a daughter, Maria. Maria is married to an Argentinean, George Perez. George is a merchant. He and Maria have little to do with the German community here in Argentina. Adolph on the other hand spends a great deal of time in this community. He is also a merchant. He owns a series of equestrian stores across Argentina and has at least one in Paraguay. He is big into polo and has several ponies.

"The Neumeyers are bankers. They work closely with the other German families and have many contacts in Germany. The Neumeyer children, four in all, make many trips annually to Germany along with the Dame Neumeyer. The old man runs a small storefront operation in the poor side of town, while the oldest boys, Hans and Lawrence, own and operate a very large bank. There appears to be a great deal of communication with a family in Paraguay as well as banking houses in Germany.

"Finally the Jurks are the smallest and poorest family. They have a modest residence near the docks. The family occupation is shipping and they operate dockside warehouses. They have three daughters, all married. Two live in Germany and one in Paraguay."

Lazaar then turned to Thomas for his report.

Thomas began his report:

"These families all came to South America either just before the Second World War, during, or immediately after. The early ones were sent here by Hitler to establish trading arrangements with South America. Later they were sent to establish a safety net then an escape route for Nazis. Finally, some were the escapees. They are supported by German dollars, at least in the beginning, although several have become wealthy with trade. There is a network that stretches over most of South America and involves transfers of dollars, some large amounts and some small.

"This we learned by research and by tapping into their banks. There is center for this activity and it is in Paraguay Asuncion. There is also some relationship with Panambi, a small town in the mountains of Paraguay."

"So what do you make of it?" Lazaar demanded. He was not much for thinking; he just wanted to be pointed in the direction of action.

"It is hard to say at this point. The Klaus family and the Neumeyer family seem to be the leaders, at least here in Argentina. I suggest we wire tap them and work their banks a little and tail all the members of these two families and see what happens. Give me a month of discreet inquiries and I think we will know something."

"Okay. I can do that," said Lazaar with a smile. "Eli, you take the tailing operation. Use all the men besides Ari and Matthew. They will work the quiet side. I will work with Joe and see what he can find out in Europe. My orders will come from him."

Thomas and Matt worked the bank and phone, both ongoing and records. They discovered that there was much contact with a family in Paraguay. Lazaar decided to visit Asuncion.

Amanda Wilhelm walked out of the record shop/ dance club and bumped into a dark man. He was short but very powerfully built. His presence was commanding. He had a force about him that drew one in. Amanda, who was tall for a woman, nearly six feet tall, with olive skin and jet-black hair, nearly bounced off the stranger.

"Excuse me," he said. "I was looking the other way and did not see you."

Amanda was flustered but tried not to let it show. "That is quite all right," she said.

"Excuse me further," the stranger said. "I am here to do business with a man named Wilhelm. Edgar Wilhelm. Might you be his daughter?"

"Why do you want to know that? If you have business with Señor Wilhelm, why not go this office and do business?"

"Because he has refused to see me twice. Now he will not refuse me," Lazaar said, showing Amanda a very ugly looking knife. "You will do as I say or you will wish you had," he said. "Now get in that blue Mercedes parked on the curb."

Amanda started to run, but Lazaar caught her by the wrist, pulled her to him, and slid the knife along her right rib. It caught neatly through her clothes and into her tender skin. She started to scream but Lazaar said, "Make a sound and it will be your last. Now get in the car."

This time she obeyed.

Once in the car the driver took off like a shot and soon they were out of the city.

Amanda stared ahead in terror. "What do you want?"

"To talk to your father, that is all. Here, call him." Lazaar pressed a cell phone into her hands.

Amanda looked out the widow and said, "I will not."

Lazaar produced the knife again and took her by the arm. He made a cut about ten inches long, starting at her elbow and ending at her thumb. The cut was not deep but it did bleed.

He then grabbed Amanda's face and held the knife to it. "The next cut starts at your eye and finishes at your chin. When I am done with your face, no man will look at you without turning away. Now make the call."

Amanda did as she was told. "What do you want me to say?"

"Tell your father what has happened then give the phone to me."

Amanda got her father on the phone.

"Daddy, some man grabbed me at knifepoint and forced me to go with them. He cut me and said he wants to hurt me some more. Daddy, help me," she said and broke down in tears.

Lazaar grabbed the phone from her trembling hands and said, "Max Wilhelm. I must talk to you. I will be at your house in ten minutes. I will enter alone. Amanda will stay in the car. When I come back safely from our conversation, she will be released. Do you understand?"

"Yes," Max said slowly. "I will expect you in ten minutes."

Exactly ten minutes later, Lazaar rang Wilhelm's door.

Max himself answered and looked over Lazaar's shoulder for a sign of Amanda.

"Come in," he said carefully.

Lazaar entered the home. The two men walked to Max's office, where they sat down.

"What do you want? You have gone through a lot of trouble to see me," he said with disgust.

"I need information and some assistance. I believed that you would not help me if I had simply asked."

"What kind of help?"

"I represent an organization that is just as anti-Jewish as yours. We, however, have not been able to kill six million of them. They stole our country before we could pick up where you left off. We would like to correct that problem.

"We have reason to believe that some German families here in South America know where there is a lot of Jewish gold. We want it."

Max's eyes did not blink. "I do not know what you are talking about."

"Shall I ask your granddaughter about that? Only I will use a knife to ask the question."

"I do not know what you are talking about," Max said. "Now release my granddaughter and leave."

Lazaar shook his head. "No, no, no, you need to answer my questions." He picked up the phone and dialed a number. "Put her on," he said when the phone was answered. He then reached down and pushed the speaker button on the phone.

Amanda could be heard crying.

Max Wilhelm went pale but said nothing.

"Cut her," Lazaar said with a snarl into the phone.

Amanda's screams could be herd reverberating around the quiet room.

"Well?" Lazaar said with a raised eyebrow. "Are you ready to help now?"

"I would help," Wilhelm said very low and very slowly, "but I know nothing."

Lazaar spoke to the phone and said, "Again."

Once more a scream rang out.

This time Wilhelm stood and without a word reached into a desk drawer.

Lazaar watched as he pulled a pistol from the drawer, but before he could raise it Lazaar shot him through the head.

He fell without a word.

"What was that?" the phone asked.

"Wilhelm being foolish. He is dead and cannot help us now."

"Wonderful. What about the girl?"

"Kill her," Lazaar said as he began a careful search of the Wilhelm home.

The next day, the headlines read "Financier and granddaughter found dead in their home. Slain by unknown assailants."

CHAPTER IV

"Thomas, you have two men at the funeral and see who shows up. I want pictures and tapes made of everyone and every word said. Then you analyze them and tell me what you found out."

Thomas and Eli went to the funeral. Eli took pictures, while Ari taped all the conversations that he could. They then returned to their safe house and worked for two full days to see what they had. They reported to Lazaar.

"We did not find a lot. The people who attended the funeral broke down into two groups: Germans and South Americans. We worked on the Germans.

"We learned that they stay in contact on a regular basses with each other.

"We learned that there are seven leading families."

"Get to it," interrupted Lazaar. "I knew this before we came here."

"Okay, we learned that their businesses for the most part interact with each other and that there is an eighth family that we were not aware of. This family lives in Paraguay. It would appear from conversations that all seven families have at one time or another visited there as a getaway kind of thing.

"We also learned that there is or was a man named Paul Latino, at least that is what they seemed to call him, who was instrumental in bringing all of them here. He appears to have had contact with them all over an extended period of time, but no one spoke of him in an immediate sense."

"So we need to find out who these new people are. Send a team to Paraguay to find out about this new man and send another team to get information on this Paul Latino, if that is his real name. I'll contact Joe and see if knows anything new."

"Yes, yes, we have kept a low profile. No, no one knows we are here. Yes, we did kill Wilhelm and his granddaughter because he would not talk to me. No one knows we were behind that.

"We have learned that there is some kind of retreat center or base or something in Panambi. We have also learned that a man named Paul Latino had or has connections with all these families. Do you know anything about him?"

"I found out," Joe said quietly, "that this Latino was the contact for the shipment of gold we are interested in. Probably for all the shipments. He may have been Hitler's own personal representative there. But that is all I know."

"We will use Thomas' skills to see if we can find this Latino, but if that breaks down we will need to use some other skills to get the answer."

Joe was very firm. "I will need to approve that BEFORE you do it. Do you understand?"

"Yes, yes, of course, don't worry. We won't make a mess here. Not until you tell us to."

Thomas was sent to scour financial records to try and find a Paul Latino. But he failed to find a trace.

On the Tuesday of the second week of efforts, one of the soldiers who was following the Klaus Edgar family reported:

"I have found another tail on Edgar besides us."

"Well, that is interesting," Lazaar said. "Who is it?"

"His name is Jon Loszin he is a small-time operator from East Germany. He used to do some freelance work for the German secret service, then after the reunification he worked for anyone that wanted him."

"Who is he working for now?" Lazaar asked.

"I do not know for sure. We put a tail on him. He is staying in a nice Marriott Hotel downtown and drives a Mercedes rental, so whoever is paying him is paying him well. He has also made a trip to Paraguay."

"That is interesting," Lazaar mused.

"I guess we need to talk with him. Pick him up and bring him to the harbor. I will have a small boat waiting tomorrow night. We can take a little cruise together."

Loszin was just leaving the Marriott when two men fell in beside him. As the doorman opened the door to his Mercedes, the two men pushed him into the backseat. One sat next to him, another drove the car, and a third man appeared to hand the doorman some dollars and then got in next to him.

Loszin was enough of an operator to know what this was about. He sat back and asked:

"Who are you working for and what do you want of me?"

"You will find out very soon, Mr. Loszin. Until then sit back and enjoy the ride."

They arrived at the docks and the four men got out, Loszin in the middle, with the third man behind Jon, poking a pistol into his back as they walked down the pier to the cabin cruiser *Lucky Dog*.

"Welcome aboard," Lazaar said.

Jon froze. "Lazaar? What are you doing here and what do you want from me?"

"Just a few questions and a quiet boat ride," Lazaar smiled.

"Come aboard, have a drink, sit down, and we will cast off." The third man pushed Jon aboard, and Eli shoved him into a chair while Thomas brought him a drink.

"Here, drink this," he said without a hint of a smile.

197 The Day the Music Died

They immediately cast off and within fifteen minutes were out of the harbor. Not a word was spoken by anyone.

Then Lazaar turned to Loszin. "Well, you have yourself in some big-time action this time, huh?"

"I don't know what you mean big-time action."

"I will not mess around.

"Mohammed, come out here." One of the solders appeared from the cabin with two buckets in one hand and a bag of cement in the other. He dropped them both in front of Jon.

"Now, you need to answer my questions if you wish to return to the shore."

Jon nodded and looked away. All he could see was miles of ocean in all directions. Nowhere to run.

"What do you want to know?"

"First of all, what are you doing here?"

"I am trying to find several hundred million dollars in gold."

"I thought as much."

Muhammad began to fill the buckets with the dry cement in the powder form.

"Tell me more details. Why were you following Edgar?"

"I arrived here a month ago and started tracking the seven main German families." His eyes continued to follow what Mohamed was doing. "I thought they might know where the gold was. I finally zeroed in on Klaus."

"Why him?"

Mohammed put water in the buckets now and began to stir.

"He seemed to be the real leader. I set up a listening device on his house and learned that there was someone in Paraguay that was involved with him."

"Did you go to Paraguay and locate this person or persons?"

Jon said, "No, I have not left Argentina."

At that, Lazaar nodded to Mohamed, who picked up one of Jon's feet and placed it in the bucket. Jon began to whimper.

"Come on, I never did anything to you or anyone associated with you. All I did was try to make a few bucks. Nothing wrong with that, is there?"

Lazaar said, "Tell me about Paraguay."

Jon tried to pull his foot out but Mohammad held it firm. Jon continued to struggle and looked at Lazaar, his eye wide. "Come on," he said, "please."

Lazaar smiled and Mohammed allowed Jon to remove his foot.

"I went up to Panambi, Paraguay, where there is a camp. There is an old mine up there and a small town with about 500 people in it. All seven families go up there at least once a year. Why, I don't know."

"Did you see anything else?"

"No, just the small town and an old mine. There are railroad tracks up to the mine, but it looks like they have not been used in years. I don't think it is a working mine."

"Thank you, Jon. You have been most helpful. One more question. Who are you working for?"

Jon said, "Some bankers from Switzerland. They want me to locate this gold and tell how to get it."

"Well, where IS the gold?" Lazaar said with a leer.

"I don't know," Jon said as Mohamed placed both feet in the nearly dry cement buckets. This time Jon was unable to get them out. He began to cry.

"Why do this to me?" he cried. "It's not fair."

"No, I suppose not," Lazaar said, "but life is not fair. Would you like something to eat before we start back?"

Jon continued to cry and beg. Lazaar sat back and ate a large dinner and drank a lot of wine while Jon continued to cry.

"Place him on the edge of the boat," he said and then beckoned for a young girl about twenty to come up on deck. He nodded to her and said, "Please him." The girl walked over and knelt before Loszin. She opened his pants, pulled out his penis, and began to suck it.

Jon cried louder, "What are you doing?"

"When you come, you go," Lazaar said with a smile that turned into a laugh....

Jon sat there, silenced by what he had just heard. His penis was already rigid.

"If you have not come before we enter the harbor, you may live," Lazaar laughed again. The crew began taking bets on when Jon would die or if he could hold out until they reached the harbor.

The girl continued to perform on him, but she slowed her head bobbing.

Jon tried to think of math problems, his grandmother, and any old lady he could picture.

He could see the lights of the harbor now.

Lazaar, still laughing, said, "Margarita, if he does not come before the harbor, he will live but you will die for being such a poor sex object." Fear crossed her eyes and she began to move faster, up and down. Soon just outside the harbor, perhaps one more mile, she raised her head in triumph.

Jon groaned and Lazaar nodded to Mohamed, who pushed the chair that Jon and his new shoes were tied to over the edge. There was splash and Jon Loszin was no more.

All the Arabs laughed. They were still laughing as they arrived at the pier from which they had left an hour or so ago.

BOOK VII: BUENOS ARIES

CHAPTER I

Argentina

September 15, 2010

David caught a plane for Buenos Aires. When he arrived, he in checked into the Hyatt and called the Israeli consulate. He gave the receptionist his name and code word and was directed to Chris Tessi. Tessi was ostensibly the head of the tourist assistance unit but in reality was the chief Mossad officer for South America. His job had been, for the last twenty years, to track down Nazis and those who had assisted them. He liked his job, liked seeing those who had hurt or killed his people brought to justice, and sometimes getting to mete out that justice. He knew who were of German descent in the South America and who had and were helping them. David made arrangements to meet him at the hotel bar for that evening.

David walked into the bar and saw Tessi standing at the far end of the bar: a short man, carefully dressed, mustache and a face that gave away nothing, including much of a smile. His eyes were brown but very flat, almost dead.

"David?" Tessi said.

"Yeah. You must be Tessi. Can we talk here?"

"Yes, if we take that back booth. I have had my men sweep it. The hotel owner is a friend of Israel."

After they had ordered drinks, David said, "I am here to track down a man named Raul Latino. At least that is name we know him by. Do you have anything on him?"

"Is he Argentinean?"

"I'm not sure. He is South American and we believe he has contacts in Paraguay, so as to his nationality, I'm not sure. He should be in his seventies by now. He worked in import/export during the war and handled shipments for the Nazis. We do not know what his cover was, but we believe he helped in weapons sales and or gold transportation."

"Hmm. That is a new name. I don't suppose you have a picture to help?"

"No. All we have is a name. What records to you have back to '44 or so?"

"Well, we have a lot. There were a lot of operatives here at that time. In fact, there still are many Nazis and their sympathizers here. We will have to go back to those we know and see where that leads. I will assign an agent to help you. His cover is that of a tour guide. He will have the names and addresses of three men that we know were key in South America during the war. A visit to them may be helpful. I'll have George Bigger pick you up at ten tomorrow. What is your room?"

"509."

"Do you require anything for this evening? A place to dine or perhaps some Argentinean entertainment?"

"Where is a good place to eat?"

"Two blocks down this street is a place called Ty's Landing. You will be able to have a pleasant meal there. If you require anything else while you are here, be sure to check with Bigger. He will know what brothels, etc., are safe for you. Good night, Mr. David, and good hunting."

After a pleasant dinner at Ty's, David fell into a dreamless sleep. He was awakened at 8:00 a.m. by his wake-up call.

He was ready when precisely at 10:00 there was a knock at his door. A tall man, dark, overweight, with a pleasant smile and knowledgeable way about him, said that he was Bigger and had come to get him.

"My friends just call me Biggs. I am here to show you the city." As he spoke, he handed David an ID card and a note that said, "Do not talk in here—the walls have ears."

When they were in George's car he said:

"I have three names for you of old men that worked for the Nazis in the forties and who know the network. None of them will be cooperative. We have only interviewed one before, and after some persuasion he did share information. That is how we know of these other two, but this will be our first interview with them. We have been watching them for years and know that they still have contacts with either Nazis or other enemies of Israel in the world."

They pulled up in front of a curio shop on a small side street. The store was cluttered and the street was crowed but not with tourists. Little children begged them for money as they crossed the street. One woman displayed a breast and made a sexual offer to the men.

In the shop there were two young clerks. Bigger said to the first one, "We want to see Neumeyer, the old man."

"He is not here, Señor. He is retired."

Bigger placed a very thin, very sharp, and very long knife next to the young man's side. Where it materialized from David could not tell.

"I'll ask just once more and then you will answer me through cries of pain. I want to see Neumeyer."

The young man, now with large eyes and small beads of sweat on his forehead, said through clenched teeth:

"Well, since you ask like that, he is in the back. Second door on the left."

"Lead the way … and smile."

When they arrived before the second door, Bigger shoved the young man through it using his head and shoulders as a battering ram. He ended up on the floor in front of an old man of eighty-plus years.

He was gray haired, thin, and meticulously dressed. He was seated in a wheelchair and was taking a sip of tea as the door crashed open and his employee was thrown at his feet. He slowly raised his eyes to look at Bigger. There was no hint of surprise or anything else in those cold, black eyes.

David pulled his gun and aimed it at the man on the floor, while Bigger just smiled at Neumeyer.

"Well, Mr. Bigger, what brings you here?" Neumeyer asked. "I have not seen you for five years. That was the last time you and your Jew friends invaded my house. What do you want before I have you removed like the trash that you are?"

"Mr. Neumeyer, you were fairly helpful last time and we expect that you will be this time."

"I am older now. There is less you can do. I care little what happens to myself now."

"That may be true, but you have a pretty daughter and two attractive granddaughters that I am sure you do not want harmed."

"You are a rotten Jewish bastard. Hitler did not kill enough of your kind. Someday someone will finish the job. What do you want?"

"We need information on a man named Latino, Raul Latino. He is or was about your age and worked in your field, import/export that is, during the war."

"Latino.... I know no one by that name."

Bigger nodded to David, who cocked his gun and leveled it at the young man's head. As he did so, he screwed on the silencer.

"I will ask once more than we will start with force. What do you know about Latino?"

"I told you Jew bastards that I know no one by that name!"

David shot the young man in the knee. His knee exploded in a cloud of blood as the young man exploded in a cry of pain, surprise, and rage."

"The next one is in his head. What do you know about Latino?" said Bigger.

The old man, shaking with impotent rage, said, "I know no one by that name, but there was a man named Raul Gomez. He was an agent that sometimes used as a code the name Latino."

"Where is he now?"

"I do not know. I have not seen or heard from him in thirty years."

David aimed the gun at the sobbing young man's head.

"Wait, wait," said Neumeyer. "There are two people that may know. They are Edward Klaus and Angelo Sausser. They are both here in Buenos Aires."

With that Bigger motioned for David to leave and the two men backed out of the small shop. Neumeyer cursed at them as they left and then reached for the phone.

"Sí, they just left, two men. They are wearing suits and they will be coming to you, I am sure," he spoke into the receiver.

David and Biggs got in their BMW and headed for the next stop. Behind them they did not notice that a nondescript Opal had begun to follow them.

Bigger explained to David when they were in the car headed for Sausser's house that these were the other two men that they had been following for years and had been tapping their phones, etc. Bigger said that he knew they were involved in smuggling and had been since 1940, that during the war they were part of a gang of German-South Americans, mostly Paraguayans and Argentineans, that were openly helping the Nazis. They had changed to drugs and other kinds of smuggling after the war. They had also been instrumental in importing people from Germany after the war. It was believed that these were former Nazis that they had imported. "They are dangerous, connected, and into God knows what," Bigger concluded.

"We treat them like the scum they are. You can see that they feel the same about us. Over the years, various Mossad agents here in South American have been killed. We believe by them or their friends.

"This Sausser is the financial man of the group. He handles all financial transactions both here and abroad. He is probably the one that we really want to talk to. We have not interviewed him before because we did not want him to know that we knew him and had him under surveillance."

Bigger turned down a narrow slum lane and stopped in front of the worst hovel on the block. He turned to David and said:

"Better have your gun ready. They will not do much talking here. We also need to move fast." Quickly they left the car and kicked the door open. Guns drawn, they entered the room.

There was not much light. Only a small candle burned in one corner. In the other corner, there was Sausser with a lifeless grin on his face that matched the grin that stretched from ear to ear on his neck. Blood covered the floor.

Sirens could be heard. Bigger turned to David and said, "Let's get out of here before the police arrive. This was a setup."

They turned off the narrow street just as two police cars careened around the corner at the other end. The Opal followed them.

"That leaves only Klaus to talk to, and we had better get to him fast."

"What do you think happened?" said David.

"It looks like someone did not want him to talk to us."

"Who knew we were going to see him?"

"No one but my boss knows I am here or why. Who in your office knows about this?"

"Only myself and Samuel my assistant. He knows my schedule and whatever else I am doing. He is Mossad, straight from Israel. His mother was raped and murdered in an Arab terrorist attack that killed five other women ranging in age from ten to forty. Each was repeatedly raped by a number of men for several hours while we negotiated. Finally, when they had agreed to end the standoff, they lined the women and girls up naked and shot them in front of our men and the TV cameras. Samuel watched on TV. Two years later, his father was killed on the Golan Heights fighting Syrians. I do not think we need to doubt his loyalty."

"Someone is on to us. I'll have to report this back to Rome. Maybe there is a problem there."

This time they arrived in front of a large hacienda with a locked gate. Bigger drove the car trough the gate.

All was quiet.

"I do not like this. There should be guards and there should be someone challenging us."

The door to the large home was open, and the two men with guns drawn once again entered the home.

They were greeted by the body of the butler. Further down the hall, a maid was sprawled out with blood covering her white uniform. As they went up the stairs they found two more bodies, one on the landing and the other in the upstairs hallway.

They could hear sobs coming from a bedroom and they carefully entered the room. There was Klaus, lying in a pool of blood that had come from the five or six holes that crossed his chest.

A younger man was holding Klaus and sobbing. He looked up at Bigger and David and said:

"Go ahead and kill me too, you Jewish scum. You finally killed him. He always said you people would get him. That was why he hated you. All of you!"

The Opal turned into the courtyard quietly. Four large men emerged from the vehicle and moved quietly toward the house. Once in the house, they pulled down masks and moved slowly and carefully up the stairs. They each carried an H&K machine pistol and appeared to know what they were doing. Once upstairs they moved down the hall to Klaus' room without a sound.

When they were only a few feet from the door, a dog appeared at the end of the hallway and began to bark at them angrily. The leader swore and without hesitation signaled to the other three to move in. He also shot the dog.

Hearing the dog bark, Bigger dropped to one knee and spun around to face the doorway. He said to David, "Get him out of here! Go to the balcony!" David, without a word, grasped the young man by the arm pulled him toward the balcony.

He had not gone more than a step before three masked men appeared in the doorway with guns blazing.

Bigger fired two shots at the first one through the door before he could lower his H&K to find Bigger. He spun backward and dropped without a cry. The next one had Bigger in his sights and he stitched a row of blood spurts across his chest. Just as the bullets were pounding him, George managed to get a shot off, which hit the large man in his right shoulder. He cried, dropped to one knee, and tried to find David with his H&K.

Before he could him, David fired and took his head off.

Number three was at the door but had been setting up to return fire on Bigger and was slow in readjusting to the fire from the direction of the balcony. As a result, David found him first and he went down in a heap.

The fourth man was kneeing at the entrance to the bedroom and shooting at David. David threw the young man he had by the arm onto the floor of the balcony and said, "Stay down!"

Lying down and peeking around the corner, David saw number four in the doorway but there was no clear shot. They exchanged ineffective gunfire for a few seconds. David turned to the young man, who was huddled in the corner with his eyes bugged out, and said, "Any way out of here besides through that door?" pointing into the bedroom.

The young man swallowed hard and choked back a scream or a sob, David wasn't sure which, and then pointed to the other end of the balcony. David could see that there was a low wall, and then about five feet from that a small landing protected by another low wall. The landing was the top of a flight of stairs that went down to the courtyard.

"Let's go!" said David. He leaned around the door and let loose a volley to keep his enemy's head down. Then dragging the other man ran for the wall and jumped to the landing. He landed on his feet and crawled back to the wall to see if they were being followed. No one was there yet. Grabbing the man by the arm, down the stairs they went.

As they reached the courtyard, sirens could be heard in the distance. They rounded the corner and David saw his car waiting for him. He grasped the other man by the shirt and said:

"You get in the passenger side and get down. If you move in any direction but the car your dead. Got it?"

The man nodded and they broke for the car.

Just as they left the corner, a hail of fire descended on them from the balcony that they had just left.

They reached the car, started it, did a U-turn in the courtyard, and raced out the way they had come in only five minutes before. As they hit the street, two police cars were heading for the gate. One policia waved at David, but David swerved around the car and took off down a side street. The police might have followed, but just then man number four appeared in the gatehouse and shot at David. The police focused their attention on him.

As they sped down the street, David grasped the cell phone in the glove box.

"Hello, this is David. I'm coming in and bringing a guest with me. Bigger is dead."

The voice, in a flat, professional tone like that of an air-traffic controller, said, "Don't bring him here. Go to 39 Annunciation Boulevard, the back door. Be sure you are not being followed."

David steered into the flow of traffic on a main street and slowed down to match the speed of cars around him.

He turned to the other man and asked directions to Annunciation Boulevard. The man initially refused to answer, but when David pointed his .357 magnum at him and cocked the hammer he gave the directions.

In thirty-five minutes, David was pulling into an open garage at the back of 39 Annunciation Boulevard. The back door was open and he dragged his guest with him into the dark house.

He was no sooner inside than he was grasped and pinned against the wall, as was his guest.

CHAPTER II

Argentina

September 16, 2010

John arrived in Argentina and received a report from Lazaar.

"We have the four German families under surveillance. All we were getting is mundane conversation about family matters then two interesting things happened.

"The first was that the Mossad came to visit the Neumeyer family. Our mikes picked up the conversation and they were asking about the gold too. We tried to follow the Jews but they lost us. That stared a flurry of calls to the other families. There is a family named Vasquez that seems to be the leader. The calls went there eventually. They made calls to a number in Paraguay and have ordered more protection from some private security people. I have had him killed to slow the Jews down. Klaus is the one we need.

"I think we need to visit them. We need to do it now."

Two hours later John, Lazaar and four operatives entered the Klaus compound. They were met by two burly, rough-looking men dressed as butlers with bulges in their suit coats. Before either could speak, they were shot dead. One team member was left to guard the exit while the rest advanced. As they entered the home, they were met by a maid. She saw their guns and opened her month to scream, but before she could two bullets prevented the alarm, one in the throat through the larynx and the other just above her right eye.

A young man came down the stairs. Before he could react, Lazaar had him by the throat with a gun to his head. "Where is Klaus?" he said. The young man, frightened, pointed toward a sitting room on the west side of the home. While two soldiers guarded the door, Lazaar and John entered the room. The room was shaded in the afternoon and had such a nice breeze that air-conditioning was not needed.

Two guards were with Mr. Klaus as he sipped his Jägermiseter. They were gunned down before they could move. Lazaar dragged Klaus' son to where he was in front of the old man. The boy was forced to his knees with the gun aimed at his head.

"John, said take a good look at your son. These will be his last seconds of life."

Klaus stammered, "Who are you? What do you want? Are you the Jews come to harm me after all these years?"

"We will ask the questions and you will answer. I assure you we are not Jews and think you should be punished for not doing a better job in the forties. I am going to ask you a question and you will answer or he will die," John said pointing to Klaus Jr.

"Where is the gold?"

"What gold?" Klaus said.

John nodded and Lazaar shot the boy in the knee. He screamed in pain.

Klaus cursed and said, "It is in Paraguay."

"How do we get it?"

After Klaus had told them what they wanted, they dragged him upstairs and put both Klaus and his son in Klaus' bedroom. Then they put a bullet in Klaus' head. As they turned their guns on the boy, he bolted. As shots tracked him across the room, he made it to an adjoining room and closed the door.

Lazaar cursed and said, "That only prolongs his life by a few seconds and increases his suffering. When I kill him, he will not die quickly." As he opened the door, a blast from a shotgun ripped the door jamb.

Lazaar jumped back and smiled.

"So the baby scorpion has a stinger? No matter he will die."

As he spoke the earpiece in John's ear crackled.

"We have company. There are two cars coming through the gate with armed men. We can slow them down, but you had better be moving."

As shots rang out from the courtyard, John told Lazaar, "Let him go. It is time to leave. We can kill him tomorrow. We have what we came for." The men collected their troops and left just ahead of David and his men.

They stopped around the corner from the compound.

"Let's just see who comes out and what they were after. That was not the police. There was no alarm set off."

"I think whoever it was wanted the same thing we did."

"Or perhaps it was just someone who wanted to settle a score," Lazaar said. He spoke into a mouthpiece, "Send a team in there. Kill all but one. I want someone to talk to."

In five minutes a car came speeding out of the compound and turned to the right without noticing the gray Mercedes.

"Follow them. They have Klaus' son in there."

The Mercedes hang behind about three cars and followed the Mossad agents to a nondescript house on a side street.

"That looks like a safe house. Do we know who those people are?" John said.

Lazaar said, "The big one works at the Jew embassy. They must be Mossad."

"So they are looking for the gold too, huh? Well, we need to cover the trail. Lazaar, I want all of the four German families dead by midnight. All of them, every family. Every member of every family, got that?"

Lazaar smiled. "I got it, no problem. Can I have some fun with them?"

"I don't care what you do but I want them dead."

That night in his hotel room with his scrambler on, he spoke to George in Cyprus. "I think we can get the gold anytime, but I don't think we should hold the gold for long. I would like to move it to a port city the same day we get it. When can a ship be in?"

"I think we can have a ship there by the first of February," George said.

"Okay. We are racing with the Jews evidently. Lazaar will cut off all tracks that lead to the mine in Paraguay. That should slow the Jews down. We will take a small team into the mountains on the twenty-fifth of January. Capture the gold and ship it on the twenty-seventh. It should arrive in on the first, be loaded, and get out of there. Where does it go?"

"I have arranged for it to be received in Pyongyang. They will take the gold and ship its value minus 10 percent to our accounts in Damascus. From there we will have full use of the money."

"Okay, February it is."

CHAPTER III

The lights came on and there stood Joseph, staring at David while his colleagues pinned his arms back. David looked at Joseph with surprise why are you holding me he asked?

"Who sent you here?" Joseph asked.

"Joseph from Rome," David replied.

"How do I know you can be trusted? Or that you are who you say you are?"

"Call Rome. I'm sure you know the number." Joseph nodded to someone in the doorway, who disappeared. He returned in a few minutes and nodded.

"Release him," Joseph said, and David was set free.

"Now who do we have here?" he said to David.

"I haven't spoken to him yet. He was with Klaus."

"Edgar Klaus was my father until you Jew dogs killed him," the young Mr. Klaus spat.

"We did not kill him," said Joseph. But we will kill you if you do not tell us what we want to know," he said quietly with a complete matter-of-fact tone, and there was no doubt in David's mind that he would do it.

"Tell you what?" Klaus the younger snared.

"Well, to start with, your name and what happened before we arrived and saved your life."

Choking back sobs, with fearful glances, he began his story.

"We had just finished lunch and had gone upstairs. My father was going to take a nap and I was going to take a shower and get ready for some appointments I had this afternoon.

"Suddenly we heard shooting from the courtyard. I ran to my balcony and saw a Dakar-yellow BMW crash through the gates. Three men emerged and assaulted the house. I ran to Father's room to warn him. I had just opened my door when I heard shots on the stairway and then Edward, Father's bodyguard, was shot in the hall outside of my father's room. Then they broke into the room and killed the two guards that were protecting Father. They grabbed me and shot me in the knee. They asked Father questions and then killed him. They turned to shoot me but I ran into Father's dressing room. He had a shotgun there and I used it. I heard more shots and then feet running away. I thought the men had left so I went to my father. He was lying in a pool of blood in his room with several bullet holes across his chest.

"He was dead before I got to him. Then the door opened and two new men were there with their guns out. You know the rest."

"Did you know the men that killed your father?"

"No. I was in my room when they came up the stairs"

"Didyougetthelicensenumberofthecaroranything else but the color that would help identify these people?"

"No, it was too fast, too unexpected."

"Why would anyone want to kill your father?"

"Why did you want to? You came to do the job but were just too late."

"No we came to ask him a few questions about his business and some of his friends. Had anyone threatened him?"

"He was always threatened."

"But lately?"

"No."

"Why was he always threatened?"

"You must know that my family has been in the import/export business since 1938 here in Argentina. During that time, all of our trading has not always been what the authorities approved of. As a result, we have done business from time to time with some ruthless and violent men. Some of these men have not been happy with our services."

"What have you been trading with?"

"I cannot tell you that."

"You will tell us all we want to know or you will wish you were lying beside your father even now.

"Bring him into the other room."

Edgar Klaus was dragged into a small room, eight by eight with very thick walls and no windows. He was strapped to the steel chair in the center of the room.

Joseph and David sat across from him in easy chairs while a third man stood by a control panel on the wall.

"Mr. Klaus," Joseph said, "I bear you no ill will personally nor do like you. I simply consider you a source of information. We will get the information we want. You can cooperate and go home, you cannot cooperate and leave here a very sick man, perhaps physically ruined, or you can not cooperate and not leave here at all. Either way, when we are done I will know what I what to know. Do you understand?"

"Yes," Edgar rasped.

"Now, what kind of import/export business has your family been dealing in?"

Edgar spat at Joseph and said, "Go to hell, you Jewish dog!"

Joseph gave a nod to the man by the wall, and he turned a knob.

Edgar screamed in surprise and pain.

"That chair you are in is a special chair that is wired for electric shock. We can shock your whole body as we just did, or we can shock selective portions." At this point, Joseph threw a glance at the man by the panel. Edgar received a powerful shock, first in his arm and then in his scrotum. "We can give you a light shock or a serious shock." Once more a glance at the panel, and another shock to his chest, which was not too bad by comparison. That was followed by an excruciating shock to his head.

"Now let me ask again. What do you trade in?"

"Almost anything: drugs, antiques, you know, artifacts that are illegal to take out of the country, and guns sometimes. Sometimes people are moved around the world by our business...."

"When did your family start this?"

"1938."

"Why did you come here?"

"My father told me that we came here to help the Third Reich. The Fuehrer needed agents around the world and sent my father here to help the Reich."

"How did he help the Reich?"

"He facilitated Nazi purchase of guns and oil and other things needed for the war effort."

"How did he do that?"

"My father told me that he would arrange transportation of payment to the various sellers of goods or services."

"How would this payment be made?"

"Usually in gold."

"So your father helped transport German gold from Germany to wherever to pay for items needed by the Reich?"

"Yes."

"How did he do that?"

"I don't know. That was before I was born.:

A glance, and a small reminder shock to the groin. Edgar screamed.

"You said you still deal in arms. How are those sales transacted?"

"Usually with wire transfer of funds."

"Who do you work with?"

He hesitated and Joseph gave the man at the wall a nod.

"My balls!" cried Edgar, "my balls!"

"I told you we could be selective about what part of your body feels the pain. Now answer the question."

"Guns and things like that are usually sold to the IRA or Arabs, or sometimes terrorist groups in Europe or Japan."

"When you deal with the Arabs, how is that done?"

"Gold is placed in Switzerland and then the dollar amounts are wired to our bank here by way of two or three other banks to keep people like you off the trail."

"Is there a Germans society here?"

"Yes." Edgar looked surprised

"Do they ever sell or buy guns or deal in gold"

"They have gold, but they do not trade in guns, at least not with us."

"You said that German war deals were done in gold. How was the gold transferred during the war?"

"Gold would be shipped from Italy to Argentina and then transported by rail to Paraguay or shipped out of Argentina by whatever means were appropriate to the sellers."

"Was gold stored here or in Paraguay?"

"Sometimes."

"Was it all shipped out?"

"I don't know."

"Where was it stored?"

"Somewhere in the mountains."

"Where?"

"I don't know. I have never been there. We do not use actual gold for payment today, not since I have been involved in the business."

Joseph nodded again to the man by the wall. Before he could act, Edgar screamed, "I don't know the answer to that question, I swear. Don't hurt me, please. I would tell you if I knew. Please don't hurt me anymore."

Joseph nodded again and then went on with the questions.

"So gold was transferred here during the war and moved from here to wherever. Sometimes the gold was stored here or in Paraguay in the mountains, but you don't know where?"

"That's right."

"Okay, now why was your father killed?"

"I told you, someone must have been unhappy with our service."

"Who could that be?"

"How would I know?"

"Well, who are your most recent clients?"

"I'm not going to give you a client list. Go ahead and kill me. If you don't they will."

"We will get a client list. And you may wish we merely killed you. But for now let's take a different tack.

"Have you had any unusual clients this last year?"

"We have been doing a lot of business with an Arab. His name is Lazaar...."

"What kind of business?" Joe's eyes revealed some interest for the first time.

"I don't know. My father would not let me in on this one. I did hear them talking about gold, but I don't know if this was payment arrangements or actual gold that they wanted moved."

Joseph looked at David but said nothing.

"Does your father know where the German gold was stored during the war?"

"I suppose so, but that is long ago."

"Do you know?"

"Somewhere in the mountains near Flint. It was in an abandoned mine, and the rail tracks led right to the mountain, which made it easier once you crossed the border. I have heard my father speak of this when he was drinking with his wartime friends."

"Do you know the names of any friends in Paraguay?"

"I told you, no names."

"This one we have to have."

"No."

Joseph nodded and the man at the panel turned the dial.

The screams were loud, long, and terror filled.

Three hours later, the man on the wall pushed Edgar out of the car in his father's courtyard.

He rolled to the corner of the building and lay in a heap, sobbing.

"Well, David, we now know that Nazi gold was moved to Paraguay, Karl Loaf Mann was in charge of storing it in a mine with railroad tracks leading up to the entrance, and that some Arabs have been asking about gold too. What do you make of that?"

"My guess is the PLO or some other crazy group is onto the gold too. They knew we are looking for it and so killed off our sources to stop the trail."

"I am going to report back to Rome. Can you continue to follow up on Loaf Mann and a possible site in Paraguay where it is or was stored?

"Yes, I will let you know in Rome what we find out.

"What about these Arabs, this Lazaar?

"Lazaar is the muscle of a PLO group. He is very dangerous and ruthless.

"I'll have the Rome office check him out. See if you can learn anything here as to what they or he is or was doing. I will leave in the morning. Good night."

"You had better stay in the embassy. It will be safer. We will get you on an El Al flight tomorrow. You never know what may be going on or how much they know."

BOOK VIII: MOLLY

CHAPTER I

Saulva

August 8, 2010

Molly had left Mark and headed for the Euro train to get her to Saulva. As she boarded the train, a pleasant-looking, well-dressed man entered behind her. They exchanged smiles. At the next station she did not notice that another man, short, unkempt, with a nasty glare, got on the train.

Molly was scared. She did not know what had really happened to her. She had boarded the train for Berlin and took her seat in the first-class section as she always did. She got out her laptop and started doing work, like always. Two men had entered her compartment and sat down. One was tall, good-looking, with a square jaw and a short haircut. The well-cut suit was obviously expensive. This was the man she had exchanged smiles with an hour ago. The other was short, unkempt, and dark with a pockmarked face. She thought they looked like a real mismatch.

"Can I help you?" she said, thinking they were in the wrong compartment by mistake.

"Yes, are you going to Berlin today?"

"That is none of your business," she said, a little angry.

"Are you Molly O'Connor?" the tall one asked.

"Who are you?" she demanded.

"I am Joseph Farok," the tall one said with an easy smile. "I think that we can do some business together."

She smiled at that.

"What kind of business?"

"I am interested in turning a large amount of gold into cash and then transporting it through several countries. I am told you now how to do that."

"Me? Mr. Farok, I am sure you are aware that such a thing is illegal. I could not possibly do that."

His smile froze.

"You are doing that even as we speak for a group of businessmen in Berlin!"

"How?" she gasped

The small man grasped a handful of her shoulder-length blonde hair and pulled her beautifully made-up face toward his ugly one. She could smell his foul breath when he said, "You had better cooperate while you can. You still may be able to take that nice job in America." The tall one was pulling the blinds on the car door as the short one spoke.

"What ... what do you want?" she cried. "You're hurting me. Let me go."

Joseph spoke again.

"We are interested in a business deal with you. You will work for us one way or another. One way, we will pay you three times what the other group was going to pay you. The other way, we will leave you for dead. Or perhaps we will leave you in a harem in the desert. My uncle would like a beautiful American blonde. You will not believe the things he will teach you there."

Scared now more than ever, she began to cry. "What do you want?"

"I want to know what arrangements you have with these men, how much you know about them, how much gold is involved, and how it was going to be moved. Then I want it moved to where I want it to be. If you cooperate we will set you free and deposit to your account in the America Bank One three million dollars. Oh yes, you must say nothing about this to anyone."

"Won't the other men know and ask questions?"

"They will not ask questions, and if you do it right no one will know about this little adventure except for us."

Drying her eyes and regaining her composure she asked, "Why do you need me?"

"We don't, but it is easier with you because we have no previous contact and we can keep this transaction outside of our normal channels."

"Okay. Three million? When do I get it?"

"As soon as we have access to the funds in our bank. We will wire it to your account."

"How can I trust you?"

With a nod from Joseph, the short one, grasped her head again and twisted her neck. He ripped the buttons off her dress, reached in, grasped her right breast, and squeezed hard.

Joseph said, "My uncle would love you. You have no choice. Trust me or I will leave you to Abdullah here." He got up to leave the compartment.

"No! Wait!" Molly cried. "I'll do what you want. I will get the money, right?"

"That's better," he said with a smile.

"Now tell me what these men told you."

CHAPTER II

Somewhere in Europe

August 2010

As she rode, huddled in the corner of the big Mercedes, Molly thought about what had brought her to this.

Molly had answered the phone three months ago to speak to Jim Luginbuhl of the Banc Swiss. He was asking about the value of gold and how one could move large amounts of gold quietly and still deposit in an account that was accessible.

She told him, "You are the Swiss banker and you should know how to keep money secret." He then invited her to dinner with him at Chat Noir on Rue Vortuer, an exclusive club in Saulva.

"Okay, Jim, what is so secret?"

"You know, Molly, I have always liked you and trusted you, right?"

"Usually when I hear that, the next request has to do with bed."

"That's not a bad idea, but that's not why I am talking to you. You've got to promise me that regardless of what you decide to do tonight you will not tell a soul about my plans."

"Okay, cross my heart," she said with an easy laugh.

"I need to move a large amount of gold from South America to Europe. No one must know about the shipment and I must be able to deposit the gold or its cash equivalent into a bank account so that I can use the funds."

"How much gold?"

"Almost a ton. I figure it is worth about fourteen billion dollars!"

"What are you going to do with this money?" Molly exclaimed, and then demanded, "How did you get the gold? Is it yours?"

"I can't tell you more until you're in. I can tell you that I have partners in banking that can give you whatever you want career wise. Plus, say a million dollars if you can help me and my friends."

"I don't know. I need to think about this. Give me a few weeks and we'll talk again."

"Okay. BUT don't tell anyone about this. It could be harmful to your health if you get my drift."

"Are you threatening me, Jim?" she said with an incredulous smile.

"No. I would never hurt you, but this information could get one killed if the wrong people knew about it."

That statement seemed prophetic as she sat scared to death in a car being driven to God knows where by God knows who.

Three weeks later when he was in Saulva again, Jim called and asked her to meet him at a very secluded bar in the south end of the city.

"Have you thought about what you want to do?" Jim asked as soon as the drinks were served and the barmaid had crossed the room.

"I'm interested but I need some questions answered as to how much risk I will be taking in this project."

"I and my friends—there are seven of us—are the only people that will know you are involved. The gold belongs to us because we found it. Law of salvage. We don't want anyone to know that we have it because there will be conflicting interest and others would want it."

"How much danger is involved?"

"None. We know where it is and we are trying to ship it to our accounts. But it is illegal to move funds like this, as you know, so there is some risk. However, all we are asking of you is expertise in how to do this, and then your silence. Your name will never show up anywhere and we will pay you a million dollars. All you are doing is selling your expertise. Isn't that what you do for the bank? This time you will be paid well for your skills."

"Okay. Let me go to work on this and I'll get back to you. I'll give you the plan and you give me 500,000. When the plan works, you give me the rest."

"It's a deal. My friends will be glad to hear you are going to help us."

It took her four months to figure it out but now it was ready. She had gone to the States and met with Charles III. She had met him through banking and admired his knowledge of international finance. When she had called him for an appointment, he had vaguely remembered her and had agreed to meet her.

They met in Café La Rouche, a small restaurant in the Georgetown area of Washington.

"Thank you for meeting with me," Molly began. "I was afraid that you would not remember me. You have been retired for some time now, haven't you?"

"Yes, a while."

"Have you enjoyed your retirement, or do you miss the action?"

"No. I had enough action when I was working. Now I just do what I like. You are in Saulva with NBD, right?"

"Yes. Did you do your homework for this meeting or do you remember?"

Charles III smiled. "You're right, I did my homework. I only remembered your name and that you were or are a specialist in international banking and financing."

"Why did you want to meet with me?"

"I am working on a situation for NBD that is very confidential. It could cause problems for some of my friends or even me if word of this meeting got out."

"Okay. I understand. What is the problem?"

"We believe that there is a large amount of gold missing from one of our banks."

"Who are we?" Charles asked.

"Well, myself and a good friend of mine. He may have been responsible for its disappearance. He did not steal it but he was careless with a client and this is the result."

"Do you want to tell me more?"

"Not really. We are not sure there is even a problem."

"Then why come to me?"

"I told him that I would try and track down the problem by working it backwards. Let's say there is a large amount of gold in South America. This man has it illegally but wants to turn it into funds he can legally use."

Charles said, "Okay. Let's suppose."

"He would have to deposit it in a bank and then move the funds once deposited out of that bank to a clean account. Once the new account was established and the money was there, then he could use it. Right?"

"That would be true," Charles nodded.

"I said that I would make discreet inquires into any bank being approached to accept such a deposit. If no one had, maybe the money is not missing. Or if I knew what banks to check with then I would know where to try and watch for the money to surface."

"Okay," Charles said, drawing on his pipe. "Where do I come in?"

"If I were this man, which banks would I approach? Who would I approach and what bribe would I use?"

Charles chuckled. "There are several banks that have done this over the years. Any Caribbean bank would be good to approach. The approach should be to the president of the bank. The bribe would be a percentage of the gold you are trying to deposit."

"That sounds easy," Molly said with a smile. "What is the catch?"

"The catch is that the bank would have to know the person they are dealing with. There would need to be prior business done or there would need to be a relationship developed. This would take time."

"How would I like find out if this were happening?" Molly asked innocently.

"You would have to find very close friends of the bank president's that would ask them for you. Or you would need to have close friends in the banks that would monitor the banks for any large deposits and transfers," Charles said.

"Well, that gives me a place to start I guess, or at least a place to tell my friend to start.

"I do appreciate you taking time to meet me and share you knowledge."

"No problem," Charles said as he put out his pipe. "Will you keep me informed as to what you are doing in this matter? I find it interesting."

"Sure. As soon as something happens, I will call you."

"Thanks again."

They shook hands and departed.

Next she made several trips to the Caribbean to find out which banks would accept a large amount of gold. This was also in the guise of security measures. She narrowed her banks to three and then got serious with them.

She met with George Washington of the Bank of the Bahamas. This meeting took place at Graycliffs in Nassau. After the meeting they adjourned to discuss it further in her room at Atlantis. This meeting, of course, was followed by breakfast in her suite from room service. George had agreed to accept the money for a 10 percent discount. He said that a ship could be used. It could dock Walker's Cay. It could be offloaded quietly and placed in a warehouse owned by the bank. They would assay the gold there and deposit the dollars to an account with them. Once she had the account, it could be wired to anywhere in the world. She said she would get back to him.

The next stop was the Bank of Jamaica, where she spent the night with their president Julian Lamos in a private suite at club Hedonism. His offer was a 7.5 percent discount.

Her third stop was the First Bank of Georgetown in Grand Cayman. After a night of dinner, dancing, and, of course, sex he was willing to go to 7.5 percent as well. Molly gave him another day of the same. A boat ride, more sexual delights, and they came to an agreement. The bank would charge Molly 5 percent. She would charge the Swiss bankers 10 percent. Molly and Wilbur Smyth would spill the other 5 percent.

Molly then had gone to Argentina and made arrangements for a train to be available on five day's notice to transport an unknown substance to the harbor, where it was to be loaded onto a ship.

Her next stop had been Amsterdam, where she negotiated with Andrew Nitsos, the owner of a fleet of merchant ships. For 200,000 dollars he had agreed to make a ship available, no questions asked, to deliver a shipment from Argentina to the Caymans.

Now all was ready. She only needed to know where and when to pick the gold up and she would have her dreams wrapped up in a bow.

She had been on her way to collect the first 500,000 when she met Joe.

"It's time to get off the train. We have a car waiting," Joe said in a pleasant voice.

"Where are you taking me?" Molly whimpered.

"To your meeting."

In the car not a word was said. There were two other men in the big, black Mercedes. Molly sat sandwiched in back between Farok and Abdullah. Abdullah constantly stroked her leg then thigh, always working higher, with a leer on his ugly face. They stopped at a phone booth across the street from the building where she was to meet Luginbuhl and the others.

After the scene at the phone booth, she was taken by car to a house on the outskirts of Berlin. Here she was dragged into a small room and left. The next day, after no food no water and not even a toilet break, she was dragged into a brightly lit room and dumped into a chair.

She was a mess. Physically her makeup had run all over her face as a result of her tears. She was hungry and thirsty. Her clothes were torn and dirty. Emotionally she was in worse shape. Scared to death not knowing what to expect had left her in a very anxious state.

Joseph Farok walked in looking fresh as a spring dawn and sat down across from her. "Did you have a pleasant night?" he asked.

"Hardly. What do you want from me? What are you going to do to me?"

"What happens to you depends on what you have to say in the next thirty minutes. I suggest you cooperate completely. Would you like some coffee, something to eat, and the use of a bathroom?"

"Yes, I would," she whimpered.

"Okay, the bathroom is through that door and the food will be here when you come out."

Fifteen minutes later, Molly emerged from the bathroom to find a small breakfast prepared for her. She was alone in the small room. There were no windows and the only door was locked. She drank the coffee gratefully and ate the food thoughtfully. *What do these men want and who are they?*

They must be Arabs and they want the gold that Luginbuhl wanted me to move for them. How did they know about it?

What am I going to tell them? That I was to find out tonight or last night where the gold is? What will they do to me? Is there really a harem?

As she tried to think through her situation, Joe Farok came in. He sat across from her and looked her in the eyes. He said very quietly.

"You are in more danger than you can imagine. You have one hope to leave here and resume your life as you knew it before yesterday morning, and that is to cooperate fully with me. I am going to ask you questions once and I expect truthful answers. Any lies or refusals to cooperate will result in dire consequences to you. Do you understand?"

Molly nodded. She had never been so scared in her life.

"What is your relationship with these 'bankers'?" He spat out the word banker.

"I was contacted a couple months ago and asked to help arrange for a shipment of gold to be moved from one place in the world to another."

"Go on."

"I agreed and then found out that they had found 2.5 billion dollars worth of Nazi gold that was stolen from the Jews during the Second World War. They told me it was in Paraguay and that they wanted me to arrange for it to be moved from there to a bank that would accept the gold. They then wanted me to transfer the dollars that the gold represented on deposit to an account with the Grand Bahamas bank. They gave me the numbers of the accounts."

"How much were you to get?"

"Two million," Molly lied, "and a job in New York as a senior vice president of Chase Manhattan Bank."

"Where is the gold now?"

"In Paraguay."

"Where?" he said, disgusted.

"I don't know. They were going to tell me tonight. You were too quick in your grabbing me," she said in an ironic tone of voice.

Joe reached over and calmly slapped Molly hard across the face.

She was thrown from her chair and spilled across the floor.

"Do not think you can talk to me like I am one of your boyfriends," Joe said angrily. "You will find that you have no rights and we will take what we want from you when we want it.

"Get back in your chair," he said.

Molly, holding her face, returned to her chair.

Joe reached over and ripped her blouse open, sending buttons flying every which way across the room.

Molly grasped the ends of her blouse and tried to pull them together, more scared now then before, if that was possible.

Joe stood over her and grasped her arms behind her back, where he handcuffed her wrists together.

Molly sat there, chest heaving.

"Now, Miss Molly, maybe you get my point. We will do what we want with you. But first I have a few more questions.

"How was the gold to be moved?"

Between sobs Molly said, "I arranged for a train to pick it up and take it to a small port on the Atlantic. From there a tramp steamer was to get the gold and transport it to Georgetown in the Cayman's. The gold was to be offloaded to the Bank of Georgetown, where they would store it in their vaults, assay it, and place a value on the deposit. I would then transfer the dollars to the Bahamas by wire."

"Okay, one more time: where is the gold?"

"Somewhere in the mountains of Paraguay. It is within two hours of the Argentina border because that is the arrangement I made with the train people."

"Who did you work with there?"

Molly had regained her composure by now and gave them the details of the transfer.

Joe stood up, pulled Molly's chin up, caressed her face and then her breast, and said, "You have been most helpful. I am sorry I cannot help you." He turned and left the room.

Moments later Abdullah walked in and began to undress while leering at her.

Molly was kept with Abdullah for two days and nights. He did things to her that she had never heard of before. After the two days, she was dressed in dark clothes and transported by car to an airfield and flown to what she supposed was an island. She was taken to another house, where she was once again used by two men for a number of days.

She was fed and given water and left alone some of the time but was never far from the abuse. Finally one night she was chained to a wall. Two women walked in and began to abuse her as well. She heard one of them call the other Sophia before she slipped into unconsciousness never to regain it in this world.

BOOK IX: CHARLES

CHAPTER I

Paris, France

August 18, 2010

The next day Charles made contact with Michael Wilson. They met in a bistro near the Ave D'Opra in Paris.

It was near sunset since Charles had taken the train from Berlin to Paris. He would spend the night and return to Berlin the next day.

"Well, Charles, what can I do for you?" Wilson was a short man with thinning hair. In his early fifties, he walked slightly bent over due to a back injury suffered while he was a paratrooper in Vietnam. He had a very dry sense of humor and usually a cigarette in his mouth.

"I want to know if the company is aware of any operations either on going or in preparation that either the PLO or the Mossad is running."

Wilson made a face like he had just eaten a sour apple.

"Now, don't give me that 'I can't tell you' bullshit," Charles said. "What I want is any operation that would take a lot of money."

"Well, you know these groups always have a lot going on. Most of their operations take money."

"No. This would be an unusually large amount of money, say around two billion. That's right, billion," Charles said quietly, looking straight into Wilson's blue eyes.

"There is nothing like that in Europe that we know about. Do you know something?"

"I'll talk if you do."

Wilson laughed. "All right. What do you want to know?"

"I told you."

"And I told you. We do know the Mossad is looking for some Nazi gold that may be in Argentina or someplace in South America. But that, we think, is just part of the Israeli government's push to regain stolen Jewish property. No big deal.

"What do you know about that?"

"What do you know?" Wilson said, his eyes narrowing.

Charles filled him in on all he knew. "My father was murdered because he knew about this or in some way was involved. That is why I am interested."

"I always liked your dad; good man and a straight shooter. I told you what we know about the Mossad. The PLO is always trying to terrorize someone. We know there is a Russian scientist trying to peddle plutonium for a nuclear bomb. We suspect that the PLO may be trying to buy it. If they were it would cost a lot of money; maybe the kind of money you are talking about.

"You are aware of no attempts to move big money across the world or Europe?"

"No. Just the usual few million that we track on both organizations."

"Okay. Look, I know I am not part of the company but you know I am informally part of the leadership through my father."

"Yeah," Wilson said slowly.

"Will you see what and if you can find out anything and keep me informed? If I get a lead on the money, I'll let you know as well, okay?"

"Yeah, I'll do that." Wilson thought for a minute and said, "This is strictly informal, right? Off the record?"

"Of course. No one will ever know I talked to you unless you want them to."

"I am being honest. We have nothing on this, but if you are right there could be something really big going down."

"Charles, you be careful. This could get you killed too."

Charles retuned to Berlin the next day.

Back in his hotel room, Charles made a few calls to his banker friends around the world. He asked if anyone had heard of efforts to move billions of dollars in gold anywhere. He especially leaned on his old friend George Washington in the Bank of the Bahamas to see what he could find out.

Charles slept alone that night.

CHAPTER II

Berlin

August 30, 2010

Charles met Jeanne for breakfast in his room the next morning.

"I have something for you on Molly O'Connor. I talked to her bank and they said that she has been working on something in Berlin the last few weeks. They also said she has flown to Argentina and the Bahamas in the last month.

"So I then went deeper and talked to some close friends of hers and finally to her current pal amour. He said that these trips were true and were related to moving some gold from South America to the Caribbean. He did not know much more than that. Except that she was working with some bankers in Berlin on this and that she thought this would get her a job as a senior VP at a major bank in the U.S."

"Well, that sounds like our money. When can we meet her?"

"I talked to Mark two days ago. I have a friend who is a coach on the ski team, and he set up the meeting. With the help of my friend, he was persuaded to supply the information I have. It took me sometime to track her down and find out more about her.

"I called her office yesterday and they said she was out. I then talked to her boss who said she has been out for two weeks and no one has heard from her, not even a call to say she was sick. This is very unusual and they are getting worried."

"Let me make a phone call.

"George Washington please.

"George? Good to hear your voice. How is all that casino money coming? You keeping good track of it?

"You know the thing I called you about a couple of weeks ago? Do you know anything about it?

"I would consider it a major personal favor and I would be in your debt if you could call me back in two hours with some information.

"Thanks."

By 1:00 p.m., Charles had his call.

"Well, it seems that the bank of the Bahamas had been approached about accepting a large amount of gold quietly. They were interested, but before they could close the deal it was withdrawn. George had talked to his friends in other Caribbean countries and found that the Bank of Cayman had agreed to accept the gold with a 5 percent discount. It seems the

Bahamas wanted a 10 percent discount and that was too much for one Molly O'Connor of NBD Saulva."

"So that's our girl."

"Yup, and those Berlin guys are our men. We need to pick them up and have a talk with them."

Charles picked up the phone dialed a number and said, "Wilson? We need to talk now. Today."

CHAPTER III

Berlin

October 1, 2010

Charles and Wilson met in a small park near the Brandenburg Gate.

"You sounded like you were onto something. What do you have?" Wilson said.

"A woman named Molly O'Connor of NBD Saulva has been working on moving large amounts of gold from Argentina to the Bank of Cayman. She has been working with seven Berlin bankers." He handed Wilson a list of the men they knew about. "Molly has disappeared."

"Hmm. This sounds like a private scam. Why don't you talk to Interpol instead of me? This has nothing to do with the company or with international spying." He laughed. "They just want to get rich."

"Well, I think that the PLO and the Israelis are onto this too. I would guess that they want the gold for their own reasons. Are you aware of any major operations that may be planned or would need large amounts of money?"

"How much money?"

"Well, 14.8 billion for sure, at today's prices."

"Wow! The Jews would want it because they would say it was stolen from them. Their operations are against either the Arabs or someone they disagree with about a particular issue, like us. So besides the fact that they would want the money, I don't know what they would be up to."

"The PLO, now they or one of their splinter groups is always looking for money to do bad things, usually to us. We are aware that there is a Russian that says he has access to an A-bomb and he has been trying to peddle it through out the world. He's tried Arab states like Syria, and Iraqi and terrorist groups like the IRA and PLO. However, to date the amount of money he wants would be far too high for most people. But if you had 100 million dollars that would probably buy it."

"Why is he running loose?"

"Well, we are trying to find out where the bomb is, if it exists, and we are waiting to see who tries to buy it."

"Do you think it could tie into this gold?"

"Well, it could. Give me a couple of days and I'll see what I can find out. But unless the gold is involved with something like this, the company will not want anything to do with it."

Back at the hotel, Charles called his sometime-friend Aaron Terrine. Aaron was a well-built man in his mid-fifties, quiet, with soft, brown eyes that belied his heart. Aaron Terrine ran the best detective agency in Europe and was also known to do an extra job if the price was right. They met in the Berlin Art Museum, the Bismarck Room.

"Good to see you again, Aaron. I have a job."

"Always like to be working. What is it?"

"First of all, I want a background check and all you can find out about these seven men. They are all bankers working for Swiss banks. Some are here in Berlin and some are in Saulva."

"Okay. That is kid's work."

"Second, I want you to find out the background on this woman. She is an American banker and I want you to locate her. She has been missing for a week. I also want to know what she has been working on and what her appointments have been for the last three weeks before she disappeared."

"Okay. A little harder but no problem."

"Finally, I want to know if the PLO is up to anything big in Europe."

"That is a little broad. Can you narrow it?"

"I can, but then that would give it away. Just see what you can find out."

"Okay. When do you want the information?"

"How soon can I have it?"

"Two weeks?"

"Okay, but no longer. Depending on what you find, I may have some additional work that is of a bit more quiet nature."

CHAPTER IV

Berlin

October 15, 2010

The next two weeks, Charles lounged around Berlin. His night were filled with Jeanne's unique brand of lovemaking and his days were spent recovering from the nights

This was the most time he had ever spent with Jeanne. It was also the most time he had spent with a woman since he had left his wife. He found that he liked being with a woman and with Jeanne in particular. They had a lot in common. She was always cheerful and upbeat, which helped him deal with his melancholy nature better. She always managed to be, do, or say just the right thing to make him feel good.

He realized that when this was over he was going to miss her. He began to wonder if maybe he should spend more time in Europe after this little adventure. Maybe something good could come from his relationship with Jeanne.

CHAPTER V

Berlin

October 24, 2010

On Wednesday the following week, Charles received a message from Wilson to meet him at the Brandenburg Gate Park again. When he arrived, Wilson was sitting on a bench by himself, feeding the pigeons.

"Good afternoon. A beautiful day, yes?" Charles said, by way of starting a conversation.

"Yes. But we need to talk. Let's go over to the Larger House around the corner. We can talk there."

When they had ordered their beer, Wilson said, "It seems you may be onto something. We do believe that the PLO is onto the gold and that they have been in conversation with that Russian scientist. So the company is interested. What else can you tell me?"

"Not much more than I did before. I have Terrine working on some background and I'll have his report next week, but in the meantime, I know nothing more than I told you. What can you tell me?"

"Are you part of the company?"

"No, but I can be with a few phone calls. You'll get no more information from me without you being forthcoming yourself."

"Okay, okay. I told you what we know. Where is this gold and how did you get onto it?"

"I got 'onto it' because they killed my father." Charles then related the details of his father's death and how he had been tracking the gold.

"So what do you know or think?" said Charles when he had finished.

"I think that the PLO is trying to get the gold to buy a nuclear bomb to be planted somewhere significant. Maybe they'll buy two, plant them both, blow one to make the point, and use the other as a bargaining chip."

"Do you know how they are doing this?"

"Of course not! We have just started to follow our sources on this in the last week. Give me a month and maybe I'll have their plot, or maybe not."

"If we follow the gold we get to the plot, don't we?"

"Yes, but let's try both ends. I'll get the company working on old Nazis in South America and you keep working your end. Let's meet here next week at the same time for updates."

CHAPTER VI

Berlin

October 25, 2001

Terrine called Charles on Monday and set up a meeting in the hotel bar for that afternoon.

"Well, Aaron, what do you have?" Charles said.

"A lot of interesting nothing. Let's start with the easy stuff. Here are portfolios on your bankers. Where they live, finances, family background, job assignments, etc. They are all working on this Jewish gold stuff that has been in the news for the last six months.

"Your girl Molly is a different story. She was working with the bankers, it appears. She had had several meetings with one of them. She made a trip or two to Argentina, where she secured a ship to be in a harbor in January to pick up an undisclosed shipment and transfer it to an undisclosed destination in the Caribbean.

"She was on her way to a meeting in Berlin when she disappeared. Charles, her body was found floating off a Greek island. Kythara to be exact. It was found last night, badly mutilated. It appears that she suffered a lot before she died."

"Do you think this is a coincidence, or was someone after what she was working on?"

"You know I don't believe in coincidence. Her 'specialty,' or at least one of them, was transference of funds internationally. She knew almost everyone in banking in the world, either because she worked with them or because they wanted to fuck her. She was not above trading sex for power.

"Her boyfriend said that she was planning on moving back to New York when she had finished the big project she was working on for these bankers in Berlin."

"Okay, what else do you have?"

"The PLO has an assault team working in Europe at this time. They are in contact with a former Russian nuclear scientist. My people say they are planning a nuclear operation of some sort. May be just buying a bomb for Saddam something like that."

"Do you think this is related?" Charles said.

"Of course, I do! Those bankers are working on lots and lots of Jewish gold. I think they found some of it unaccounted for and decided to keep it. O'Connor was to help move it. The PLO found out and now they want it to finance this major operation, which I think is independent of any Arab country per se."

Aaron looked around carefully and then asked:

"Okay, do you want anything else from me?"

"No. Thanks for what you did." He slid an envelope across the table and smiled.

"You know, there is one more thing. Why would they kill my father?"

"Well, if you read the dossier on O'Connor, she knew your father. They had worked on a couple of projects together when she was in New York. My sources did not have the details. Your father, when the company was tracking movement of money, did some research together with her, since that was her expertise. One of her stops in the last six months was Washington. Do you suppose she asked your father for help on this? Or maybe she thought he was still with the company and was tipping him off?"

"Could be. Although I did not see her name on his appointment calendar, I went through that very carefully for the last twelve months."

"Maybe she used another name for the meeting, if there was one, or maybe it was arranged to be an accidental meeting.

"Anyway this gives me a place to start thanks," Charles said. "Maybe we'll meet again."

BOOK X: SOPHIA

CHAPTER I

Rome

October 27, 2010

It was 8:30 p.m. when Sophia was introduced to Glenda Durst in the elegant restaurant of the Kouklis Hotel. She was introduced as a newspaperwoman from the *Dearborn Reader* in Detroit, Michigan (a very pro-Arab paper, since Dearborn is the largest Arab population center outside of the Middle East).

Glenda was cordial but not forthcoming. Over dinner Sophia, David, and Glenda talked about the "cause." Sophia asked about so-called terrorism, and they discussed how that was important to the cause of Arab freedom.

In a low voice, when David was talking to the waiter, Sophia asked if she could meet Glenda later alone. Maybe in her hotel room? "My room is here. It would just take a few minutes."

Glenda nodded and they squeezed hands under the table.

Around 1:00 a.m., there was a knock at Sophia's door and Glenda entered the room. "What did you want to see me about?" she said.

"A couple of things. One business and one personal. Can I fix you a drink?"

"Vodka straight up if you have it," she said.

As she handed her the drink, their hands touched just a little too long and the stare was a little too deep.

"Well, what is it that you want?"

"You can check me out with David. I am not only a newspaper person I am liaison for the Diaspora terrorist group. You have heard of it, yes?"

"Yes," she said warily.

Glenda had reason to be wary. The Diaspora was responsible for some of the bloodiest acts of terrorism that the world had seen. They were so aggressive that the PLO had disavowed them, and now most of their support came from Algeria. They had blown up two airliners, killing a thousand people and two what they termed traitor politicians. Killing a whole planeload of innocents to get one man each time. They had also bombed buildings in Europe and the East and committed at least four assassinations.

"I am going to ask you two direct questions. You can answer them or not, whatever," Sophia said looking straight into Glenda's eyes.

"First, we know that you are working on a nuclear device and have a team in training to use it. What do you plan on doing with it and can we be part of this?"

"And your second question?" Glenda said without a hint of emotion.

"Do you like women? Because I am attracted to you." As Sophia spoke she dropped her hand to Glenda's leg.

"You know I cannot answer the first question without authorization from others. As for the second," she patted Sophia's hand and moved it up to her face, where she kissed it. "What do you think?"

Sophia stroked Glenda's face and then ran her fingers along her collarbone and came down to cup her breast. As she did this they embraced and kissed. The kiss became long, deep, and moving. When they broke, they looked into each other's eyes.

Glenda broke the stare first, drew in a breath, and said, "Not on the first date." With a smile, "I'm not that kind of girl."

"Can we meet again?" Sophia said, her hand lingering on Glenda's leg.

"I would like that. Say tomorrow night at the Taverna below the Acropolis?"

"Say 9:00?"

At 9:00 the next night, Sophia met Glenda. The Taverna was a quiet place, good food, dancing, dim lights. Through the large windows that lined one wall, the Acropolis could be seen. Lighted for the tourists, it provided a beautiful backdrop. It was also a place where the couples on the dance floor were often of the same sex.

Glenda and Sophia dined, danced, and drank.

Around midnight Sophia, while dancing with Glenda, whispered in her ear, "Let's go back to my place. Is the second date too soon?"

"Second dates work for me," she said, slipping her tongue in Sophia's ear.

By 5:00 a.m. Sophia's bedroom was a mess. The sheets were askew, and there were two empty vodka bottles as well as an empty champagne bottle. Sophia and Glenda were naked, wrapped around each other, touching and cuddling. Dawn was creeping around the edges of the Athenian skyline.

"Good morning," Sophia said, seeing that Glenda's eyes were open. "How did you sleep?"

"Little," said Glenda with a seductive smile. "How did you learn to do all those things?"

"It's not hard if you think about it and are willing to try new things." She winked as she spoke.

"Well, I need to see you again. How about tonight?"

"How about today?" Sophia said.

"No, I would like to but I have some things I must do today. I know a little island we can sail to and spend the day on a secluded beach or walking through a six-hundred-year-old town. We can sit in little bistros and while away the day. I can do that tomorrow but I have to work today."

"Work? What do you have to do?"

"You know from David I work with the PLO. Well, I am on assignment and I have some loose ends to tie up."

"Can you tell me?"

"Of course not. The Israelis are everywhere and they would kill me or my cell if they knew of us. The best way to make sure that doesn't happen is to make sure no one but those who need to know, know about what we are doing."

"I understand that. But you know I am a reporter. Does not the PLO want publicity?"

"We get plenty of that. And we will get plenty more when this new thing happens."

"If I knew, I could make sure there was really good coverage, like having the news crews in place to get it all from the beginning or get a manifesto or whatever just before or just after. The press can be useful. I can be trusted not to publish before I am supposed to. Check me out with David."

"This is too big and there are too many important people watching me. I cannot tell you."

"How about a hint?" Sophia said as she tilted her head slightly to look into Glenda's eyes.

"Or why don't you talk to whoever you need to and see if you can bring me in some way?

"I do know how to show gratitude, you know. Sophia smiled and slipped her mouth over Glenda left breast. The result was immediate.

"Well, let me see what I can tell you. I'll see you tonight?"

"Yes, of course. Why don't you pick me up here and then we can see what we want to do."

The romancing of Glenda went on for three weeks. They were together every night and nearly every day. They went dancing, went to plays, visited small Greek islands, and made love in more and more imaginative ways every night. But Sophia was getting no information out of Glenda.

Finally, on a Wednesday after a month of dating, Glenda decided to open up a bit. They were on a warm beach on a small island bout thirty kilometers from the Greek mainland. The island was about one kilometer square, and they seemed to be the only people to have found it.

They had just finished swimming and were toweling off. Both were nude and were enjoying watching each other's bodies.

Glenda said, "This has been a great month. I love sex with you. You are so inventive and have such a beautiful body." She reached out and caressed Sophia's back and then ran her hand over her shoulder and down onto her breast. "Have you ever tried sex with someone about to die or someone who is dying?"

"No. Is that good?" Sophia said, her eyes filling with excitement. "Have you?"

"Once. It was great. Their fear heightens all the responses. Would you like to?"

"What do you mean?"

"David's group has captured an Israeli spy. She is twenty-four, small, and pretty. The men want to use her and then kill her when the information we want is gained. David said we could have her if he could watch. Does that bother you?"

"Of course not. He can join in if he wants to. But where can we do this?"

"That's the problem. I would have to bring you into the circle that knows about operations at the highest levels. Can you be trusted?"

"You must know the answer to that or you would not be talking about this to me."

"True."

"If you trust me enough for this, why not let me know what you are doing here in Greece?"

"Let's see how our little game goes and then we can talk."

That night Sophia and Glenda met David on Kythara, another island. He took them to a smelly, fisherman's hut. Inside it was cramped with sophisticated communications equipment. Through a trap door in the floor, he led them to the girl.

She was indeed pretty. She was tied to the wall naked. She was blonde with small, pink nipples and beautiful skin and legs. She made Sophia catch her breath.

"Well, I saved her for you two. Help yourself to the bar and I am going to sit down over here and just observe," David said, his voice heavy with excitement.

Sophia smiled, placed her arm around David, and said, "Not just observe. You undress and join the party."

When they were done with Molly, Glenda slowly strangled her as David finished inside her for the last time.

Later they sat around drinking. They became very drunk on the sex, each other, and the liquor.

Finally Sophia asked, "So, what is so big you can't tell even me?"

Glenda said, "David does not know either. But I will tell you both." She was drunk, laughing, and feeling very confident.

"My team will be planting a nuclear device in New York on February third next year."

"February third? That is only six months way. Where are you going to get such a device?"

"We have already agreed to buy it from a Russian who already has it in Poland."

"What did or are you to pay him?" asked David.

"Fourteen point eight billion in gold!"

"Fourteen point eight billion? Where are you getting that?" questioned Sophia.

"We have a source in South America that will deliver the gold to our bank account on the second day of the year. My squad will then pick up the device, set it in place, and wait for the fun to begin."

Sophia was shocked into silence as was David at the immensity of what they planned.

Glenda said, "It should devastate every thing for fifty miles around that Jew city. What a glorious day that will be!"

"Which Jew city?" Sophia asked.

"New York will get the first one."

"First one?"

"There are two. One to demonstrate what we have and what it will do; the second one is to make the deal with. We will target either Washington, D.C., or the city where the peace conference will be taking place. Either way, February 6 is the end of New York."

The next day Sophia left Athens for Rome.

BOOK XI: THE ENDS BEGIN TO MEET

CHAPTER I

The Bankers

Berlin

October 16, 2010

Luginbuhl did not hear from anyone for more than a week. On a Wednesday he had had to go into the bank. At 1:30 his phone rang.

A voice said, "Leave the bank immediately. When you leave the bank, turn right and walk until I pick you up."

Luginbuhl did as he was told.

He walked for three blocks until a gray Mercedes slid to a stop next to him as he waited nervously for a traffic light.

"Get in," a dark man said as the door opened.

Luginbuhl did as he was told with a quick look around.

Once inside the car, it took off at a high rate of speed.

The dark man in the seat next to him said in a voice lined with ice, "We want the gold."

"So go get it," Luginbuhl said, thinking that this would start the negotiations.

Lazaar reached over and without a word stuck his finger deep into Luginbuhl's eye.

He screamed in pain and shock.

"You need to understand the position you are in. We want the gold. If you tell us now where it is, I will let you and your family live. If you do not cooperate, you will die in the next five minutes." He began to screw the silencer onto a pistol he produced from his coat.

"It does not matter to me. My men are killing Kitchton's family as we speak. B's is next, and so on. Every five minutes that goes by, another family dies. When they are gone, we start on the six of you."

"Can't we cut a deal?" Luginbuhl gasped through his pain.

"I have given you the only deal you will get. You have three minutes to save B's family."

Luginbuhl said. "Okay, what do you want to know?"

"I want to know where the gold is exactly."

Jim told him.

As he began to talk, the dark man (Lazaar) nodded to a man in the front seat, who placed a call.

"Okay, you just saved B's family as well as the others. Now I want you to call the others and have them meet you at the Berlin Zoo in one hour."

"What else do you want?"

"I am going to kill all of you."

"What?" Jim said incredulously.

"I am going to kill all of you."

"I won't do it."

"Yes, you will. The choice is simple. I kill all of you or I kill all of you and your families."

Luginbuhl though for a minute and then made the calls.

CHAPTER II

December 10, 2010

Vladimir and Michael met with the dark man that Vladimir had met in the bar in Siberia.

"We are here. Where is your money?"

"What bank do you want it deposited in?"

"Here is the deposit information."

"Do you have the packages?"

"Yes. They are here in? We will need fifty million deposited by tomorrow. Once that is done, we will leave for Budapest. Before we arrive in Budapest, we will take a side trip to Gdansk. We have arranged for the packages to be stored in a shipping locker. With the proper papers, you can have them loaded onto a ship and delivered anywhere you want. When the rest of the money, one billion, is deposited into our account, we will send you the papers you will need to complete the shipping of the packages."

"We will have the gold in two weeks. Where can I reach you in Hungary?"

"This is the hotel where we will be in Budapest. I will wait to hear from you."

CHAPTER III

South America

Peru

December 22, 2010

Lazaar, Farok, Eli, and Thomas met in a safe house in Peru.

Farok looked at the other two men and asked, "Are you ready?"

Lazaar answered, "I have a strike force of fifty men that are the best in the world. They are scattered through out the city. Say the word and we go."

Eli said, "I have personally gone into the mountains and mapped out the location. There are about 500 people in the village and mine area. There are no more than five guards on duty at any one time. It has been fifty years and they have never had a problem, and they expect none now. The guards are more for show and to keep away local banditos or communists that might want to finance their revolution with the gold. All told there might be sixty fighting men in the whole compound."

Farok looked at Lazaar. "Do you have a plan?"

"Of course. We helicopter our men in about two in the morning. The guards change at 3:00 so the current shift will be sleepy and the new ones will still be in their beds. We do an air assault and take the guards out quickly. Remember, there are only five. We have four of our men already in place as workers. They will gain control of the vault ten minutes before we arrive by air.

"We use our other men to control the crowds. I think we grab Hauptman out of his house at the same time. He tells his people that we are the ones they have been expecting and to load the gold. They load it onto the train and we leave."

"Where does the train come from?" Farok asked.

"It brings supplies every two weeks from Argentina," Thomas said

"So does that mean we take the train to Buenos Aries, Argentina?" Lazaar asked.

"No," Joe said. "The bankers were going to take it out that way. If anyone else figured out what they were doing then they would expect us to go that way.

"It will have to move by ship. I have decided that we should use a port on the west side of South America, say in Peru. If someone like Hauptman wanted to stop us, they would look for the closest port rather than the west coast. If we take it out of Peru, Korea would be the nearest ally that we take it to. They would be happy for the gold and could move the value to our accounts in Libya with no problem. From there we can move it to our scientist via Swiss accounts. I have arrangements for a ship, the *Arab Destiny*, to be in Peru and take the gold out that way.

"I will make arrangements for our friends in Pyongyang to be ready to receive the gold. John, you need to go to Callao, Peru, and make sure there is no foul-up. We will need a berth for the ship, and it will need to be ready when we arrive with the gold. I want the ship loaded in a couple of hours and out of the harbor in two and a half."

"I can do that," said John. "Don't worry. The ship will be there the day before you strike. I will take care of the harbor people. We will be able to clear the harbor as soon as the gold is loaded."

"Okay then," Farok said, "can we go in ten days?"

Lazaar and John both nodded. No problem they said.

CHAPTER IV

Charles

October 16, 2010

Wednesday, as the bankers were dying, Charles and Wilson met in the park as before.

"Well, what have you learned?" Charles asked.

"There is an operation on and it does involve nuclear weapons. They have their best operatives on this one. The Mossad is aware of the gold and, although they would not say this, they are tracking it too. They are unaware of the nuclear plans but are scared enough of the possibility to cooperate on a mission to get the gold and stop the nuclear weapons exchange.

"We have formed a team composed of two of their people, two of ours, and you, if you want to be included. This is probably why your father was murdered. They meet on Thursday, tomorrow morning, in the Israeli embassy at 8:00 a.m.

"I'm off this now, except as directed by the committee that you are part of, so we do not need to meet again. I'll pass this information you and Terrine dug up on to the right people. I'll also see if anyone in Washington has heard anything of Molly, gold, or bombs. Good luck and be careful."

Wilson left the park and stepped into the street. Charles heard machine gun fire and screams.

When he got outside, he saw Wilson lying in a pool of his own blood along with two passersby. They were all dead.

Charles backed back into the bar and moved to the back door. He exited quietly, located a cab, and went to the U.S. embassy. He did not return to his hotel even for his clothes.

He stayed in the embassy for the day waiting for the committee to meet.

Since the operation had now gone hot, the operatives did not want to meet in the embassy. Instead, they set up a meeting in the suburbs at a safe house thirty miles south of Berlin.

Charles arrived by unmarked embassy vehicle and entered the house. There he was introduced to Don Moore, a rather heavy man, round-faced, cheerful, with slightly thinning hair, around fifty-eight. Jeff Seymour, a young man in his late twenties, about six feet, 200 pounds. Charles could tell by the cut of his sport coat that he was in shape. He was dark with black hair and eyes to match. He smiled but not in his eyes. Machmoud Perzinii, a slight man, about five foot ten, small, thin, well dressed. He looked more like a shopkeeper than an agent. Finally there was Mike Bordeaux, a small man, overweight. He remained seated when he was introduced. It was clear that this man had the power in the meeting.

"Well, now that we are all here, let's get down to business," said Bordeaux. "Here is what we know. The PLO is working on a deal to get a nuclear device, actually two such devices. They plan on planting the first one in a major world city, probably New York or Washington, D.C., and the second in another such city. They will detonate the first device to demonstrate that they mean business, and the second will be a threat to get what they want from Israel."

A look of shocked horror crossed the faces of the three Americans, who had not known the extent of this plan yet.

Bordeaux went on. "They will finance this operation with the gold they get from the missing Nazi gold shipment of 1945. They have located it in Paraguay and are on their way to capture it. They will ship it by train to the coast, and from there by ship to a friendly bank. Once they have use of the gold, they will pay a Russian scientist who has the devices. Incidentally, there maybe more than two."

"It seems like you know plenty about this plan. Why do you need us?" Moore said.

"Because, while we have pieced this together and have teams on the scene, there is still much we do not know and help that we need."

"For example?"

"Where exactly is the gold? How to they plan to move it? When are they transporting it? Who is the scientist? Can we capture the devices ourselves? Our own intelligence is a bit short on answers to these questions."

Charles said. "May I be of some help in this matter?"

Moore and Seymour nodded.

"I believe that I know where the gold is, or at least who does know exactly where it is. Molly O'Connor, an American, was going to transport it from Argentina to the Caymans. The gold was to arrive by train from Paraguay and be loaded onto a tramp freighter for transportation."

Seymour said, "O'Connor has disappeared."

Perzinii said, "Correction: she has been found dead in the Aegean Sea just last night. If she is the one knowing the whereabouts of the gold she will not be talking."

Moore said, "Well, we know it was in Paraguay. I will have our satellites note all the train lines from Paraguay to Argentina. We will then search them until we find the ones that begin in the mountains. Then we can send teams to check each one out."

"How long will that take?" Bordeaux said.

"Three weeks or less, depending on the number of likely train lines we find."

"That may be okay, but one week would be better."

"I'll see what we can do. We can also put out a worldwide alert for information on gold shipments, special trains, ships contracted for a run from Argentina to the Caymans, etc. Maybe that will turn something up."

"Okay, that will be helpful."

"Do we have a clue as to where the Arabs will go with the gold? Also, can we assume that they will use Argentina as well?"

"I think we can assume that since it is the fastest and most direct route from Paraguay to the coast that they will use it. Also, they must know what Molly planned and so why not use what she set up? Their work would already be done."

"Okay. We will set up patrols on the Argentinean coast with subs, planes, and some surface vessels. If we identify a suspect ship we can stop it."

"Stop a ship on the high seas?"

"Well, let me rephrase that. Would it not be possible for the Mossad to have a ship or two off the Argentinean coast, and when we've identified a ship, this pirate ship with no markings could make a stop?"

Boudreaux smiled, "Yes, I see what you mean and that should not be too hard to arrange. Machmoud you will see to that."

Machmoud nodded.

"That should capture the gold, but I have a couple of questions about the gold," Seymour said.

"First of all, who gets it? Second, what can we do about those nuclear devices, if all that stands between them and the PLO is money? When we foil this plan there will be another."

"Good point." Boudreaux said. "But we do not know who or where this mad Russian is and we need help to find him.

"Israel believes that the gold is that of the Holocaust victims. Israel has provided a sanctuary for those people from 1948 on and believes that we are entitled to those funds."

"You want the U.S. government to help Israel get gold bullion for itself? If it were to happen, can we assume that Israel will one, pay the U.S. government the cost of capturing this money, and two, ensure that these nuclear devices are recovered and placed in the care of the U.S. government?"

"I will have to check with the proper officials but I believe that we could strike a deal along those lines."

"So where do we go from here?"

"I will contact you in a week or less with what data we are able to unearth through our system," said Moore. "In the meantime, I suggest we all get busy. We need to find a mad scientist and a mountain full of gold in less then fourteen days."

CHAPTER V

Berlin

October 18, 2010

Charles left the meeting and caught a train for Zurich. He arrived at the University of Saulva station by 3:00 that afternoon. He hailed a cab, which took him to the Swiss Banque du International and his old friend Harold Cole. Harold, a tall, thin man in his late sixties with gray hair combed discreetly to the side, was dressed in dark suit with a white shirt and black and red tie.

"Well, Hal, don't you look professional?" Charles said. "How have you been?"

"I've been good. Sorry to hear about your father, though. How are you doing?"

"Okay. As good as one might expect. His death was unexpected, you know. Sometimes I think I will just call father and see if he is free for lunch then I remember that I can't do that. Very sad that we have to lose those that we love, don't you think?"

"Yes. Both my parents are gone now and I feel the same way. That is something you never get over, just learn to live with.

"What brings you to Zurich and to me? I know you must have a reason."

"Yes, I do. I am doing some investigative work for old friends. Please don't ask me who."

"Okay, what does that have to do with me?"

"Well, if you were a Russian and had several million dollars to deposit in a bank, how would you do that?"

"I assume you mean not a Russian bank?"

Charles smiled. "Of course, not a Russian bank. I assume this man or woman lives in Russia now and would want to place this money in an account that he could access from anywhere in the world. The account would need to be a secretive, which is why I am in Switzerland, and cooperative with his special needs, whatever they may be."

"Well, most any bank in this country could do what you've described. However, there are two that do a lot of Russian business and have branches in Eastern Europe. They are Clariden of Liechtenstein and the Bank."

"Is it possible for me to get information on an account from either of these banks?"

"Not legally. I assume you knew that. But a discreet inquiry from myself could get some information. What do you want to know?"

"I want to know if … well, I am looking for a Russian who has opened a small account. This man is a former scientist so I assume that he is not financially astute. He would have opened an account in the last twelve months. The deposits would be small, but the account is about to come into a large amount of money from probably the Near East."

"You know more than that?"

"No, that's all. Can you find anything out?"

"Well, that is pretty vague, but maybe. I'll get you of list of new Russian accounts with small sums of deposit that are a year old or less from both banks. But I warn you that that could be a lot of names."

"That may be enough. Thanks, Hal, I owe you big-time for this. When I can, I will tell you how important this is. When get I get these names?"

"Give me ten days. Call me and tell me where I can send the list."

"I'll do that. Thanks again."

Charles called Jeanne and had her take the next train to Zurich. *If I'm stuck here for a few days I might as well enjoy myself,* he mused.

Jeanne arrived on the late train from Berlin. She was glad to see him.

They spent the next six days wandering around Zurich doing tourist things. They ate in fine restaurants danced till dawn and then made wonderful love.

On the seventh day as they took a private boat trip around the lake, complete with a picnic lunch, they talked more deeply than they had the previous few days.

"Charles, what are you going to do when this is over?"

"What do you mean?" he said.

"When you track down the gold and get the people that killed your father, are you just going to go back to Washington and fly out of my life again?"

"I hadn't thought much about it," he said. These last few months, I have grown fond of you. I have come to look forward to being with you. To sharing, talking, laughing. I have just not thought of what I would do next."

"I don't think I could deal with you leaving without seeing you regularity. I have grown very fond of you too, maybe even more than that," she said with her head bowed.

Charles took her by the chin and raised her lips to his. As he kissed her he thought, *Could I be falling in love?*

He had promised himself never to love again after his disastrous first marriage, but is this different? Could he go back to Washington and pick up the strings of his life? Go on like these months had not happened? Could he live without her?

Of course he could. He did before. But would he want to?

He looked into her eyes and said, "I know that I will never be the same and that I never want you out of my life again." They embraced and returned to the boat. Nothing really resolved except an awareness for both of them that maybe there was something between them that could grow.

Coming into his hotel after the day spent on the lake with Jeanne, Charles found a note waiting with the concierge. It said: "9:00 a.m. Strudelhaus. Tomorrow. HC."

At 9:00 a.m. Charles was in the Strudelhaus waiting for Cole. Cole came in looking very pale. He said, "Good morning, Charles. I have what you want but it has caused an uproar. There has been an attempt on my life. You will need to get me somewhere safe for a while."

"I can do that," Charles said. "Is there a back way out of here?"

"Yes."

"Let's go."

They reached the back alley and turned south to the side street where Charles had his car waiting. As they passed the front of the Strudelhaus, two large Arab men were entering the building with bulky coats. Charles shuddered.

Two blocks down the street, he stopped at a pay phone and placed a call to the local CIA office.

"I need a pick up ASAP. This is number 8891. I'm at 1260 Rue de Krest."

Five minutes later, a big Mercedes swung into view. One large man got out and walked over to

Charles. "What time do you have?" he said, his hand inside his coat. "8891," Charles answered.

"Let's go."

Once in the car the driver asked, "Where to?"

"This man needs to be safe for a while."

"Got it," the driver said.

Charles turned to Harold.

"What did you find out that caused all this trouble?"

"The Russian's name is Michael Vladimir. He goes by the name Val Isaac and is in Vienna. He has made contact with the PLO and has made a deposit of ten million U.S. dollars in the last month into his account. He opened the account early in the year with a couple of thousand dollars. When I ran the check for small accounts it came up. When I took a closer look, I saw the recent deposit. I then started asking questions of my friends around town and found out about the PLO. I have an address but I would bet he is not there now."

"Do you know anything else?"

"Isn't that enough?"

"Yes. It's plenty. Thanks, old friend. Let these men know whatever you need or want and you will have it. If they are slow in helping you, call my Washington number and I'll be sure you get what you need."

Charles said, "Take me to the airport and give this man anything he wants, and I mean anything. He has a blue clearance.

"Do you have a secure phone?"

The large man handed him a cell with a scrambler.

Charles called Moore and related the information he had received. "You had better move fast. There has been an attempt on my source's life, and Vladimir may be on the move."

BOOK XII: SOUTH AMERICA

CHAPTER I

Four hours later, Weiss received word that he was to go to Paraguay by way of Paris and be sure he was not followed. He would be joined by Sophia and David.

Sophia, David, and Weiss met in the hotel bar in Paraguay. They compared notes and set up a plan to get the gold. They now knew where it was and who was in control. They also knew they were in a race with the PLO.

Sophia was to make arrangements to have a ship waiting in an Argentinean harbor to accept the gold and set sail. They were to be cleared to leave the harbor within two hours of the gold being loaded, and there was to be no questions asked about what was being loaded.

Weiss was to have the train at the mine on the second of February. He was also to have clean sailing into Argentina.

David was to get the gold.

Sophia contacted Rome and made arrangements to have a tramp steamer arrive in the harbor on the thirty-first of January. This was an Israeli ship with an Israeli crew. These arrangements were made with the use of her scrambled cell phone.

Sophia went to Rosario, a city on the cost with a small harbor. She learned who the harbormaster was and the head of the customs office by hanging out in The Anchor, one of the bars on the waterfront that was frequented by ships captains. A little flirting and touching obtained this information.

She then zeroed in on the harbormaster, Emanuel Garcia. She met him first in his office when she came in to ask for some instructions.

"I am looking for the harbormaster. I believe his name is Garcia," she told the secretary. The secretary regarded her with suspicion as she took in her attire. Sophia was tall and blonde, which made her striking anyway. But today she had on a tight black suit. The suit was businesslike except for a couple of things. First, she wore no blouse under the jacket and so displayed interesting cleavage. Second, the skirt was just a little too short, again displaying her beautiful legs. And finally, the whole ensemble was very tight.

Emanuel Garcia fell over himself to offer her a chair and a drink. While he walked behind her he stole a peak down her blouse and then sat across from her so as to take in her lovely legs. Garcia was fifty-five, overweight, bald with a moustache. He had a wife (the third one) and three children, each by a different woman. He had his job by virtue of being distantly related to the governor of the province. He had been in the position for fifteen years and was looking forward to retirement in the next five if he had enough money.

Garcia had lost a lot of money that would have been his pension to each of his wives. He also gambled with the abundant sailors in a closed section of an old tugboat that was dry-docked at the far end of the harbor. While he loved gambling, he did not do well.

He also loved the women and paid large sums to various waterfront sluts for their services. All in all, Garcia was lonely, horny, and broke. Sophia made not only his interest rise.

Sophia began by saying that her father owed several tramp steamers and that her family was putting Rosario on the port of call list. What did she need to do to have a berth waiting for their ship, *The Golden Lady* (named after her, with a smile) on January 31?

Garcia, watching her legs, said, "The thirty-first. There will not be much room. I doubt that I can get you in on that day."

"Now, Mr. Garcia, it is very important for us that we stay on our schedule. Isn't there something that I can do to have you make room for us?" She uncrossed her long legs and shifted, giving Garcia a good look at a lot of leg.

His throat went dry and lustful thoughts filled his dim mind.

"Not only do we need a berth, we are also accepting a cargo from a train on the third of

February and we need to load it immediately and be able to sail within two hours of loading."

Again Garcia said in his most official voice, "That will be impossible. There are no crews or equipment available until the end of February. This is a small port. Secondly, customs will need to inspect the ship and cargo to give you clearance to leave the harbor."

Sophia reached into her purse and pulled out a thick wad of American dollars and displayed them to Garcia.

"We understand that service is expensive. I have been told that you are the man that can make things happen here, is that not true?"

As Garcia looked from her purse to her face, he noticed that the top button of her suit was now unbuttoned and that a very large portion of a very beautiful breast was on display. Speaking was difficult but he said, "Ms. Renoir, it is impossible."

Sophia stood, dropped her hand on his shoulder, and then caressed his neck.

"Is there some place more private where we can talk?" she purred.

They adjourned to a quiet bar of a small, run-down hotel two blocks from the waterfront. Between a few drinks and an hour in one of the rooms, Garcia agreed to have the berth ready and a stevedore crew with equipment ready. He also agreed to bribe the customs officer for the departure arrangements.

It was January 15. Sophia would need to make calls on him at the hotel at least weekly just to stay in touch until the ship arrived. She would also provide 300,000 U.S. dollars to grease the wheels of Argentinean Maritime procedures.

Weiss contacted a transportation firm that did business with Israel. They put him in touch with Eduardo Aviles of the Paraguay Railroad. Mr. Aviles required 200,000 U.S. dollars to arrange for a train to get into the mountains on January 29.

Aviles also made the arrangements with the Argentina Railroad to have the train cleared through to the harbor. The train would cross the border on the thirtieth and arrive in the harbor on the thirty-first of January.

Weiss' next stop was the border guards. First, on the Paraguay side, a friend of Aviles was spoken to. He agreed to process the train for 20,000 U.S. dollars. He also provided the name of his counterpart on the Argentinean side. They met in a small bar. Aviles, Michael Torres, and Weiss. Here, another 20,000 got the shipment into Argentina.

Weiss and Sophia reported to Rome that the way was clear. Rome contacted David with the green light.

CHAPTER II

On the twenty-sixth of January, John, Lazaar, and a tactical strike group of ten heavily armed men arrived at the mines in Paraguay. They had been helicoptered to the back side of the mountain, and then they hiked overland to the mine compound.

Lazaar said:

"Only token guards and no real security. Looks like about 500 people live and work in the compound. My spies say that there are five guards in the vault that holds the gold. The rest of the people are employed to make the compound look like a viable operation. I suggest we disguise our men and let them infiltrate. When we are all in the compound, they will secure the perimeter. Four will take the guards' quarters (I think killing them quickly will be best), and then you and I will visit Herr Hauptman and his family. The other two will take the vault.

"Okay, that should work. I suggest we strike at 5:00 tomorrow morning. Most will be asleep. We will need to hold the compound for twenty-four hours and then roll. We will need the people to load the train."

"Do you need to kill everyone?"

"No, just the guards. Hauptman will help us control the rest of the population until we leave. When we go, we blow the tracks and communications behind us and, of course, kill Hauptman and his family."

Lazaar nodded. "I'll get my men moving. Shall I set up our tent?"

"Yes, we will have a few hours to wait and we might as well be comfortable."

At 5:00, Lazaar and John arrived at the compound to find their men in place. The doors were open and the perimeter guarded by their own men. The four assigned to the guards' quarters were quick and efficient. Using Hock and Klegger automatics with silencers, they made short work of the guards and their families. No one even woke up.

The men assigned to the vault also had no problem. The guards, while awake, were inattentive. They were easy targets for well-trained professional killers.

Hauptman was awakened from his sleep next to his wife by Lazaar's command.

"Get up, swine, we need your services."

"What? Who are you?" Hauptman asked sleepily

"We have come for the gold you keep in the vault room. Listen well and you may live. Say or move the

wrong way and your family dies in front of your eyes."
As he spoke one of the men entered the room with
Hauptman's two daughters and son at gunpoint.

"What do you want me to do?" he said, still
genuinely shocked.

"To start with, your wife and daughters can fix
us breakfast and some coffee. We will give you your
instructions over food."

As they ate, Lazaar gave instructions.

"You will tell your people to load the gold onto
the train that will arrive in four hours. Make up some
believable story as to why and where it is being
moved, enough to get the work done with no one
causing trouble. Our train will arrive at 10:00 a.m. I
want the train loaded by 4:00 p.m. We will leave at
6:00 p.m. Anyone who causes us the least delay will
be dealt with. You understand?"

Hauptman nodded his head.

John got his radio out and gave the signal that
would bring the train to the mountain and sat down
to wait.

Hauptman called his foreman to his office at 8:00
a.m. and told him to have his crews prepare the gold
for shipping. "Have everyone you need ready. A train
will arrive in a few hours and the gold will need to be
loaded quickly so it can depart on schedule."

"No problem," the foreman said and went to get
his job done.

The train arrived at 10:00, right on time, and was loaded by 4:00 p.m.

Lazaar reported to John that the train was ready to roll.

"We will leave at 7:00. I do not want to be waiting at the port. I want to arrive, load, and leave."

"We have received word that the ship *Arab Destiny* will arrive on time and be expecting us at 2:00 p.m. tomorrow. What do you want done here to wrap up?" Lazaar said.

"Get everyone into the mineshaft. Then destroy the mine."

"Can my men have some fun with the ladies first?" Lazaar asked with a leer. "After all, we have two hours to wait."

"Not this time. I want nothing to go wrong. You and your men will be handsomely rewarded for your work here. You can have all the women you want when the gold is safely in our banks."

By 6:30, all the people in the small city had been rounded up, placed in the mine shaft, and the charges laid.

"Okay," John said, "let's roll.:

As the train pulled out of the small town, John nodded to Lazaar and the detonator was charged followed by a long, muffled explosion from the mine.

Five hundred people died.

CHAPTER III

David set up a team of Mossad operatives. They arrived in Paraguay on the nineteenth of January. David had the site under surveillance and had taken photos from every conceivable angle.

On the twenty-third he met with the team.

"Here is the map of the layout of the compound. You can see that it is lightly guarded.

"It would appear that the cover was to make it look like nothing unusual. Fifty years of no contact has made it look very mundane. An old SS colonel is in charge. His son and grandson share the responsibility. They reported to Argentina. However, the men they reported to are dead. Killed, it appears, by the PLO. Since their deaths, guards have been doubled. They have twenty men that work three shifts, roughly seven men at a time, with a barracks in the northwest corner of the compound. I do not know what alarm system they have. I have seen only small arms for weapons.

"I think you ought to try and get inside and see what exactly is there. Is that possible?" said Sheldon Safer. Sheldon was a big man, full bearded, and who looked every inch the combat veteran that he was. Sheldon, or Shelly as his troops called him, had been involved in nearly every Israeli operation in the last twenty years.

"I don't see how. I can't just walk up and introduce myself. And we have no contacts with this colonel or his family. The Argentineans would have helped but they are dead."

"Okay, we will just have to go with it as is. Here is what we will do. We will use two helicopters. You will need to have the train ready to roll into the compound at exactly 5:30 a.m. We hit at 5:00 a.m."

At 5:00 a.m., just moments before dawn on the twenty-seventh two Blackhawk helicopters with no markings slipped over the mountain. One hovered over the barracks and blasted it with six missiles, destroying the building and all inside. The other, coming from the northeast, first raked the inside of the compound with machine gun fire and then both set down and disgorged fifteen heavily armed men. They met little resistance. In fact, they met no resistance. The place was empty.

David and Safer carefully entered the mineshaft but found no one and nothing. Then around a curve in the shaft, they saw a few bodies next to what appeared to be a cave in. The gold was gone!

Safer looked at David; David said, "The gold was here. I was watching the mine until fifteen hours ago and the gold was here!"

"Well, where is it now?" Shelly asked.

"Someone beat us to it."

"Why don't we use the helicopters to find where they went? They can only be a few hours ahead of us." As they spoke, Weiss and the would-be gold train arrived in the compound. Weiss was filled in and said, "We have come up the only reliable train route from Argentina to this mine. They did not take the gold east. They must be going north or west. South would be too long."

The Blackhawks were airborne in minutes. As dawn broke, they were following the train tracks that led away from the mine. They came to a divergence and the choppers, split one going southeast and the other north.

Charles:
CHAPTER I

Charles was taken to the airport, where he was placed on a company plane and flown to Berlin. In Berlin, an armored Mercedes took him to a CIA safe house. Moore met him.

"You will be staying here until this is finished. I have had your clothes brought here."

"What about Vladimir?"

"We just missed him. We got to the address but he had left only minutes before. We do know that he has a mother in Budapest and a son in Athens. We have tails on them and taps on the phones. We should be able to track him down through one of them."

"I can have Jeanne find and monitor his transactions from his bank account. That should give us a handle on where he is."

"Are you sure she can do that? We have tried but get no cooperation from banks the other side of the old Iron Curtin."

Charles placed a call to Jeanne.

"Charles, where are you?" she said worriedly.

"I can't say exactly, but know I am safe. This thing is coming down now."

"Be careful. I don't want to lose you just when I found you," she said.

"Okay. I need your help. Can you talk to someone at the Magyar Ncmzeti Bank in Budapest and set up a watch on the Michael Vladimir account or accounts?"

"Yes, I think so. I know those people. What do you want to know?"

"I want to know when any deposit is made, or a withdrawal. I would like to know where the withdrawal was made and, as close as possible, where Vladimir is. What would be great is, if there was a large withdrawal or transfer, if they could hold it up and give us time to get there so as to apprehend him when he arrives at the bank expecting his money."

"I don't know about that one. I'll call my friend at the bank and see what I can do. How can I reach you?"

"You can't. I'll have to call you. Will a few hours be enough?"

"I should be."

"Okay, I'll call back in three hours."

"Charles," Jeanne said in a low, meaningful voice, "I love you. Don't let anything happen to you. We have some things to settle."

He hung up without another word. Charles paused for a minute, thought about Jeanne, and then pushed her out of his mind. Turning to Moore he said, "I think we can get a handle on Vladimir. What is going on with the gold?"

"While you were gone, we located the mine in Paraguay where the gold is," Moore said. "It is just outside of a small town called San Pedro. The Israelis have a raid ready to go tomorrow morning just before dawn.

"From here, we will be in communication with the operation."

Charles called Jeanne within three hours to the second. She got the phone on the first ring. "Yes, Jeanne speaking."

"What did you find out?" Charles said without preamble.

"They will do it. Fredrick Baja is president of the bank. We have been friends for years. They will monitor the account and, if possible, let us know if they can get him to come in. Where can I reach you with information? This will not be able to wait for a call from you unless you plan on calling every ten minutes."

"You're right. Moore, can we have a number for Jeanne to call?"

Moore gave her his classified cell number.

"Thanks, Jeanne. Let us know when something happens."

"I will."

He hung up before any personal conversation could take place.

It was early afternoon in Europe when Moore and Charles sat down to listen to the operation.

They found they were a day late. The helicopters swept in and found that the gold was gone, and no one knew where.

David reported that they were searching the rail lines down to various Peruvian ports in search of a possible train with the gold. So far they had nothing.

In a few hours, now early evening in Berlin, a report came that a train was spotted headed toward Callao, a Peruvian port city. At least they thought that was a likely destination. The train had crossed the border from Argentina into Bolivia and was heading for Peru.

Reports from the Weiss informed them that there was an Arab ship in the harbor named *Arab Destiny* and that it was waiting to be loaded. Now the PLO's plan was evident. They had beaten the Israelis to the gold and were heading for Callao.

The Mossad
CHAPTER I

Weiss called Rome and informed them of what had happened. He asked for the operatives in Peru to meet him in Lima. By then the choppers needed to refuel, and so they had returned to base.

In Lima, Robert Sillos was alerted and told to find the gold. He at once sent his men into the waterfront to find a ship waiting to be loaded, with clearance to sail already arranged. By the evening of the thirtieth, he had learned that a ship by the name of *Arab Destiny* was waiting to take on cargo. With some not-so-gentle persuasion of the harbormaster, he learned that the ship was ready to sail upon the arrival of its cargo. The cargo was due to arrive the next day. Loading was to commence immediately, followed by an immediate departure. Although this was unusual, so was the amount of bribe money paid to the appropriate authorities.

Sillos told Weiss, David, and Safer:

"They are expecting a shipment by train tomorrow and will leave the harbor immediately upon loading. Customs says that it will be carrying grain from the high plateau, but I think this is the ship you want. It appears to be heavily guarded, and while it appears to be a tramp steamer it has a very fast engine and maybe even deck guns."

"Can we get a man on board to check it out, or better, as a crewmember?" Weiss asked.

"I am trying to get one of our men onto the ship as we speak, but this crew is tight and tight-lipped. They have not been allowed shore leave, and no one on the waterfront knew exactly what it was about. This is the first visit to Lima by the *Arab Destiny*. It has been in port a week."

Safer said, "I think we need to get to it. If they are waiting for the gold train we do not have long."

Weiss ordered David, "Stake out the train yard. Check the schedules to see what trains are due in from the east tomorrow.

"Sillos, you work the waterfront to see what you can find out about the *Arab Destiny*." Weiss ordered, "Get me a map of the waterfront area with the train tracks and loading docks indicated."

By 10:00 a.m. the next day, David reported that a train from the east was due to arrive at loading area 8 by 1:00 p.m. Safer reported that the *Arab Destiny* was to be prepared to load at that dock at that time. The *Destiny* was cleared to leave port by 4:00 p.m.

The support team of fifteen men was not due to arrive until noon.

"It will be very hard to have our men in position and ready to attack before 4:00 p.m.," David said.

"Yes, and what do we attack? The ship with frontal assault? The loading team?" Weiss said in frustration.

"The train is the most vulnerable aspect of the operation. If we could hit the train before it gets here, we would hold the gold," Sillos said.

"Yeah, but how would we transport it after we got it?" David asked.

"We could just steal the train and head it back to Argentina, where we have our plans ready to transport," David said.

"That is a good idea. There would be no logistical problems in getting the train back to Argentina and on the right track, but I think we could overcome them. The Arabs would not know we had the gold until the train was a couple of hours late.

"We could grab the train, move it to a landing field, and fly the gold out of here rather then taking the time and effort to get it back to Argentina," Weiss said warming to the idea.

"Before we can have out men here and in position the train will be in port. If we were to hit the train, we would have to be on our way now. The earliest we could hit it even on the run would be noon. The train will be in the outskirts of the city by then," Sillos said.

"There will be no planning, just a hit and run. We would need to get control of the engine and divert the train while we finished off whatever guards they may have on board," Weiss said thoughtfully.

"I don't like it," Safer said. "Too quick. No planning means failure and death to many of our brave men."

"Okay. You're right," Weiss said, disappointed. "If we only had more time."

David suggested, "Maybe we could delay the train. We could get it lost in the switchyard outside of town and that could take a couple of hours."

"We could also blow some track," Safer said. "We have time to do that if we move fast. Takes no special planning to blow a few hundred feet of track. That would stop the train for as much as a couple of days. That would mean it would be sitting on the rails and vulnerable to attack. We would only need twelve hours to set up a strike, and that would give us the time we need."

"That might work," Sillos said. "I have a couple of demolition people here. They could be ready to move in thirty minutes." "Do we know the route the train will take?" Weiss asked.

"It will come out of the mountains on one of two lines," Sillos said, producing a map. "The lines merge twenty miles outside of town. After that there is only one line coming into the train yards. If we were to blow the line, it would need to be after the junction and before the town."

David, looking at the map, said, "There appears to be little population in this area here between n and m. Somewhere in here would do."

"Okay," Weiss said to Sillos, "get your men on it. They would need to blow it before dawn."

Safer said, "We'll get it done. I'll report when we are in position."

After Sillos left, Weiss and David continued their conversation. Weiss said, "We need to know where that train is now."

"The only way we can find out is to tap into their communications. I don't think we can pick it up by chopper and I also don't believe that we have enough data on it to track it through the railroad records."

"Yes, before we could locate it would be here."

"Our only hope is in delaying it."

"In the meantime, do we agree if the train somehow gets here, there is no way we can attack the ship while it is loading or is in port?"

"No," David said, "that would be impossible."

"Then I am going to call Rome and see if we can get some back up oceanside."

Weiss had just got off the secure line to Rome when an ashen-faced David reported, "The train is here."

Charles:

In Berlin, Moore's cell phone buzzed.

"Moore here," he said gruffly, not wanting to be disturbed from the monitoring of the Israeli progress in South America.

"This is Jeanne. Is Charles there?"

"Charles, it's for you," Moore said without another word.

"Yes?" Charles said.

"Charles, I have something for you."

"Go ahead," he said.

"Vladimir has asked for a withdrawal to be sent to him at a hotel in Gdansk."

"What is the hotel?"

"The Helious on Helielusza Street."

"When did he ask for this transfer, how much, and how did he request it?"

"He cabled the Bank of Budapest an hour ago and requested that 30,000 U.S. dollars be sent to him by cable through the bank of Gdansk. It is to be deposited to an account there. The account is in the name of Michael Yakov. He wants confirmation sent to him at his hotel when it is done."

"What is the bank doing?"

"Waiting for me to tell them what to do."

"Okay, hang on just a minute he said excitedly."

Charles relayed the news to Moore and asked what to do.

"Tell her to have the bank make the transfer around 4:00 this afternoon. That will give me time to get our people to the hotel."

Charles relayed the message.

"Thanks, Jeanne. When this is over I'll tell you how important what you have done is."

He hung up.

Moore was on the scrambled phone already, ordering a team of operatives to pick up Vladimir before 4:00, thinking he would be waiting at the hotel for the confirmation of the transfer.

"Why do you suppose he is sending money to another account?" Charles asked.

"I don't know. He may have someone with him, or he needs to get some cash and this is either a dummy account or a trusted friend's," Moore said.

"Either way, we will have a background check done on this Michael Yakov."

Moore called in one of his men and ordered a search of all available records for Yakov.

By 1:00 p.m. the search was completed. They had come up with nothing in Poland for Yakov, but there was a Michael Yakov who also was a nuclear scientist and had been stationed in Kazan, where Vladimir also worked.

"The plot widens," Moore said. I think it would be safe to assume that there are two of them. We are still working on Yakov's background but we know he has family in Poland and has traveled there often."

"Well, that explains why they are in Gdansk and why money is going to Michael."

"Or does it?" Moore said. "Why would you need 30,000 dollars?"

"To travel," Charles said, matter-of-factly.

"No. Because that much money would be difficult to cross the border with. They are out of Russia. All they have to do is go to Hungary or Czechoslovakia and they can cross into the West. The Bank of Budapest would send money to a German bank with no questions asked, where as a Polish bank will not.

"So they must need the money for something in Gdansk."

"Yes," Moore mused. "What could it be?"

"Well, Gdansk is an industrial city with lots of shipping companies. The banking world is always jerry-rigging some way of underwriting either the steel industry or the shipping arrangements there. Not being able to deal directly with their banks is a pain in the ass."

"Well, they are not building anything," Moore said.

"No, they already did that," Charles mused. "But they do have to get it to the PLO. How would you do that?"

"I would store it somewhere I could tell my buyers to pick it up. That way I don't have to worry about getting busted on delivery. In fact, I could be in the West enjoying my money regardless of what my buyers do with it."

"Would Gdansk be a place for this pick up?"

"Sure. You could rent a warehouse and tell your buyer where to go to get it. The buyer could just arrange shipment of lot number or whatever on a ship or train or plane on a certain date. No one would hassle it until you got to the country it was being shipped to. Here you would need to control customs. But if you are the PLO, you send it to Libya or Syria and there would be no problem."

"So now we need to find which warehouse the package is in?" Charles asked.

"Yes, we do. We will need to know what their plans are. So we will have to question them after we pick them up. The arrangements may already be made. I will need to tell our people to get them out of Poland to a place we can talk with them."

Moore placed a call and gave the instructions.

He was told that a team of four operatives was in Gdansk and was en route to the hotel.

"When you get Vladimir, you will have to find out where Michael is and get him also. We will need them both in Sweden for a conversation as soon as possible," Moore told his men.

The Mossad:

"What? How can that be?" Weiss exclaimed in dismay.

"I don't know but my people at the dock just reported that a three-car train arrived at the loading area 8 where the *Arab Destiny*, which is taking on cargo, met it," Sillos said.

"It is now 12:30. They will be leaving at 4:00?"

"That is when they have clearance to sail."

"Can we get the clearance revoked?"

"I doubt it. Safer has the contacts for that. He is setting up the attack on the tracks for later today. I doubt he can be reached for a few hours. I'll try, though. But even if I reach him, we can't him back here before 5:00 p.m., and that will be too late."

"Well, call him anyway. Use a cell if you have to but get him. See if he can get the ship held. Maybe he can do it by phone or intermediaries."

At 3:30, Safer checked on that. He had the departure approval denied pending a customs inspection of the *Destiny*, which could not be done until tomorrow morning by the customs people.

Weiss smiled broadly. "At least we can do something right," he said.

"Now, how do we stop this ship from sailing at all?"

"Well, we could launch an attack on the ship herself and either capture her or scuttle her," Sillos said.

"We could set up an ambush and take her on the high seas," David said.

"We could simply sink her on the high seas," Weiss said thoughtfully.

"But the idea is to get the gold for ourselves. Failing that, we will deprive the PLO of the gold as a second outcome." Weiss went on. "So I guess we should try and capture the ship. We can do it here or on the high seas.

"What assets do we have available on the high seas?" Weiss asked David.

"Nothing. Everything we had was set up on the east cost of South America, thinking they were going that way. It would take too much time to get anything to this; even aircraft to sink her would be a challenge."

"So what do we have here for an attack?" Weiss asked once more.

"We have our operations team of fifteen armed men ready to go," Sillos said.

"Where are they now?" Weiss asked.

"They are on their way back from the train assault position at San Quean in the mountains. They should be here in the next thirty minutes."

"If we were to attack the *Arab Destiny* how would we do it?"

Sillos said, "I have a map of the harbor. We could get a small group, say five men with in by skiff with another three in reserve. We would need to use another five men to seal off access to berth 19. They could do it here where the road is very narrow. Five men could hold the position for thirty minutes probably. After that there would be enough police, army personnel, and weapons to force passage.

"We would also need to send what we had left, the two commandos plus the three of us, to gain control of the harbormaster's center. That would shut down communications. The team that takes the ship would need to sail it out of the harbor. With control of the harbormaster's center, we might be able to slow sea-based pursuit until we were in international waters.

"We do have two land-based choppers that could help with that cover as well. They could give air support until they were out of fuel and then ditch. We could recover the crews," David added.

"That sounds like a workable plan. How soon can we have it ready to go?"

"The men will be here any minute now," Sillos said. "We can work out the details with the men in about an hour. It will take another hour to get the equipment and men in place. It is now 4:00 p.m. We could be ready to go by 6:00. It is getting dark about then, so if we wait another hour we can strike under cover of darkness about 7:00."

"Okay," Weiss said, "get it done. Keep me informed. I'm going to contact Rome and let them know what has been happening."

The Russians
CHAPTER I

Vladimir was drinking vodka in a run-down, waterfront bar. He was alone but waiting for Michael to join him.

Michael walked in, sat down, and asked, "Where is my vodka?"

Vladimir laughed waved for the waitress to bring two more vodkas. He turned to Michael and said, "Well?"

"It is done. The packages are in locker 329 of the warehouse at 1110 Stephan Street. They will stay there until the shipper comes with the key to pick it up. No one knows or cares what is in there. Now all we need is the money to pay the rent on the locker—10,000 rubles—and then to fly to Budapest."

"I have the money being delivered to my hotel at 4:00. Let's pick up a couple of bottles of vodka and wait for the delivery."

"Let's don't wait alone," Michael said. "I think we can find some female companions to wait with us, and then we can celebrate the beginning of our new lives with them. I have not had a woman less than thirty or less then 200 pounds since our last trip to Sweden."

Vladimir smiled. "Okay, that does sound like a good evening. Do you know where to find these ladies?"

"Sure. I saw a lovely one on a corner a block up. I bet she has a friend."

"Okay, let's go see."

The two men ordered three bottles of vodka to go and started to walk up the street. They found the lady in question two blocks up.

Michael approached her. "Good afternoon, are you looking for some company?"

The woman was twenty-five, blonde, thin, but looked much older. Her eyes were tired and her walk was slow. Her skin was thin, pale, and wrinkled.

She gave Michael a careful, apprising once-over and said maybe. "But I have bills to pay, you know?" Michael smiled and said, "We have plenty of money."

"We?" she asked. "I only do singles."

"Do you have a friend?" Michael asked. "We would prefer it that way too." She gave them another once-over and said, "Yeah, I can arrange that." She reached into her purse, pulled out a cell phone, and talked for a few minutes.

"Erica is available. She is my age, dark, with bigger breasts. Are you interested?" Michael nodded. "Okay, where shall she meet us? Have her come to Hotel Hehelius at 4:30."

The three of them walked down the street together, leaning on each other, each man touching the woman and kissing her as they went.

Vladimir dropped his keys as he rounded the corner to the hotel. It was three thirty. Out of the corner of his eye he noticed two well-built men with bulky coats trying to look inconspicuous. "Keep walking," Vladimir whispered under his breath.

"What? Why?" Michael said, starting look around.

"Don't do that!" Vladimir hissed. "Look at those two men across the street. They don't belong. They look like KGB."

Michael took a sidewise glance and agreed. "Also there are two men in the hotel doorway."

Both men buried their faces in the whore's hair and began to kiss and fondle her as they continued by the hotel.

"That is a setup," Vladimir said. "Who knows we are there?"

"No one," Michael said. "Just the banker."

"The banker. He must have betrayed us. Let's pay a visited to the bank."

Michael handed the girl 100 U.S. dollars and said, "Thank you but we do not require you now. Something has happened to change our plans."

She shrugged and walked away, putting the bills into her coat pocket.

"Now to the bank," Michael said.

They took a cab to the bank and walked in to the manager's office. The secretary tried to stop them but they brushed past her.

"Okay," Michael said, "I am Michael Yakov I have come for money that was to be transferred here for me from the Bank of Budapest."

"Certainly," the manager said, looking from one angry face to another. "Let me check on that." He walked out to the head teller window and then returned with a slip of paper. "Certainly, Mr. Yakov, I have 30,000 dollars here for you, but the instructions said to deliver it to the blank hotel, and the delivery is on its way."

"Well, we are here and want it now."

"Right here, right now," Vladimir said, glancing out the window nervously.

"Okay, do you have identification?"

Michael showed him his Russian scientist ID card and pass for international travel, as did Vladimir, and the cash was dispensed to them.

They left the bank and went into a bar around the corner. They ordered vodka and then motioned for a bartender to come over.

"Is there someone here we can trust to run an errand for us?" Vladimir asked.

"Yes, yes, Justin is a good boy. He can do whatever it is you want."

"Get him over here," Vladimir said, placing a ten-dollar bill in the bartender's pocket.

He gave Justin a fifty-dollar note and handed him an envelope with ten thousand dollars in it. "Take this to 1110 Stephan Street. Give it to the man behind the counter. Return to me within thirty minutes with a receipt and I will pay you another 100."

Justin's eyes grew large at that much money and he ran out the door heading for Stephan Street.

He was back in twenty-five minutes, and Vladimir gave him 200 more dollars.

The two men left the building.

"Where to?" Michael said.

"The train station. Let's get a train for Budapest and from there we will arrange the rest of our money and to be moved to the West, and then we shall follow."

"The West," Michael said thoughtfully. "Good food, pretty women, warm weather. We are indeed fortunate."

The Mossad:
CHAPTER I

By 5:00 the men were just finishing up the strike plans when the phone rang.

David picked it up. "Shit! The *Destiny* is leaving port!"

"How can that be?" Weiss exclaimed, once more distraught.

"She finished loading and pulled away from the loading area to return to her berth assigned by the harbormaster. However, when she got to her berth she kept on going. She was at the mouth of the harbor before anyone realized she was trying to leave. They sent the navy but she was almost to international waters before they got a cruiser out to her. She opened fire on the cruiser and poured on the stream. After a few exchanges of shots, the cruiser gave up the chase and let her go. She is steaming west about twenty miles out as we speak."

"Can we follow her, David?" asked Weiss.

"We can get the choppers fired up and see what we can do," David answered.

"Let's get started with that," Weiss ordered.

Twenty minutes later, they were over the Pacific and had the *Destiny* identified, seventy-five miles off shore now, still steaming west.

"Keep her just on the horizon. We do not want to get too close," Weiss said to David.

After two hours their fuel was spent.

"Time to go. Bring them home," David said.

"Okay, let's mark the position and see what Tel Aviv or Rome has for suggestions.

"Maybe the American Navy can help us, or at least track her with a satellite?"

"I will make the calls," Weiss said.

CHAPTER II

David called the secret number on Moore's cell at midnight Peruvian time. It was 7:00 a.m. in Berlin.

"We need help," David said. "All our ships are on the east side of South America. We have no assets on the west side. They left Pisco, Peru, a few hours ago. We can't reach them. We have a heading but that is all. It is doubtful that our air force can attack them or even find them."

Moore said, "Not to worry. I can track the ship, but what are we going to do when we find it?"

"We want that ship!" David said in a fierce stage whisper.

"Call me back in half an hour," Moore instructed.

He made a call to the Pentagon and asked for satellite photos to be faxed to him in Berlin. Twenty minutes later, the fax line began its noise of beeps and tones.

Moore grabbed the photos from the machine and laid them on the table. Charles could see a circle around a dot that was a ship. In the series of photos, one could clearly see its track.

"Intelligence says it looks like it's headed to North Korea," Moore said. "That makes sense," he mumbled to himself.

"What do we have in the area west of Peru?" He turned to Joe Shovels.

"We have some destroyers and a sub or two," Joe said with a shrug.

"Is it possible to remove our markings from a sub at sea in a few hours?"

"Probably."

"Get it done. I want a sub with no markings between Hawaii and Japan in the next twenty-four hours." Moore looked at Shovels. "Get it done! No excuses!"

At thirty minutes exactly, the cell rang again.

"David," Moore said, "we know where your ship is and we think we know where it is going. We will meet you in Hawaii seventeen hours from now."

"Let's go to Hawaii," he said to Charles.

As they were in flight in a U.S. Air Force aircraft, Moore received another call on the cell.

"Yes?" he said.

"Great! I thought you guys knew what you were doing. I don't want excuses, I want results. Where is he now? Okay, I'll get back to you."

He turned to Charles. "It seems our boys failed to get Vladimir or his buddy Michael. He was not at the hotel; the address that we had from the bank was an empty nest. All our people found was a whore who said she was waiting for her date. The money was disturbed at the bank. Thirty thousand dollars. To a Michael Yakov and Vladimir X. They have disappeared."

"How did that happen?"

"The bank manager said that they arrived in the bank around 4:00 p.m., and said there had been a change in plans and they wanted to pick the money up there. They had proper ID, so he paid them."

"So where are they now?"

"We don't know. I would assume they are headed for Hungary and their money. From there they can cross into the West with ease."

"The Hungarian bank will send money to a Western bank with no problem," Charles added then said, "Let me call Jeanne. We can still track the money."

"Jeanne, we missed them in Poland and we believe they are going to Hungary for a crossover into the West. They will want their money. We still need to track the dollars. Call your friends and alert the Western banks to the possibility of a large transfer of funds from Hungary to a bank somewhere in the West. It could be anywhere."

"I'll get on it first thing in the morning," Jeanne said a bit sleepily.

"Thanks, Jeanne," Charles said and broke the connection.

In fifteen hours, they had landed in Honolulu and were meeting at the Lanaklian Hotel with their Israeli counterparts.

The Russians:

Michael and Vladimir arrived in Budapest around dawn. They left their first-class train accommodations and checked into the Intercontinental Hotel.

They napped, had room service bring them a nice breakfast, and then went to Chain Bridge over the Danube. It was 11:30 a.m.

Vladimir and Michael appeared to be admiring the beautiful Danube. The man feeding the pigeons said, "Did you enjoy your trip from Gdansk?"

A little surprised, Vladimir said, "Yes, we did."

"Were you successful in your business there?" the old man questioned further.

"Yes, we were."

"Then when can I get my packages?"

"When do we get our goods?" Vladimir retorted.

"We owe you one billion us dollars minus the 500 million upfront money you were already given.

If you go to the Bank of Budapest, you will find that we have deposited 100 million dollars your account. You will get the other billion dollars one week from today. We will make another deposit when we pick up the packages you have for us. Another deposit when it arrives at its destination and a final payment when you give us the codes to activate the packages. This is as it was agreed, no?"

"Yeah, that's right. Take this deposit slip to locker 329 on 1110 Stephan Street. I suggest that you pick up the package and get on a ship immediately with it. We may have been followed in Gdansk. We are not sure."

The old man accepted the deposit slip and spit a stream of tobacco juice on the sidewalk. "We will be careful and in touch soon. Where can I reach you in three days?"

"The Hotel Intercontinental is where we will stay until we hear from you further."

The old man simply walked away without a word.

Vladimir and Michael made their way to the Bank of Budapest. They asked to see the manger. When they were alone with him Vladimir said, "We want to verify the balance in our savings account."

The manger said, "Certainly," and tapped a few keys on the computer. "Your balance is 10,008,000 dollars. Is that all?"

"No, that's not all," Vladimir said. "We are expecting further transfers of large sums of money. We are establishing an export business and will need to be able to accept and to move large sums of money. Where do you suggest I establish an account in the West?"

The manager swallowed and said, "Any bank will do. But for security and efficiency I suggest a bank in Liechtenstein. There is only one bank there that I can deal with and that bank is Claridan."

"Thank you," Vladimir smiled. "That is the bank we have already chosen. Can you transfer funds there upon request?

"Please make the arrangements," Vladimir said and handed the manger a 100-dollar note. "For your troubles," he said with a smile.

South America:

"Here is what we will do," Moore told Weiss. "But you will owe us big for this."

"Okay," Weiss responded, wondering just how much this would cost.

"We have a U.S. sub that can stop this *Arab Destiny* on the high seas. The ship will have no markings of any kind. You will arrive in three small boats to board the ship. Once aboard you will sail it for four hours south, where you will be met by another unmarked cargo ship that will transfer the cargo from the *Destiny*. The *Destiny* will then be scuttled and the crew put off in lifeboats.

"You will sail the cargo in this unmarked ship to the U.S. naval base in Diego Garcia. You will need to have an Israeli plane there to meet the ship and accept the cargo."

"Where will this take place and when?" Weiss asked.

"Three days, at first light. The *Destiny* will be three hours off the cost of Japan, just outside of most shipping lanes. Here we will stop her. You will need to get a merchant marine ship from Japan today and put to sea. Here is the name of a discreet captain. His ship is ready to sail. Here are the codes and frequencies for communication with the sub. You need to have this ship at sea in the next five hours."

The information was handed to David. He was told to take charge of the operation and to be sure he and at least six of his crew were on board the merchant vessel.

"Now what do you want from us?" Weiss asked.

"We want a Russian scientist named Vladimir. He has at least two and maybe more nuclear weapons for sale. We want the weapons and we want him. That is what the Arabs planned to do with the gold. He was in Gdansk but he is on the run now."

Moore handed a file to Weiss. "Here is all we know. We want him fast. We don't care if he is dead or alive, but we do need the nuclear devices. We believe they may be stored in a warehouse or some other kind of drop in Gdansk. If you kill them, we will not know where the devices are, so be careful, at least initially."

"Okay," said Weiss. "Anything else?"

"Your government is aware of what you and we are doing?"

"Yes," said Weiss.

"Then you need to communicate to them that we expect them to pay the expenses of this operation. We also will expect your president to attend a peace conference in Washington, D.C., with our president and various representatives of the PLO."

Weiss' smile froze. "I don't know if I can guarantee that," he said icily.

"There is a secure line in the other office. You may make a call. We need the answer," Moore said.

Fifteen minutes later, Weiss was back. "The PM will attend the meeting, but there is no guarantee of an agreement, is that understood?"

"That will be acceptable," Moore said with a smile.

"Now, let's see if we can get this *Arab Destiny*."

Jeanne

Jeanne could not go back to sleep. She tossed in her bed for a few hours and then got up. She fixed herself a cup of tea and sat down to drink it. She looked out her window at the predawn darkness and thought. She thought about Charles. She thought about where her life was going, and she thought about money being moved around the world.

Charles. So strange that he had come back into her life. At one point she thought that he might be someone that she could build a life with. But he had never seemed interested in anything more than an evening. Yeah. He always treated her well, and although there were months between contacts with him he never made her feel used or taken for granted. But he would never really give himself to her. Even when they were making love he was not quite there. There was always something held back.

These last few months, though, that was not the case. They had seen each other often and this time there seemed to be a real touching of their selves as well as their bodies. Could there be something here?

She would have to leave Europe to be with him and return to the States. But that was all right. She could be a stepmother to his children. She doubted that they would ever have children but that was all right too. Being with Charles, whom she loved, would be a safe, warm place to grow old.

Well, now that you have that settled, she told herself as she fixed another cup of tea, *you could only hope that Charles feels the same way. He was rather short on the phone the last two times we talked, as if he did not want to go beyond basic conversation. What could that mean? He did not want to talk? He did not feel the same way she did? Was he just wrapped up in this gold thing? Well, it could be any or all of the above,* she thought.

"Where is Vladimir?" she said out loud, startling herself. "Where could he go? The money was in Budapest. Thirty thousand was sent to Gdansk, but the bulk of it is still there. So he plans on having the money transferred to a Western bank. Which one would be the easiest?"

Well, Swiss banks are easy, she mused, *but he would need to come personally to open the account in order to establish recognition procedures. Liechtenstein would also be easy. Both countries maintain open relations with Eastern Bloc banks. Wait! Liechtenstein has a small bank that has been accused of being a depository for Russia money and they are easy to access from abroad.*

Jeanne moved to her computer and went online. Europe was just waking up, but she sent out several messages to friends in Germany, France, Belgium, England, and Liechtenstein. Then she waited to see if she got a reply. By now it was 6:00 a.m. in Berlin, so she showered and prepared for the day.

Jeanne returned to the computer in forty-five minutes and two of her friends had responded to her e-mail. The first one, Charles Britt of France, filled her in on Liechtenstein banking law and procedures. It fit. E-mail and phone calls could be used to open an account with two Liechtenstein banks, and both of these banks had Eastern Bloc money.

Next Stacy Shaw, a compliance monitor for the Liechtenstein government, responded with information on how secrecy is maintained by the banking community. She also provided names of people in various banks that she thought would be approachable to get information from. Stacy wrote, "As a compliance monitor I can't say these two are open to bribes but there have been rumors over the years. My office has investigated them on several occasions and there is nothing we can prove but I think there is something there."

Jeanne checked to see if she was online and she was in luck.

"Thanks for the info," she typed. "Can you give me their numbers or places I could meet with them?"

Stacy responded with two numbers. "Terry David hangs out at the casino two blocks from the bank. He gambles nearly every day and it is said he likes the ladies.

"Bill Labean is very serious but loves photography. He usually can be found at Vaduz Art Gallery either buying or talking about art."

"Thanks," Jeanne typed back. "One more question. Does there need to be cash to open an account?"

"What do you mean?" Stacy said.

"Well, if I knew was going to have funds, could I open an account with a zero balance and then transfer the funds at a later date?"

"Only at the two banks I told you about, and such an account is only allowed for thirty days."

"Could I get a list of new accounts?"

"LOL," Stacy typed back. "That would defeat the purpose of banking in Liechtenstein, and if my office found out someone gave that to you it would be their head!"

"Thanks anyway. I'll see you when I am in Liechtenstein again. Have a good day."

So someone could open an account by phone without funds at Clariden or Swiss Nationale, she thought. *Maybe I could get this Terry or Bill to help me but how? Bribes would work but they don't know me, so I would need someone they trusted to offer such a bribe.*

Jeanne picked up her phone and called Charles Britt. "Chuck, I need your help," she said without preamble.

"Okay, nice to hear from you too," he said laughing. "What do you need?"

"I need to know if someone has opened an account in either bank in the last thirty days."

"You know you can't get the info."

"I know it is illegal for a bank to release that. But what if I had someone on the inside get it for me?"

"That's illegal! No one would do that. If you got caught, they would go to jail, or at least it would be the end of their career."

"What about a guy named Terry David? Do you know him?"

Chuck laughed. "Yes, I know him. He is a character. He is the poster boy for living large. He is big, conspicuous, and never does anything in a small way. He brags about how much gambling he does. I have spent a lot of time with him at sporting events and in casinos all over the world. He is a fun guy to be with. Something is always happening.

"Why do you ask?"

"Well, I have heard that he is not above bending the law."

"I have heard that too, but he is careful."

"Chuck, could you arrange a meeting for tonight with him and me? You can come too. I need to convince him to get the list I need."

"Okay, let me call him, but don't expect much."

"Chuck, set this up and I owe you big-time."

"I'll see what I can do," he said as he hung up.

Jeanne had just arrived at her office when her phone rang.

"Jeanne, this is Chuck. You owe me. He will meet you tonight at the blank casino at 8:00 p.m. I'm coming too."

"Great," she said.

Then she pushed the intercom for her secretary. "Lynn, I'm going to Liechtenstein for the rest of the day. Please cancel my appointments for today. I will be back by noon tomorrow."

Jeanne caught the 11:00 a.m. train to Liechtenstein.

The Mossad

David and three other commandos rappelled onto the deck of the tramp steamer *Spartan*. The captain, Dennis or Denny Johnson, was about sixty-five. He was five foot nine with sliver hair a weather-beaten face and cold gray eyes that had seen many miles of ocean go under the keel of his ships over the last forty-five years.

David had had an agent in Japan visit Captain Johnson in the ship's office yesterday. He told Johnson that he needed his ship and crew to rendezvous off the cost of Japan with another ship and receive a cargo transfer at sea. "Can you do such a thing?"

"Yes, yes, I can do it if the weather is not too bad. But that is unusual and probably illegal. What do you want me to do?"

The agent opened a briefcase with 500,000 dollars in it and set it on Johnson's desk.

The old skipper's eyes grew large. "Now I know it is illegal."

"We do not want to answer questions. We will give you coordinates and six of my men will join us at sea. I have twenty other passengers that will come aboard in two hours. We will then steam to another set of coordinates, where you will accept the contents of another ship's hold and place it in your hold. You will then steam to a place I will tell you of at the time. This should take no more than seven days. There will be another half million when you return here."

Johnson scratched his chin. "Well, I don't know. That sounds very risky and I'm sure there is more to that then you are telling me. I'll have to think about this."

The agent leaned across the desk. "Don Moore gave me your name and said you would be interested in such an operation."

"Oh! Don, Huh? Now I know this is risky. Last time I worked with him I was nearly killed. I said I would never do it again."

This time the agent said, "You know too much now. You really don't have a choice. We sail in two hours. Get the ship ready."

Johnson's eyes grew cold and small. "Whatever you say," he said, "but this will never happen again."

Once David joined the ship by rappelling from a helicopter, he and his team leaders took over the captain's cabin and began to pore over maps and plans.

Johnson was forced to bunk with the first mate and grumped continually about this and the whole operation, but he was perfect as a seaman. The ship got to where it was supposed to be when it was supposed to be there.

David reported to Weiss and Moore back in Hawaii that they were in position. "I figure to be just over the horizon from the position of the *Destiny*," he said.

The next morning at first light, 200 miles off the coast of Japan Moore, Townsend and Weiss sat down to watch in real time the satellites covering of the attack on the *Arab Density*.

The Destiny

Eight days later, the *Arab Destiny* was near the cost of Japan on route to Korea, when suddenly two jets buzzed them.

John went to the bridge.

"What and who was that, Captain?"

"Two planes, no markings, buzzed us. That was a warning."

The radio hissed to life

"Merchant vessel *Arab Destiny,* you must heave to and prepare for boarding or be destroyed. Confirm my orders please."

"What do we do?" John said.

The captain shrugged. "I think we heave to, call for assistance, or prepare to fight. We do have some guns that can be uncovered. There are only two planes."

Lazaar arrived on the bridge. "We have two 'copters on the horizon heading this way. I could not make out any markings."

"Well what do you want me to do?" The captain said.

The radio repeated the demand as one of the planes dived across the bow and the other screamed down the length of the ship at about fifty feet.

"I say fight," Lazaar said. "There are only two. We could get the first one for sure before they knew what happened."

"Okay," John said grimly, "get the guns ready."

The third time the demand came, one of the planes again swept across the bow of the *Arab Destiny*. This time it was met with a hail of small-arms and four-inch cannon fire, scoring a direct it. The plane exploded.

The gun was turned for the second, but this time the second plane had stayed at altitude in a wingman's traditional role of guarding the leader. Without further warning it dove, coming in from the rear, strafing the deck.

Screams of shock and agony told the bridge that men had been hit.

Captain Johnson demanded a damage report.

The first mate reported no serious damage to the ship. Three men hit and two dead.

The plane climbed, circled, and dove again. This time a series of flashes were seen on its wings.

It pulled up out of range of the ship's guns. Four explosions racked the *Destiny*. Several bursts of flames came from various parts of the ship.

As damage crews went to their stations the captain took in their reports.

"We have several fires burning and some damage below the water line. We may be able to control the fires. I think we can still make Korea; it is only six hours of steaming. Is that what you want me to do?"

John nodded.

Before he could speak, a third attack was underway from the plane, and the ship was hit twice more; however, the plane was hit as it pulled out of the attack. Trailing smoke, it hit the water and disintegrated.

The helicopters now took up positions on either side of the *Destiny* just out of gun range.

This time the first mate reported, "Our engines are out and our emergency power will not keep the pumps working for long. The chief engineer says at least four hours if we can fix them. That is too long. The ship will sink within sixty minutes of the emergency power failing."

The captain reached for his PA mike and made the order to abandon ship. He also opened the radio and said, "Helicopters attacking the *Arab Destiny*. We are dead in the water, taking on water, and will sink. We are abandoning ship. I beg of you to cease your attacks to allow my crew to escape."

The voice on the radio said, "You have twenty minutes and then I finish destroying the ship."

Twenty minutes later the crew sat huddled in four life boats while two 'copters, obviously military but with no nationality markings, circled overhead. Suddenly a submarine, again with no national markings, surfaced next to the *Destiny*. A boarding party led by Jason Rolland, chief petty officer, went onboard and began a search of the ship.

Lazaar, John Farok, and five of their team had not left the ship but were on the bridge.

"Okay," John said, "we will need those ships here in the next hour. This tub only has two hours to live. With some auxiliary power and pumps we might save her, or at least keep her afloat long enough to transfer the cargo."

Lazaar said, "We have company. Get your weapon ready."

They waited until the onboard party was exposed, spread out across the deck. Rolland had just reached the bridge deck when Lazaar nodded to his men to open fire.

Rolland was the first to die. He never knew what had happened. Three other members of the boarding party were cut down before they could find cover.

The remaining ten marines returned fire. From the deck of the submarine, the 60-caliber guns opened up. The blast took out the three men on the starboard side of the ship next to the sub.

The boarding party had worked its way around to the port side. As the two remaining PLO soldiers moved to the port side to have cover while firing at the sub on the starboard side, they were cut down. That left Lazaar and Farok on the bridge.

The marines worked their way up to the bridge deck as the firefight went on. Finally Bob Root, a gunny sergeant, got a burst into the bridge. Lazaar was hit with three shots, all in his stomach and chest. He collapsed in pain and curses, and was soon unconscious.

Farok threw down his assault rifle and cried, "Don't shoot! Don't shoot!"

He was taken into custody.

The submarine then sent over engineers and a power line. The pumps on the *Destiny* were started once more. The list began to improve.

On the horizon another ship, again without markings, appeared and made for the *Destiny*. This was Johnson's ship. Within an hour, the gold was ready to be transferred from the *Destiny* to the *Wolverine*. Just as the booms began to work there was an explosion from deep within the *Destiny*. She suddenly lurched to port and dipped at the bow. A second explosion was heard and felt from the stern of the ship. The *Destiny* righted herself then split in two. The crew on board dived for the water. Within sixty seconds the *Destiny* and the German gold shipment from April of 1945 was under the Pacific Ocean. The bottom was two miles below.

Four of the six crew members were picked from the water.

"Shit! Goddamm!" David screamed at Johnson. "Do something! Don't let it sink! We need that cargo!"

"What do you want me to do?" Johnson said. "I can't hold a ship together that's been scuttled. They obviously left a surprise for us when they left the ship. Nice move. We never suspected it."

"What are we going to do about the cargo?" David asked again.

"Nothing we can do at this time," Johnson said. "I guess I will pick up my crew in the water and their crew from the lifeboats."

Jeanne:

Jeanne arrived in Liechtenstein by 1:00 in the afternoon. She went immediately to the bank and met a friend of hers from the U.S. banking system.

"Good to see you, Beth," Jeanne said brightly. "How is banking in the secret kingdom of Liechtenstein?"

"Oh fine. The work is boring but you meet some very rich men," she said with a wink.

"What have you been up to?"

"The same old thing. I am getting ready to go home and try to settle into a nice banking slot with lots of money and no travel."

"Any men in your life?" Beth asked.

"Not really. There is someone I am interested in but we will see what will happen.

"How about you?

"No, just interesting times with interesting men.

"Beth, what do you know about Terry David?"

"Terry? Ha! He is fun but don't trust him. He will show you a good time, but he only wants a good time. Are you interested in him? How did you meet him?"

"I haven't yet and I'm not."

"What do you mean?"

"I would like to meet him. He has some information that I need in a really big way."

"Banking information? Forget it. He can't and won't tell you anything about his clients. Not even the government can make him."

"I know that but this is really big and I only need a little bit of help."

"He won't tell you anything, even if he knows and even if you sleep with him. He would be all done in banking anywhere in Europe if it got out that he broke confidence."

"Well, tell me this. What is his position?"

"He is director of operations."

"Which means?"

"He runs the bank right under the president."

"Then he knows or can find out anything about any account?"

"I suppose so, but forget it he will not give information out."

"Okay. Well, thanks for the information. When will you be in Berlin again?"

"Not for a few months," Beth said.

"Well, call me when you are coming. I will arrange a fun evening for us. Including some interesting men."

Before Jeanne met with Chuck she called Charles again.

"Charles, I am meeting someone in a Liechtenstein bank that I think can be very helpful but he is reluctant to talk. Is there something I can get from your friends to help me?"

Charles got Moore on the phone.

"Where are you staying Jeanne?"

She told him, "I am staying at the Marriott."

"Okay, I will have two men meet you before you go to your meeting. They will have everything you will need to get information out of anyone."

Later that day, Chuck Britt took Jeanne to Mr. David's office.

"Terry, there is someone here that wants to meet you."

Jeanne flashed her most alluring smile and said hello as she was introduced. Terry looked her up and down appraisingly and then said hello with a very gracious smile.

"What can I do for you?" he said with just a slight bit of innuendo.

"Well, I am with Bank One Europe and wanted to talk about some affiliations that we might do together."

"What do you mean?" Terry said, growing thoughtful, business-like.

"Well, we do a lot of business with key U.S. banks and you, I understand, have good relations with banks in the old Soviet Bloc countries. As you know these banks do little business with Western banks due to history. U.S. banks have governmental handicaps that have not yet been removed so they do not have access to these developing economies.

"What I propose is an affiliation whereby our bank works with yours to put money from the East to work in the U.S."

"Well, that sounds interesting, but why can't I just contact Chase Manhattan myself?"

"Because there are levels of relationships that are needed to really make money in this field. I have them including an inside contact with the CIA. I can guarantee not only a relationship but also an inside one that will be very profitable."

"Well, I don't see any reason why we can't talk about this. What kind of money arrangements do you have in mind?"

"Oh, a percentage of the action for your bank and my bank and the client makes good investments with good returns."

"Okay, run a scenario by me. I'm listening."

"Suppose a person in Russia had a great deal of money, say millions. He wants to get it out of Russia and into the West. Currently he would need to move the funds to a bank in Poland or Hungary. From there to one in Switzerland or Liechtenstein. Then he would have to invest it in Europe or a third-world country, since access to U.S. investments is limited and at a disadvantage. With what I propose, the money can be moved through my bank to Bank One in Columbus, Ohio, and from there to any use anywhere in the world the client might want to use it for."

"Okay, but he can do that now."

"But not so easily, and the rates he gets will be several points below what I can do as well as at an unfair exchange rate.

"On a hundred-million-dollar account this could be the difference of ten million dollars. A difference that we could help the client with. Put a million into each of our banks while adding eight million to the client. Of course, this edge would make your bank more inviting for this kind of money than, say, a bank in Switzerland or even another Lichtenstein bank."

"Yes, that is true. I like this."

"Jeanne, you are as attractive as you are intelligent. Would you like to have dinner with me tonight?"

"Yes, I would," Jeanne said.

"I will pick you up at your hotel at 8:00. Wear something comfortable. We will go dancing after dinner," he said with a sly smile.

Jeanne wore something comfortable. It was a wraparound dress with a slit up one leg nearly to the top of her thigh. Not only was she showing a lot of leg, but a lot of cleavage was on display as well.

After dinner and dancing, Terry brought Jeanne home around 2:00 a.m.

"We have not talked business at all," Jeanne said with a slight slur in her voice. This was a put-on since she had been dumping her drinks all night. "Would you like to come up to my room and see if we can strike a deal?"

Terry's eyes lit up. "That sounds wonderful," he said.

In Jeanne's suite, Jeanne offered him more drinks. These, however, were laced with a substance that would put him out. Once he was out, Jeanne called in the agents that had been assigned to her by the CIA.

They took Terry into the other room, where they administered a drug that caused him to talk freely and answer questions. A tape recorder was set up and his conversation regarding his bank, boss, employees, and customers was recorded.

Finally, most of his clothes were removed and he was awakened to find himself in bed with a nude Jeanne and a terrible headache.

"There you are. Awake finally!" Jeanne said. "Would you like to do it again? You are such an animal and sooo creative," Jeanne said with a sly smile.

"I would love to," Terry said, confused, "but my head is about to explode. What time is it anyway?" he said.

"About 4:30."

"A.m.?" Terry asked incredulously.

"Of course. You have been asleep about an hour after the last romp."

"I must get home, get cleaned up, and get back to the office by seven," he said.

"But we haven't finished our business," Jeanne said.

"Oh that. I think we can do a deal, but I can't talk now. My head hurts. Can you come into the office tomorrow about noon? We can have lunch. And maybe more of this," he said with a smile.

"Noon will be fine," Jeanne said.

CHAPTER II

Noon came and Terry eagerly waited for Jeanne to show up.

One o'clock came and he continued to wait. No Jeanne.

By three he gave up.

At four he left his office for home and an early bed. His last thoughts before going to sleep were of Jeanne. *Where did she go?* he thought.

Jeanne was back in Berlin by four and on the computer provided by the CIA. She was reviewing all the accounts of the Liechtenstein Bank courtesy of the information provided by Terry the night before.

Around 10:00 p.m., she found what she was looking for.

"I think I have it," she said to herself. "Here is an account set up by Michael Yakov and another one by Alexander Vladimir with a few thousand. The money was transferred from the Bank of Budapest to the

Bank of Liechtenstein in the window we are looking at. There is an order opening further transactions from Budapest.

"Now I need to get to the Bank of Budapest and see if it matches with our man."

By 3:00 a.m. Jeanne knew that it matched.

"Okay, all we have to do is monitor this account for activity and it should lead us to our man," she said excitedly.

Three days later, a transfer of ten million dollars was made.

The next day, a notice was received that Mr. Michael Yakov will arrive in person on the twenty-third of January to provide further instructions to the bank regarding his account.

"Since this is a change in the standing instructions, it will need to be in person. All we have to do is stake out the bank and we have him."

CHAPTER III

On the twenty-third of January, David, Charles, and three heavies were waiting at the Liechtenstein bank.

They followed everyone that did business with Terry that day. There were five men and three women; all were followed and apprehended. Each was followed until they got into a cab or onto a side street, then two agents walked up and took them aside. They asked what the person was a doing in the bank, reviewed their passport, and got the home address. They also took the account number and relayed it back to Jeanne at a computer on the other side of town.

The third man was pay dirt.

As he got into a cab, two agents got in with him and the doors locked.

Michael looked up in surprise and said, "I have this cab. You will need to find another."

"We need to ask you a few questions," the first man said.

"Questions? Questions about what? You can't do this to me," he said and started speaking in rapid Russian.

However, Bobby Perkins and Chas Fedorca spoke Russian and answered his somewhat obscene comments in his language.

"What were you doing here today?" Chas asked.

"None of your business. I am not in Russia now and you can't make me talk to you."

Bobby said, "We have all day and night if that is what it takes. Or you can simply answer the questions."

"What are the questions?" he said suspiciously.

"Your name, your passport, and your account number; that is all."

"Why my account number?"

"We need to check it against a list we have of possible fraudulent activities. Someone is trying to steal money out of the bank via computer manipulations." They produced bank security ID.

Reluctantly Michael provided the information. It was relayed to Jeanne.

"That's him!" she nearly screamed. "That's him!"

"Okay," Bobby said. "You will need to continue with us."

"Why? I gave you the information you wanted."

"Because you are Michael Yakov, a former Soviet nuclear scientist, and you have sold nuclear devices to the PLO."

Michael went gray but did not speak.

Chas stuck a syringe into his arm and Michael was asleep.

They took him to a safe house in Belgium near the harbor of Antwerp. There he was given another shot to make him talk.

There were two devices, each packed in a crate in the Gdansk shipyard, waiting to be picked up for delivery to Morocco. That was all he knew. There was another scientist involved with him in the scheme. He was still in Gdansk, watching the crates. They were to be picked up sometime after the first of February. After ten million more dollars were deposited to Vladimir's account.

The Last Russian

Agents in Gdansk picked up Vladimir's trail without him knowing it. Vladimir spent most of his time in bars and with ladies that could be purchased. He stayed close to the warehouse district. He checked his messages regularly at the hotel where he was staying.

Growing tired of waiting, the word was given to pick him up. The two agents, Joe Urbanik and Paul Ross, waited until he was leaving a bar around 2:00 a.m. with a street whore.

As they fell in step with him, Paul grabbed the whore by the arm, slipped a few bills into her hand, and said get lost. He then grabbed Vladimir's arm and they steered him toward their car.

"Hey, hey, what is going on Vladimir?" slurred through the alcohol.

"We are taking you for a little ride," Joe said. "Just go along and it won't hurt a bit."

Vladimir was drugged, put in a box, and then put on a plane, which landed around dawn on an island in the Mediterranean. He was transported to a safe house in the Mediterranean, where he was reunited with Michael.

Joe and Paul remained in Gdansk and continued to check the hotel for messages.

CHAPTER II

Now it was a waiting game. When would they be contacted?

The contact came on the tenth of February. The coded message said for Michael to meet Assad at a restaurant on the twelfth at noon. He was to wear a brown suit and carry a blue umbrella when he entered the coffee shop and take the last booth on the right wall.

Agents got there early and staked out the coffee shop and then Chas went in dressed in the designated manner.

A dark man, one that the Mossad recognized as Joe Farok, joined him at the booth.

Joe stared the conversation. "There has been a change in plans. We cannot pay you the other billion at this time but we want the shipment."

"No money, no shipment," Chas said. "That is all I have to provide the life I want."

Joe said, "You will have to trust us. We can deposit five hundred million today and the rest after the operation is successful."

Chas shook his head.

Joe said, "Look, I am not playing games here. We have had a problem with the arrangements we had for the gold, but when we are successful we can pay you. We need the shipment now."

"No. No money, no shipment."

"What would your government say if they knew what you did?"

"You won't tell them."

"No. Not today. But we might decide to if you do not cooperate. We need the shipment. It is of no use to you except to sell to us. So take the five hundred million and the IOU."

"Make it five hundred million and another 1.5 billion IOU and I will give you the location of the shipment."

"We can get three but not five."

Okay, five and a 1.3 billion IOU."

"Deal. How do we get the shipment?"

"First the money."

It will be deposited this afternoon in the Bank of Budapest as has been arranged before.

"Okay, we can meet tomorrow when I have confirmation. Then I will hand over the papers you need to pick it up.

We can meet tomorrow at the Opera Bar around the corner from the Opera House Bar. Do you know where that is?"

"Yes," Chas said. "Tomorrow at 2:00 p.m."

That night, the CIA and Mossad set up their plan. "We will want to get the devices first thing in the morning in case anything goes wrong. We have a ship in the harbor, the *MV Wolverine*. We will take possession of the cargo in the wheelhouse and the ship will sail at 4:00 p.m.

"We will have a stake-out team that will apprehend the people that come to get the cargo and the ship that they are from. We can turn them over to the Polish government. I think they would like to have the pleasure of taking credit for the bust.

"We will have a team ready to follow Joe Farok. We have wanted him for a long time and now we can get him and those he is working with. Without a doubt he will leave the country after he makes the deal. We will follow him, tap any call he makes, and arrest everyone he comes in contact with. Joe and his buds we will take to Israel and decide there what to do with him."

All went as planned in getting the devices into the *Wolverine* and the *Wolverine* out onto the high seas. Once in open ocean, she ran into the middle of a NATO task force on maneuvers, which provided an escort back to England. From there the cargo was transferred to a U.S. Navy ship and taken to an unknown port in the U.S.

At two, Joe showed up at the Opera Bar.

Joe said, "Have you received confirmation of the transfer?"

"Yes," Chas said. "Here are the documents you will need to pick up the cargo in Gdansk."

Joe smiled, shook Chas' hand, and left.

He went to his car, where he made a call to Rome, relaying the information to so and so. From there he went to the waterfront.

There he met a tall man in the Anchor Bar. He gave him the documents and got back on a plane for Berlin.

As he left the plane in Berlin, three agents met him and took him into custody without a fight.

In Italy at the same time, the Imperial Building was raided. Twenty men were arrested and transported to Tel Aviv, where they were reunited with Joe.

Charles was informed three weeks later that they had been neutralized. For the next several months there was a series of accidents, suicides, and other strange deaths of nearly 100 people who had been associated with Joe and Saladin. This included Glenda and a David Albert, who appeared to have died in a boating accident.

All in all, the PLO operations in Europe were nearly decimated.

Michael Yakov and Alexander Vladimir were given jobs in the U.S. nuclear research center but were never out of CIA surveillance. They were very happy to be in America and to be working again. Five years later, they became U.S. citizens.

Israel mounted a salvage operation off the coast of Japan to recover a ship they said they lost. To date this has not been successful, but the work continues.

Charles married Jeanne and they live in Virginia, where they do contract work for the CIA in the area of computers and international banking.

About The Author

Lynn A. Eastman was born in Flint, Michigan, in 1948. The city of Flint was the home of Buick and the famous sit-down strike that formed the UAW. By the time he was a teenager, the hits of Motown were playing across America, and Lynn's proximity to Detroit created a fascination with both fast cars and rock and roll. These roots influenced the title of his first novel, *The Day the Music Died*.

Lynn graduated from the University of Michigan in 1970 with a B.A. in counseling, and then attended Central Bible College in Springfield, Missouri, where he obtained a degree in religious education. Lynn received his graduate degree from the University of Michigan and holds a masters degree in counseling and psychology. He has been married to his high school sweetheart, Jeanne, for thirty-five years, and they have two children.

Eastman and his wife were foster parents during the late 1970s, and their experience caused them to see a need for improved services in this area. Lynn discussed his concerns about the need for improvement in foster care with a local probate judge, who said, "I agree with you completely. Why don't you start a good program?" This conversation inspired him to become the founder of a therapeutic foster care program that has expanded into several states.

Eastman currently serves as the executive director of the agency and he spends much of his time traveling to the various offices. The travel time allows him the opportunity to develop plots and create his fiction. Lynn is also an avid world traveler and he interweaves the places and experiences he has had into his novel.

When he is not traveling, Lynn loves to spend his weekends attending University of Michigan football games at "The Big House" with his children. His son Zachary designed the cover for Lynn's novel.

Printed in the United States
24855LVS00001B/1-30